PRYDE'S ROCK

Lesley at Darian

love

Mabel

xx

Recent Titles by Malcolm Archibald

PRYDE'S ROCK

Malcolm Archibald

This first world edition published in Great Britain 2007 by
SEVERN HOUSE PUBLISHERS LTD of
9–15 High Street, Sutton, Surrey SM1 1DF.
This first world edition published in the USA 2007 by
SEVERN HOUSE PUBLISHERS INC of
595 Madison Avenue, New York, N.Y. 10022.

British Library Cataloguing in Publication Data

Archibald,   Malcolm
   Pryde's rock
   1.   Engineers - Fiction
   2.   Landowners - England - Northumberland - Fiction
   3.   Northumberland (England) - Social conditions - 19th century - Fiction
   I.   Title
   823.9'2 [F]

   ISBN-13: 978-0-7278-6459-8 (cased)

All Severn House titles are printed on acid-free paper.

Typeset by Palimpsest Book Production Ltd.,
Grangemouth, Stirlingshire, Scotland.
Printed and bound in Great Britain by
MPG Books Ltd., Bodmin, Cornwall.

For Cathy

Prelude

Coast of Northumberland, September 1777

'Breakers ahead! Breakers ahead!' The seaman's voice rose to a squeal as he scrambled downward, bare feet slithering on the ratlines. He thumped on to the deck and pointed urgently ahead.

'What?' Peering through the open door of the deckhouse, the master focussed his tired eyes past the masts to where the bowsprit bobbed to the chopped North Sea waves. 'Sweet Christ, it's the Black Corbie! Larboard the helm!' Naked save for his woollen underwear, he took two long strides to the wheel and added his weight to that of the helmsman. 'Larboard, for the love of God!'

The helmsman screamed at the sight of waves splintering against pitiless black rock. Silver-white spindrift rose to the height of the foremast, hung for a second as if in agonized hesitation, then swooped downward to the frothing sea below. Blinking against the battering spray, the helmsman hauled desperately at the varnished spokes of the wheel, repeating the same copulative expletive as if it were a mantra of divine protection.

For an instant the ship seemed to hesitate, her masts trembling and her bowsprit rising inexorably skyward. Veins bulged prominently in the master's temple as he struggled with the wheel, roaring orders in a voice that was hoarse with fear. The ship danced a terrible jig as a succession of waves smashed against the hull, and then the mizzen topgallant staysail exploded in a welter of tattered canvas.

'All hands! All hands!' the master yelled, but the wind captured his voice and whipped it away into the wicked

1

blackness of the night. The muscles of his forearms writhed as he strained against the spokes of the wheel. 'We're doing it, Abe, see!'

A voice bawled forth as a seaman prematurely celebrated the imminent landfall.

'Then we'll rant and we'll roar like true British seamen,
We'll rant and we'll roar all across the salt seas
Until we strike soundings in the Channel of old England . . .'

The voice faded away as a wave broke amidships and thousands of gallons of cold North Sea water surged across the deck. There was a crack like the advent of Armageddon and Abe screamed as the wheel spun beneath him. A spoke smashed into his chest, breaking his third rib and thrusting a jagged end of bone into his lung. He fell, writhing, screamed again as the ship heeled violently to starboard and the deck tilted at a terrifying angle.

'Abe!' The master swore, but he could not leave the wheel to help the stricken helmsman. He had to concentrate on the growing angle between the bowsprit and the breakers as he eased the ship away from danger. Closing his eyes, he redoubled his effort on the wheel, pushing against the pressure of wind and water.

The singing seaman began to scream as danger sobered him. 'God save us all, but it's the Corbie!'

'Abe!' the master shouted again as the helmsman rolled down the now steep deck, his hands scrabbling for a hold on the planking. For a second Abe stared into the master's eyes, silently pleading for help that could not be given, then the ship lurched sickeningly and threw him over the side. There was no scream.

'Abe!' the master yelled for a third time. He knew that the seaman was beyond aid. The sea had taken him, as it threatened to take them all. He grabbed at the wheel and swore as the spokes spun madly through his hands. 'Steering ropes have snapped,' he said, and raised his voice above the howl of the gale.

'Abandon ship. Everyone! *Abandon ship!*' He staggered as another wave broke on the stern and waist-high water flooded forward, knocking him to the deck. A line snapped aloft and began to flog against the mainmast, while a block crashed to the deck from above, rolling madly as the ship pitched. The singing seaman began to wail in terror.

The master hauled himself to his feet. 'Sarah! Get the children!' Gasping, he pushed astern to the wildly flapping door of the deckhouse. 'Sarah!' He looked to his wife, hating himself for ever agreeing that she should accompany him on this final part of the voyage, aching with fear for her safety, while still hoping to save as many of his crew as possible.

'Martin!' Sarah held a child in each hand. Seawater had plastered her nightgown to her plump body and smeared her hair across her face. She fought to control the panic in her eyes, but her chin remained as firm as ever. 'Are we going down?'

The sight of his wife steadied Martin. He was never more proud of her than at that moment. Drawing strength from her presence, he took a deep breath and stepped forward, even as the ship staggered under a succession of blows. A terrible splintering from aloft told of a spar snapping, and blocks thundered down on to the deck. 'It's the Corbie, Sarah.'

For a second Sarah closed her eyes and her grip on the children tightened. For a second the fear showed in her face. 'Then we're in the hands of the Lord.'

He reached for her then and they touched, man to woman, husband to wife, soul to soul, until there was a sound unlike anything they had heard before, the tearing of canvas and wood as the ship squealed on to the dripping fangs of the Black Corbie. The foremast was gone, its stump a sneering reminder of a once-proud ship. The bowsprit rose in a tangle of rigging and splintered wood as a wave broke explosively on the exposed keel and spray hammered at the standing canvas. With a sickening groan louder than anything that had gone before, the mainmast broke twenty feet above the deck and the wind flogged the ropes into a devil's dance against what remained.

'Oh, pity help us,' Sarah prayed. Releasing herself from the comfort of her husband's arms, she clung to her children, closed her eyes and fought the tears that threatened to render her useless at this time when they needed her most.

The mizzen yard broke free and speared downward, to be temporarily halted by the mizzen brace, and then it spun, smashing through the deckhouse. It lifted the master off his feet and hurled him against the stump of the mainmast. The snap of his ribs could be heard even above the tortured whine of the wind, and bright blood burst from a mouth that was now bereft of teeth. He lay there, a broken and bloodied thing that screamed its agony until the next wave cleansed it over the side.

'Martin!' Sarah's horror was brief. Born to the sea, she steadied herself with the realization that she must mourn later. First she had to try and save the children. That was her duty now. One glance at the ship assured her that there was no hope of remaining on board. The impact of the Black Corbie had broken her back, her masts were gone and the sea was beginning to pound her to pieces. Sarah could see only one member of the crew, and he was clinging to a hatch cover in frenzied terror. Fragments of cord and canvas bobbed amidst the frothing waves.

The children were wriggling, squalling their terror at this bedlam that had broken their ordered lives. 'Keep still!' Bracing herself on the sloping deck, Sarah shook them into silence. She heard the seaman give a despairing yell as a wave prised him from the hatch cover and nodded grimly. 'That will do,' she said, and, balancing both children in the crook of her left arm, she grabbed a coiled line from the outside of the deckhouse and inched forward.

For a seaman's wife and daughter it took only seconds to lash the children to the scarred wood, but the cover was heavier than she had imagined. She could not manoeuvre it to the side.

'Jesus save us!' Sarah bent over the hatch cover and pushed, feeling muscles tear deep inside her. Pain lanced through her, but the cover scraped over the deck. 'Sweet Jesus,' she prayed aloud, 'I don't ask for myself, but save my babies, please save my babies!'

As if in answer, a wave recoiled from the Black Corbie and hammered against the stricken hull, shoving it upright for a second before hissing in retreat. The ship seemed to judder, and then lurched down again, thundering into a trough of the waves. The jerk scraped the cover across the deck until it lay poised with one end over the side. Sarah looked and screamed her horror.

Despite her double-planked hull, black fangs of rock had pierced the ship in half a dozen places, one thrusting deep inside her hold to penetrate a cask of whale blubber. The greasy mess spilled out, fouling the waves. What remained of a seaman lay directly beneath Sarah, one leg rent loose and his belly torn open so the bowels and intestines coiled around his writhing body. Beyond that was the rock, jagged and strung with seaweed, half hidden beneath breakers and a haze of leaping spray. There was only death out there.

Sobbing, Sarah bent to the nearest child. 'I'm sorry, my angel, I'm so, so sorry, but maybe Jesus wants you with him now.' She kissed him lightly on the cheek just as the storm redoubled its efforts and a succession of mighty waves smashed against the tortured hull. Lifted bodily and tossed against the Corbie, the ship broke in two, with the aft section separating with an eruption of savage splinters. For one terrible second Sarah saw the ship's surgeon hanging on to a spar, his mouth open in an agonized appeal for help, and then the sea sucked him down. While two thirds of the ship remained on the rock, the stern spiralled clear, tumbling over and over in the ugly green waves to the north.

Sarah screamed, slipped on the greasy wood and rolled over as the hatch cover slithered into the sea. For what seemed like a lifetime she clung to the wooden frame as the waves pounded her, but with her nails scraping shallow grooves in the varnish she hauled herself to the second of her children. A dark mountain of water threw the hatch cover high in the air, where it hung for an instant before crashing back down. Sarah screamed again, gasping and choking as cold water surged down her throat into her lungs, but she kept hold of her child. There was an ugly roaring in her ears, a burning in her chest as she gulped the bitter water, again and again. She knew that she was dying but somewhere inside her was the thought that if she swallowed all the sea her children would survive.

5

'Gentle Jesus, save my babies. That's all I ask.'

Then the hatch cover broke surface and she saw safety ahead.

It was a light, flickering through the dark, yellow and vague, but it promised hope and life amidst this horror. Sarah lifted her hand in hopeful appeal, then realized that she had only one baby. The ropes that had held the other had parted during the frenzied journey from the ship. 'My baby, oh Jesus, guard and protect my baby.'

Another wave thundered against the hatch cover, lifted it and drove it toward land, with Sarah clinging to her remaining child as the pain of torn muscles wrenched at her. She coughed up blood and bile and salt water. The light remained, a symbol of safety and a promise of salvation. There was a line of breakers ahead and the cover was tossed upside down, scraping Sarah against harsh sand, tearing her nightdress and ripping the skin from the left side of her body. She tightened her grip on the child as the waves receded and she lay moaning in the surf of a bay, with the blaze of lanterns bobbing toward her.

Capable hands hauled the cover further up the beach, out of the pounding waves, and a broad face loomed over her, its features obscured by the yellow light of the lantern. Sarah heard concern in the voices as strong hands took hold of her. Unable to speak, she shook her head, clinging to her baby, until a knife sliced the ropes and freed both. Still holding her child, Sarah felt herself lifted further away from the sea and laid in the shelter of a twisted tree.

'A woman.' There were two people present, one man and one woman. 'And a baby.'

'Anything?' The voice was hollow in her ears.

'Aye.' The woman's face came closer to Sarah, inspecting her. 'Three rings. Nothing else. She's in her nightclothes.'

'Get them, then,' the man said, and Sarah felt something tugging at her fingers.

'They won't come. Her fingers are swollen.' There was a second's pause, then a sharp agony that caused Sarah to scream anew. 'I've cut the fingers off.' The woman's voice was casual.

6

'Nothing else? Here, let me see.' Sarah writhed in horror as the man wrenched away her clothes and inspected her naked body. 'No. Nothing here.' His laugh was crueller than the worst of the sea. 'Sometimes they hide things next to their skin. Not this one.' He dropped Sarah back on to the sodden sand.

'Will I cut her throat?' The woman pressed the blade of her knife under Sarah's ear.

'If you like, but she's dying anyway.'

The woman peered into Sarah's eyes. 'Aye, like enough. Come on, there may be more.' She led the way back to the surf, the yellow circle of light from her lantern bouncing against the beach.

Sarah turned on her side and reached for her baby, which lay squalling and unheeded on the sand. For a second she pressed the small body to her own, praying and sobbing as blood flowed from her mutilated hand and seeped from her mouth and ears. She was only dimly aware of the figure that loomed over her, but tightened her grip as the hands tried to remove the small body. 'My baby!'

'Mine now,' the voice said.

One

Northumberland, March 1804

Matthew grunted as another rut in the road threw him against the thinly padded interior of the coach. The man who sat opposite him swore and huddled deeper inside his thick travelling cloak. 'About time somebody did something about these roads,' he muttered, gripping his silver-topped cane, presumably in case it was stolen.

Matthew did not reply. He had heard that same phrase a score of times since the coach had left the Black Bull in Newcastle hours ago, and hundreds of times since it had left the Green Dragon in Bishopsgate. He stared out of the mud-spattered window, gloomy with tiredness despite the excitement at this new adventure. The sights and sounds of London seemed very far away up here in this bleak northern land of hills and moors and rain. He accepted that ruts and mud were as much a part of travelling as inconvenience and sour-tempered companions. They were barely worth mentioning.

He held his tricorne hat firmly in his lap, kept his feet rigidly together despite the cramp that gnawed at his left leg, and watched the progress of a single raindrop amidst the hundred that rolled down the window. Travelling was an interminable bore, with people becoming more uncouth the farther the distance from London, but if he concentrated on some complex algebraic formulae, the journey might pass more pleasantly.

The coach slowed as the horses struggled up a twisting incline that set the passengers at an acute angle and tried the patience of the driver to the utmost. Matthew glanced out of the window again and saw nothing but moorland, rising to ugly heights that seemed to stretch away for ever. Even the sheep appeared downcast in this dirty landscape.

'You'll partake of some snuff, sir?' The third passenger, a middle-aged woman, offered him a pinch from a silver and tortoiseshell snuffbox. When Matthew shook his head she smiled, sniffed up a generous amount and sneezed violently. Matthew turned aside, for once agreeing with his male companion's muttered expression of distaste. The fourth passenger was a Scottish Presbyterian lawyer with a face so humourless it seemed that his chief form of recreation was sucking the sourness from a lemon. He made no comment but reached inside his cloak, produced a small Bible and buried his long nose between the pages.

The coach lurched again, its two tons thumping into yet another rut so the axle creaked under the strain. The impact threw the woman forward, snuff spilling from her snuffbox on to Matthew's cloak. She clutched hold of him for support as he helped her retake her seat. 'Don't you have springs on your coaches up here? I do believe that this vehicle still uses thorough braces!'

The woman eyed him as though he were a Frenchman. 'You're from the south,' she accused. 'I thought you had a most unusual accent! Not from London, surely?' Her eyes were bright with renewed interest as her male companion grunted and stared pointedly at the fresh snuff stains on Matthew's cloak. The lawyer did not look up from his Bible.

'Indeed, ma'am.' Matthew regretted his lapse. He had no desire to converse with strangers in a coach, no matter for how long he was forced to endure their company.

'My brother was in London once,' the woman continued. 'He said it was a large city, but very noisy. You may have met him? A tall man with whiskers? His name was—'

'London is a very large city, ma'am,' Matthew interrupted rudely. 'There are many tall men with whiskers, so it is unlikely that I would remember him even if we had met.'

'Foulmire Cross!' The driver's roar saved any need for further conversation. 'Half an hour while we change the horses. Next stop Alnwick!'

Used to the perpetual bustle of southern coaching

9

establishments, Matthew was surprised at the grim silence of the inn at Foulmire Cross.

The Lord must have been in a sour mood when he created the forsaken fells that impeded progress from south to north. Virtually devoid of trees, they were riven with dark gullies through which torrents broiled, while a perpetual wind cropped the grass and heather. Relenting only slightly, He had allowed a pass through these hills, but tempered His mercy by scooping out the land to form a bowl of tepid marshland. Ever the optimist, Man had planted an inn at the summit and hacked a road just below the ridge of the hills.

Now a toll bar stretched across the road that led to Scotland some tens of miles to the north, and travellers stopped at the inn for their final sustenance in England. Matthew opened the door of the coach, groaning as he stretched his cramped legs. The building looked villainously bleak, with two storeys of dark whinstone and an arched doorway leading to a courtyard.

The perpetual drizzle only smeared the dirt on opaque windows, but the smell of food made Matthew realize that he was hungry, and the woman who adjusted her white cap at the door was curvaceous and could have been fetching, if she only washed once in a while.

The toll keeper pulled his tricorne hat firmly over his eyes and jammed a long-stemmed churchwarden pipe between his teeth. 'Spoken for,' he said, noting the interest in Matthew's eyes.

Matthew ignored him. 'Guard!' he ordered. 'Get my luggage out. I'm leaving the coach here.'

'May the good Lord protect you,' the lawyer broke his silence for the first time since he had boarded at York.

Matthew would have taken the mail-coach for preference, but the Edinburgh Diligence was cheaper, if slower and less reliable. He watched as the guard checked his waybill to ensure that Matthew was not mistaken about his destination, then opened the hind boot and hauled out his luggage: one large leather portmanteau with his name neatly printed on top, and a smaller iron-bound case that was securely locked.

'Careful with that, damn you!' Matthew strode forward as the guard gasped under the weight of the case and nearly dropped it on to the straw-strewn cobbles. 'What do you have in there? Cannonballs for Boney?' The guard did not look discomfited at being sworn at. 'Instruments. Delicate instruments.' Matthew took charge of his case and waited for the guard to hand down his portmanteau. It was unusual for a coach even to carry a guard, but when his cloak fell open, this man had a brace of pistols under his belt and Matthew had already noted the blunderbuss on his seat.

The guard made no attempt to close his cloak. 'Captain Ellwood is notorious in these parts,' he explained, and added, 'he's a highwayman,' as if talking to a child. Matthew nodded. The roads around London were infested with highwaymen, but he thought that the gentlemen of the road would have but meagre pickings here.

Carrying his luggage inside the front door of the inn, Matthew deposited it on the stone floor beside the curvaceous woman. She dropped in a slow curtsey. 'I'd like a room for the night, please,' he said curtly, 'and supper.' The woman disappeared into the recesses of the inn, her long apron rustling with every step. The place smelled of damp, horses and cooking. Raucous laughter sounded from within and the lanterns guttered foully.

'Come in, sir.' The smile of the woman compensated for most of the inn's shortcomings. 'You'll be a visitor to these parts, then?' Her accent was hard to Matthew's ears, but she lifted his heavy case with ease and guided him into a taproom where the tables were laden with food and maidservants bantered with half a dozen hirsute men who may have been cattle drovers or shepherds, and smelled like a combination of both. One spoke about the small fair at Hagshaw, and how he preferred the great Whit Fair, when the weather was better.

'Yes, I'm moving on tomorrow.'

'I'm sure you'll be very comfortable, sir.' The woman brushed her hip against Matthew as she passed, smiled an insincere apology and pulled out a chair. 'Moving on where, sir, if I may ask?'

11

After so many long hours in the coach, the plate of thick broth was more than appetizing. Matthew lifted his spoon. 'Onswick. Down by the coast.'

Matthew could feel the sudden interest in the room. The conversation ceased abruptly and two of the hirsute men turned to stare at him.

'Onswick? There's no coach runs there, sir.' The woman raised her eyebrows. 'Will you be hiring a horse?'

'I will,' Matthew confirmed as he addressed the soup. 'You do have some to hire, I presume?' He was gripped by sudden anxiety in case these northern inns did not have such facilities. 'This is a coaching and hiring establishment?'

'Of course we can accommodate your wishes, sir.' The woman stumbled over the syllables, as if she had learned them many years ago and had rarely used them since. 'I'm sure we can come to some arrangement concerning the cost.' She leaned closer, whispering confidentially, 'We'll put you upstairs, sir, for tonight.'

The woman helped carry his luggage to the room, touched his arm and left. The room was gloomy, with cold ashes still in the grate and no covering on the floorboards. At one time somebody had given the plaster walls a thin coat of white-wash, but now dark mould was showing through. Matthew sighed and glanced outside. The rain was becoming heavier, splattering against the multi-paned window, beyond which moorland rolled upward to the dimly seen ridge. It looked grim and bleak and harsh. Matthew sighed. Poets would no doubt find such scenery romantic, but he doubted if Wordsworth or Coleridge had ever spent the night in such a dismal inn, or had their senses assailed by the mingled stinks and sounds of a crowded stagecoach.

Pulling shut the curtain, he heard a murmur of conversation in the creaking corridor outside, turned down the cover of his bed and frowned. The insect that leaped on top of the once-white sheet was surely not alone, so he decided to sleep in the chair instead. Better to spend a night in discomfort than to provide sustenance for untold numbers of vermin. Where there were fleas there might also be lice or bedbugs or who knew what other infestations.

He watched the single candle flicker and prepared himself for the night. He could ignore the clatter of feet on the corridor floor, the blare of the horn as the mail-coach visited, the ringing clamp of hooves and rumble of iron-shod wheels on cobbles, but his mind was busy with work. He had been set two linked but distinct tasks, and although it was two years since he completed his apprenticeship, this was his first endeavour with no supervision. He knew that the next few weeks would stretch his skill to the utmost.

Stripping off his clothes, he washed in the ewer of tepid water, pulled his nightshirt over his head and doused the candle before lowering himself on to the chair with his travelling cloak pulled over him. It was not the most comfortable of sleeping places, but he had known worse. Ignoring a sudden outburst of revelry from the taproom beneath, he composed himself for sleep. The hooting of an owl somewhere outside seemed only to increase his sense of isolation. London seemed very far away.

It was dark. Matthew lay for a moment, unsure where he was or what had wakened him. Not noise, for he was used to that, but a presence, something that should not be there. He listened intently, trying not to move as he kept his breathing level. The floor creaked under the weight of a body and Matthew threw aside his cloak and sat up. He could feel the rapid beating of his heart.

'Who the devil's that?'

There was more noise; the scrape of feet on the floor and Matthew strode forward.

'I said, who's there?'

Reaching out, he grabbed hold of something that felt harsh and slightly sticky. He heard hoarse breathing and pulled the person toward him. 'Now we'll see!' Matthew threw back the curtain so a faint glint of starlight penetrated the room, illuminating what seemed to be a tall man with an unruly mass of hair. 'Name yourself, fellow!'

The man moved in his grip and pushed hard so that Matthew staggered backward. Something caught the back of his leg; he put out a hand to regain his balance, tripped and

13

sat back heavily in his chair. The shadowy man merged into the darkness.

'Who's that, I say? Declare yourself, sir!'

There was the patter of footsteps, an echoing bang as something heavy crashed to the floor, then the door was flung open and somebody hurried out. Matthew had another glimpse of a lean figure in a short coat with that unmistakable explosion of hair, then he rose and plunged into the corridor, shouting, 'That man! Stop, I say! Stop, thief!'

As Matthew ran along the corridor, each door opened and confused faces peered out at him.

'What's all the noise, fellow?'

'Can you not keep quiet?'

'What the devil do you mean by that racket?'

There were voices raised in surprise, anger and consternation as seemingly every guest at the inn demanded to know who was making all the noise. Unheeding, Matthew strode on with his nightshirt flapping around his knees and his bare feet pattering on the floorboards. He rattled down the stairs and stared around the taproom. Glowing cinders were all that remained of the fire and the tables were empty. A grey hen that had once contained whisky lay on its side on the floor.

'Are you all right, sir? Why all the commotion?' The landlady appeared from a side doorway, carrying a candle in a pewter holder. Her hair was tied up in paper and her nightgown ended at shoes that she had pulled on to the wrong feet. She placed anxious hands on Matthew's shoulders. 'Is there something that I can do for you?'

Matthew pointed into the dark. 'There was a man in my room, madam. Some man prowling around.'

'A man, sir?' The woman placed the candle on one of the tables, its pool of yellow light chasing away all the mystery of the night. 'Surely not! Did he harm you, sir? Or take anything? I don't like the sound of that, not at all.'

'Harm me?' Matthew shook his head. 'No. No, I'm unharmed. And I have not checked to see if anything was taken.'

'No? Nobody passed me, I'm sure.' Her voice rose a little.

'Perhaps you had a bad dream, sir?' She nodded reassurance. 'Come along then, and we will see. Come on.' The landlady's voice was soothing and her hand warm on Matthew's arm as she escorted him back up the stairs into the babbling crowd of guests. 'It's all right, everybody. This gentleman has had a bad dream. Go back to your beds now, and sleep tight. Come along, sir.'

When the landlady lit a second candle, Matthew saw that his leather portmanteau had not been touched, but his case lay on the ground. Presumably that had been the loud bang that he had heard. Kneeling, he opened it quickly and scanned the contents, aware that the woman was watching but more concerned with any possible damage to his possessions than with her inquisitiveness.

'All right, sir? Is there anything missing?' Holding her candle high, she peered over his shoulder. Matthew felt her pressing against him.

'No. Nothing missing,' Matthew confirmed. 'I think that I disturbed him before he could take anything.' He could hear the inn settling down as the guests returned to their rooms.

'A bad dream then.' Dismissing Matthew's theory, the landlady nodded her understanding. 'It happens sometimes in a strange bed and after a long journey.' She glanced at the obviously unused bed. 'I'll be saying goodnight then, sir, but if you're still afraid, the key is hanging on a hook behind the door.' There was a moment's hesitation before the landlady stepped outside.

She closed the door firmly and Matthew could have sworn he heard a derisive laugh as her footsteps pattered back along the corridor. It was only then that he became aware of the black smear of tar on his hand. That had been the slight stickiness he had felt when he grabbed hold of the intruder. What sort of man would cover his clothes in tar? Frowning, he scraped his hand as clean as he could and washed in what remained of the water in the ewer before locking the door and sinking back on to the chair.

He had been warned that people in the north were wild and unsophisticated, but he had thwarted the attempted theft without much difficulty. Matthew opened his portmanteau and pulled out the pistol that had cost much of his fortune. A man at home with mechanics, Matthew had insisted on a Joseph Manton, and now examined it with pride.

Matthew had worked with Manton at one time as an apprentice, and knew that he was probably the finest pistol maker in the world. After personally helping select the most suitable piece for his purpose, Manton had ushered Matthew to the range that sat beneath his Mayfair workshop. Only when he could hit the bull eight times out of ten did Matthew leave. His logical mind enjoyed the mechanics of Manton's craftsmanship, while the mathematic precision of angles of aim and allowance of windage were pure pleasure. Only now, with the possibility of death or injury so far from home, did the reality hit. This smooth handled, efficient machine might save his life.

He loaded with care, pouring powder down the muzzle and tapping home the ball with the small metal ramrod that sat under the barrel, before adding the wad to wedge the half-ounce of lead in place. Cocking the pistol, Matthew placed it on the floor between his feet, settled back in the chair and knew that he was ready if the intruder returned.

A hubbub of noise awoke him. Cursing, Matthew stooped to scoop up the Manton, opened the door and peered outside. The man who cleaned the boots was rushing from room to room, arguing with the washerwoman with her pile of clean linen. A porter carried out baggage and trunks to the mail-coach, whose guard was blowing his long horn with such gusto that an entire rookery took to raucous flight. A barber's boy carried a splashing basin of hot water and a handful of cut-throat razors as he scurried behind his master, whose bag leaked a fine line of hair powder along the floor.

'Good morning, sir,' the landlady greeted him brightly.

'Morning,' Matthew returned automatically. He glanced outside.

The hairiest of the drovers kicked at his dog, which barked madly at a small herd of lowing cattle, while in the far corner of the courtyard a blacksmith hammered at a

16

horseshoe. Sparks hissed against his long leather apron. Matthew shook away the sleep and breathed in air that was crisp and cool.

The smell of breakfast drifted from the taproom and Matthew was able to wish his fellow travellers a good morning, all but forgetting the distractions of the previous night. There was loud laughter and boisterous good humour, a drover teasing him about his nightmare and another wondering if the good lady of the house had comforted him to sleep. The Scottish lawyer looked up disapprovingly from his bowl of barley gruel and said nothing.

'You're going to Onswick, I heard?' The carter was burly, with flaxen hair that hung over a face already flushed with beer. 'Well, God speed you, fellow.' Others in the room echoed his laugh.

'Why?' Matthew asked. 'What's the matter with Onswick?'

'You don't know the stories, then?' The carter had obviously enjoyed a good breakfast. 'But I won't frighten you, what with you being a Londoner. I'll just say that if you walk into Onswick sane, you'll walk out mad as a winter-born hare.' His glance around the company at table brought instant agreement.

'Aye, man, they don't like strangers in Onswick. They'll give you the Onswick stare.' The drover who had enquired about his sleep demonstrated with a squint-eyed scowl that had his companions nodding. 'It's not a place I'd go to. Even the kyloe would avoid Onswick. You'll leave mad, right enough.'

Matthew smiled, shaking his head. 'And have you been there?'

'Not I,' the drover said, spearing a fat piece of mutton on his plate.

'You surprise me, sir, for you show all the attributes of lunacy.' This time the drover was the object of the table's amusement, joining in with a fine display of good humour. Morning seemed to have dissipated all the suspicion of the night as Matthew ate well, finishing with a mug of small ale that tasted stronger than anything bearing a similar name in London, and called the landlady to see about hiring a horse.

Matthew was surprised to learn that Northumberland had a tradition of horsemanship. Both the landlady and the groom were knowledgeable as they showed him over their selection of animals.

'Do you want a fast horse, sir, or a stayer? Something sturdy for long distances, or showy, for speed?' The landlady's eyes twinkled. 'Is it a young lady that you have come to visit, sir? If so, she will want to see a tall, fast thoroughbred. Like the rider, if I may be so bold?'

'Not a lady.' Matthew shook his head. 'A stayer, sturdy and docile. I don't want a bone-setter for I do not intend to enter any races.'

The landlady consulted the groom before pointing to a medium sized, undistinguished looking brown mare that stood in a stall at the back of the stables. 'That's the one for you, sir. We call her Sally.'

'Sally it shall be,' Matthew agreed, patting the horse.

With the rain clearing overnight and the sun dappling through flitting clouds, the moor seemed a different place to that of the previous evening. Rather than bleak, the broad reaches of heather invited investigation, while the herd of dun cattle plodding south invoked a sense of timeless continuity. What had seemed forbidding to a tired traveller was invigorating to a man awakening to a fresh adventure.

Matthew's eyes followed the line of hawthorn trees that straggled to the crest of the Heights, where a great iron beacon probed upward. If the French should land, that beacon would be lit as part of a chain that stretched from Dover to Edinburgh, rallying the Volunteers and Militia and warning the country that there were French to repel. After meeting the customers at the inn, Matthew rather pitied any Frenchman who tried to conquer this part of the country. Smiling, he blew into Sally's nostrils, fondled her ears and touched his heels to her flanks. However backward their innkeeping, these northerners certainly knew how to care for their animals. Sally was as well groomed and as fit as any animal he had ever seen.

It was pleasant to ride on such a morning, with his portmanteau and case secure by his side and the road not too muddy beneath him. He remembered the directions that the landlady had given him. Follow the road along the base of Hornshope Heights, pass the estate of Harestone and continue down to the coast. 'Two hours of a journey on horseback,' she had said, 'given fair weather.' Then she had paused. 'But watch for highwaymen and the like. It's a strange place, the Heights.'

Matthew had nodded and tapped the butt of his pistol. 'I'll watch,' he said. After surviving the environs of London, where highwaymen literally queued up for the privilege of holding up a coach, the odd felon in the north would hardly be a threat. All the same, once he was clear of the inn he checked the pistol was loaded and that the flint was dry.

Now, with a bite in the March air and birdsong sweetening the sky, he could enjoy this ride. The vibrant sun was barely above the Heights shadowing the road, with patches of spring frost glittering and ice rimming the most shallow of the puddles. These hills were unlike any he had seen in the south, nearly bare of trees, perhaps a thousand feet high and riven with gullies gushing with clear water that sometimes overflowed on to the road.

Skylarks trilled above and rabbits broke across the path, jinking from side to side in their frantic search for shelter before one of the patrolling buzzards swooped. Matthew followed the road, avoiding the worst of the potholes, and grunted when he reached an abrupt gap in the Heights, through which a road trailed south. He could see the pillared gates of a country estate.

'Harestone, no doubt,' he told himself, and heeled his horse onward. There was a rare copse of trees here, and an isolated spur of the hills that would make a fine vantage point. On an impulse, Matthew fastened Sally to one of the trees, and extracting his spyglass from his case, clambered up the spur.

The grass was slippery beneath his riding boots, the wind chill around his ears, and he had to use one hand to keep the tricorne hat from blowing off his head. Unused to such violent exercise, Matthew was panting long before he reached the summit, and allowed himself five minutes in which to recover before he extended the spyglass and peered eastward.

There was a group of Scots pines on a knoll nearly opposite him, and past that, continuing in an irregularly decreasing
ridge, the Heights thrust into the sea only a few miles ahead.
Beyond the point was a group of islands and rocks, which
Matthew studied before he scanned the shoreline. He saw
low cliffs and a straggle of trees whose skeletal branches
clutched at the high sky, but there was no sign of any village.
He frowned, wondering if he had somehow missed the track.
There was farmland and the slow moving shape of sheep; a
handful of black cattle and a wide scattering of cottages with
low stone walls and roofs of heather thatch. Blue smoke
smeared each habitation and such people as he could see
looked cold and miserable as they trudged round-shouldered
across the landscape.

On an impulse, Matthew swung the telescope back toward
the Harestone estate. He watched a lone horseman ride along
the base of the hill and enter a steep-sided grassy hollow, a
basin in the hills. Although his position allowed him to see
into the hollow, Matthew guessed it would be invisible from
any lesser height. When the rider dismounted and threw back
her cloak, Matthew realized that it was a woman.

Moving his position, Matthew slipped on the wet grass,
swore and recovered, but his flurry of movement had alerted
the woman, who glanced up, hastily recovered her cloak and
was back on her horse in an instant. Wondering what activity
he had interrupted, Matthew hurried downhill to Sally in
case the woman should ride up and demand an explanation.
He had broken no law, but as a stranger, he thought it best
to withdraw. Kicking in his spurs, he pushed Sally along the
road.

As his altitude dropped, the heather changed to rough
grass, home to sheep and the occasional hare. He rode on,
slightly worried that there was still no indication of any
settlement. Where he had expected a church spire or the roof
of a manor house, there was nothing except the road, which
seemed to stretch onward until it disappeared into the sea.

Matthew breathed his relief when the road suddenly dipped
and he saw a collection of cottages clustered by a tight cove.
He halted for a second, looking through the haze of blue

20

smoke to the confusion of rooftops and beyond to the sea. This was his destination. Matthew stopped and took a deep breath. Here was his destiny; what happened in Onswick could determine his future life.

Two

Onswick, March 1804

Lightly snapping the reins against Sally's neck, Matthew
began his careful descent of the twisting road. There
were two dog-leg bends to negotiate, then a steep slope with
a breath-catching drop to his left, and finally a dark area of
stunted hawthorn trees, among which a score of finches chattered and bounced. Only then was he among the first of
Onswick's homes, with the pistol loose under his cloak and
his eyes wary for danger.

It was not what he had expected. After hearing the stories
at the inn, he had imagined a place of ramshackle huts
populated with scarred people armed with muskets and
cutlasses. Instead there were prosperous looking cottages
standing without design or plan, some companionably
close, as if to discuss the events of the day, others in aloof
isolation. Many had well cared for gardens, with walls
built of a curious yellow brick, while the roofs were a
mixture of reed thatch or ochre pantiles. Even the decoration spoke of individuality, for some were brightly
painted, others coated in tar against the weather, but a
profusion of small and shining windows stared cheerfully
at him.

Down here, chimney smoke hung low and blue, while a
profusion of children and dogs gambolled in the narrow
streets. A queue of women gossiped at the well, men carried
fish baskets toward the harbour, or rolled kegs over the
ground, while the iron clamour of a blacksmith's shop echoed
from the cliff walls.

'Excuse me,' Matthew addressed a weathered looking
man, who grinned gap-toothed at him without a hint of the

introversion he had come to expect in rustic clumpertons. 'Could you direct me to the inn?'

The man nodded, bright eyes scrutinizing him. 'Down by the harbour.' A jerk of his thumb indicated the direction. 'You'll be the Londoner, then?'

'Indeed.' Matthew could not hide his surprise. 'How did you know that?'

The man's grin widened, his eyes never straying from Matthew's face. 'I heard tell. It's a long way from London, mister. You must have important business to travel so far.'

Matthew chose to regard that as a statement rather than a question. 'A long way indeed. Down by the harbour, you say? Thank you kindly, sir.'

Each house that Matthew passed bore some reminder that they were by the sea. The first had a pair of ship's lanterns hanging outside; the door of the second had once graced the cabin of some shipmaster and a collection of creels crowded the front of a third.

Although Onswick was not a large village, navigation was difficult in the tangled streets. There were small terraced rows mixed with individual cottages, winding lanes that seemed to lead nowhere, open spaces beset with upturned boats and sheds, then finally a broader road that ended at the stone built harbour. Half a dozen open cobles bobbed in the shelter of the harbour wall, while a dark hulled coaster discharged coal into an open cart, to the accompaniment of mingled curses and caustic humour from the crew. A litter of creels and baskets, nets and oars spread along the cobbled pier, while a creaking sign swung over the doorway of a two-storey building. 'The Mermaid's Arms', it proclaimed, together with a vivid picture of a green-tailed mermaid whose arms were extended to embrace the fortunate to her ample bosom. The remains of last season's woodbine clung gamely to a lattice that clambered up the walls.

'And you'll be the gentleman from London?' the innkeeper greeted him. 'Your room is all ready.' He was a tall man, neat in his dark clothing, with hands too large and rough for his profession. 'My name is Anderson, Billy Anderson.'

Matthew watched the stable boy care for Sally before asking how Anderson knew that he was coming.

'Oh, we all knew you were coming. We just did not know your name Mr . . .?

'Pryde. Matthew Pryde.'

There seemed to be a long gap before the innkeeper spoke again. 'Mr Pryde, sir.' His eyes surveyed Matthew from the top of his tricorne hat to the scuffed riding boots. 'If you'll follow me, I'll show you your room. Will you be staying long, sir? Or are you just resting from a longer journey?'

'I may be staying for some time,' Matthew told him cautiously.

They entered a kitchen that obviously doubled as a parlour. It was comfortably furnished with a well-oiled table and hair-bottomed chairs, while a long-case clock welcomed them with a melodious ticking that augmented the crackle of the fire. An old man glanced up from a newspaper that looked to be at least a week old, acknowledged them with a wave of his pipe and returned to his reading.

'You'll be snug as a bug here, sir,' Billy Anderson assured him.

Matthew nodded. The Mermaid's Arms seemed a world away from the inn at Foulmire Cross. Only the slightest tension pervaded the atmosphere of prosperity. 'Your inn has an interesting name,' he said.

'Yes, sir. An old legend of a mermaid that haunted the bay.' Anderson smiled. 'Old women's stories, sir, but we like to keep traditions alive around here.'

There was a cheerful bustle and pleasant aromas from a back kitchen, and the sound of a woman's voice rose in song. Plump and cheerful, the singer bustled past Anderson to replace patterned plates in the Dutch dresser that occupied most of one wall. Noticing Matthew, she smiled and curtseyed, before hurrying back to her work.

Matthew followed Anderson up a flight of polished wooden stairs to a large room that overlooked the harbour.

'Will this do, sir?'

Matthew tested the sturdy Dutch bed that squatted beneath

a brass ship's lantern. It felt firm, and when he lifted the coverlet there was no sign of unwanted livestock.

'It will do very well, Mr Anderson,' he approved. 'I intend to be some time. Unless I can lease a house in the area?'

Anderson screwed up his face, as if in deep thought. 'Begging your pardon, sir, but there's little call for leased property here. Her Ladyship is quite particular about that, meaning no offence. We don't get many visitors in Onswick, you see. Not much here for them.' Anderson dismissed the entire village with a single shake of his head. 'We used to have a few fish merchants and shipowners, but you don't appear to be a nautical gentleman, sir, if you'll pardon me for saying.'

'Nautical? No, I'm not.' Matthew allowed the innkeeper to carry his portmanteau while he carefully placed his case on the table that stood in the centre of the room. 'So you don't know of a house to lease?'

'I'll watch out for one.' The innkeeper held Matthew's eyes with no pretence of servility. 'Will that be all, sir?'

'For now, thank you.' Matthew nodded. 'I'll take a walk around the area and will eat on my return.'

'As you wish, sir. You be careful now. The cliffs can be dangerous, and the tides are fickle at any time of year.' Again there was that hesitation. 'Do you wish a guide?'

'No, I want to go myself.' Matthew had no desire to have a local reporting his every step to the village. 'I do wish a key for my room though.'

'You'll find a key on the table, sir, beside your case.' Just for a moment, Anderson's eyes probed the case, and then flicked back to Matthew's face. 'One thing, Mr Pryde; avoid the cove just to the north of Onswick. Especially if the bell rings.'

'Avoid the cove?' Matthew repeated. 'And why is that, pray? Local smugglers?' He injected as much sarcasm into his voice as he could, which the innkeeper parried with a small smile.

'No, sir. The smugglers would work if you were present or not. The cove belongs to Her Ladyship's daughter, and nobody else is allowed there. Best do as she wishes.'

About to argue, Matthew saw the concern in Anderson's face and nodded instead. 'Thank you for the warning, Mr Anderson. Her Ladyship appears to be very important in Onswick.'

'Yes, sir. Remember; don't go near the cove if you hear the warning bell. Indeed,' Anderson smiled, 'it would be best to head indoors if you hear the bell. Safer, sir.'

'Safer?'

But Anderson had already left the room. Matthew looked outside, following the line of the coast northward as he wondered who Her Ladyship's daughter might be, and how disregarding her wishes could possibly be dangerous. The boom of surf against the harbour wall drifted through the open window.

Leaning to one side to counterbalance the weight of his case, Matthew headed south toward the cliffs where the Hornshope Heights plummeted into the sea. Passing upturned cobles and the ridge of seaweed that marked the high tide line, he stopped among the bent grass that occupied the space between the beach and the cliffs, lowered his case and listened to the suck and surge of the sea.

Spray rose high as waves battered against the offshore rocks. There was a group of fisherwomen plucking mussels for bait and handing them to children to be shelled, while a man cleaned his longline. A second man was hurrying along the beach, clutching a cloak to him as he walked in a clumsy, round-shouldered gait.

Onswick crouched at the far end of the beach, untidy beneath its haze of blue smoke. The square tower of the church rose above every other building, a sign that, however atheistic France may become under its republican regime, England would remain in the sight of God. The beacon on top was a reminder that at times even the Lord might need some help.

Matthew smiled, reassured at the essential normality of a village he had been warned might be barbarously unfriendly. Lifting his case, he turned away from Onswick, faced the tumbled rocks that marked the tail of the Heights and wondered what Mr Denton would think of him now. He, who had called upon a sedan chair at every opportunity, was now gasping like a grampus as he slogged over the crumbled rocks, cursing the case whose weight threatened to tip him into the sea.

Matthew swore at the green slime and birdlime that made the rocks slippery. He blasphemed as he stumbled over a loose stone, but persevered, clambering ever upward until he reached a vantage point from where he could look out to sea. The cliff had eased into a broad, weather-smoothed ledge where a conveniently placed boulder could serve as a seat. There was another beacon here, a simple iron tripod topped with a brazier that was prepared with wood and coal and protected with a canvas cover. Matthew considered that this beacon would be an unpopular posting on a wet night, but dismissed the thought, placed his case on the ground and eased the cramped muscles of his arm.

He could hear the roar of waves breaking on the group of small islets and rocks, and saw the spray and spindrift thrown high into the air. Opening his case, he removed the brass spyglass. As he focussed, the islets leaped into view, a confused mass of sharp rock and frothing water, black and green and silver, with seabirds perched on the extremities and tendrils of seaweed rising with each wave.

There was one sizeable island of perhaps half a mile in length, supported by a group of sea stacks, and two small islets with near-vertical cliffs. In between was the surge of the sea, tidal races meeting their own backlash in a frenzy of foam that made Matthew shudder. He had heard that two score ships had foundered here within living memory, and nobody knew how many more in the preceding centuries.

'The Black Corbie.' The voice came from his elbow and Matthew looked around in surprise. 'Not one of our Lord's most beautiful creations.'

Matthew recognized the man who had been hurrying along the beach. He was tall and slim, with an old-fashioned cloak that flapped around his legs and an even more old-fashioned feather-top wig that seemed to balance precariously on his head.

'Positively ugly, I would say,' Matthew agreed.

27

The man nodded. 'In some eyes, maybe, but everything has a purpose.'

'Perhaps so.' Matthew watched a cormorant suddenly plunge from the edge of the Corbie, to reappear seconds later with a fish squirming in its mouth. 'The birds seem to approve.'

'All God's creatures.' The man started, ducked away suddenly and began to scrabble on the ground at Matthew's feet. 'Don't move, sir. Whatever you do, don't move!'

Matthew stood still as the man plucked something from between his shoes. 'Are you all right, sir?'

'All right? Of course I am. Did you not see it? Look.' The man arose and proffered his cupped hand, in which sat a small beetle. 'Is she not beautiful?'

'Lovely,' Matthew agreed, recoiling a little. The creature was black and shiny, with many legs.

'Lovely indeed. I shall take her home forthwith and identify her.' The man adjusted his wig, which had tilted in his sudden swoop. 'I don't recognize her at all. It is my aspiration to discover some new species, you see, and give it my own name.' Pulling a small jar from his pocket, the man placed the beetle carefully inside.

'Create your own immortality, then,' Matthew said, and the man smiled. 'If I see any more interesting insects I will tell you.'

'That would be most kind of you.' The man sounded genuinely grateful.

Matthew continued to examine the rocks. 'Do you know the Black Corbie well?' He flinched as a wave rose full fifteen feet into the air and thundered on to the furthest edge of the rock. Even at this distance he could feel the vibration. Viewed through the spyglass, spindrift seemed to hang like an opaque curtain before the wind blew it away and another wave rose in turn.

'We all know the Corbie,' the man said soberly. 'I am afraid that it is part of our existence.'

'You've been out there?'

The man shook his head. 'I have not, but some of the fishermen lay lobster pots around the lee of the rock. A dangerous

28

occupation, but lobster is quite a favourite in Onswick.' He paused for a second, and Matthew recognized the first of the delicate questions that would attempt to draw from him the purpose of his visit. 'Do you enjoy lobsters where you come from? London, isn't it?'

There seemed to be a long, level area on the large island, although the sluicing of the sea made it difficult to tell exactly what was rock and what was undulating weed. 'London, yes. And no, I've never eaten lobster. Eels, though, and oysters.' He lowered the spyglass, realizing that he would have no more peace in which to work.

'You should try them.' The man tucked his jar into some private corner of his cloak and extended a hand. 'I'm Charles Grover.'

'Matthew Pryde.'

It must have been the sudden increase in the wind that made Grover wince, but the shock remained in his eyes while he held Matthew's hand. The words seemed to come slowly to his lips. 'Have you visited this parish before, Mr Pryde?'

'Not ever, Mr Grover,' Matthew assured him. 'I grew up beside the Thames, not the North Sea. Why do you ask?'

Grover shook his head, using his left hand to clutch at his wig, which had again begun a slow slide down his face. 'For a minute there I thought that I recognized you. Perhaps I saw you in London.'

'That must be it, then,' Matthew agreed, gently removing his hand from Grover's grasp. He did not like to pull the longbow, but he was not inclined to discuss his life with a stranger.

Grover took a step backward. 'Now, Mr Pryde, we do not get many visitors up here. Is there a specific reason for your journey? Something that I can help with?' There was sudden animation in the ascetic face. 'Perhaps some aspect of natural history? Are you of a scientific bent, Mr Pryde?'

Matthew shook his head, strangely sorry to see the enthusiasm fade from Grover's eyes. 'No, Mr Grover, I am afraid that I have little interest in natural history.' He snapped his spyglass shut. 'However, perhaps you can help me with some advice?'

'Of course!' Grover was all eagerness. 'Just ask.'

'I would like to visit the Black Corbie by boat. I would like to land on the largest island and have a closer look. Who would be best capable of taking me?'

'Why, Mr Pryde, what a strange request. Most people try to avoid the Black Corbie, not seek to land there.' Grover shrugged, which was an unusual gesture for an Englishman. 'The Corbie is a dangerous place, but I am sure that if you offered suitable recompense, one of the fishermen would oblige. You could try Mr Megstone – Robert Megstone; he's a daring fellow if any is.'

'Robert Megstone. Thank you.' Matthew stored the name in his memory. 'Well, Mr Grover, I think I've seen enough here for the present.' As Matthew replaced the spyglass in his case, Grover scrabbled around the rocks, prising up loose stones in his search for insects.

They walked back together, with Grover varying between silence and bursts of volatility in which he spoke about the bird life of this part of the coast, the unseasonably pleasant weather and the course of the war with France. 'Lord Chevington's Yeomanry are busy galloping their horses, pinking turnips with their sabres and shouting, "Cut them down, the villains, the hounds of hell!" They say that there is an army of invasion poised on the coast of France, ready to board ships at a minute's notice.'

'Do they, indeed?' Matthew pretended surprise. 'And who says this, pray?' He waited until Grover had chased some small creature along the beach, only to be foiled as it burrowed into the sand and disappeared.

'Why, everybody, Mr Pryde. The news is all over the parish.' Grover came closer and lowered his voice to a whisper. 'They say that the French prepare the way by sending spies over, to search for possible landing sites.'

'Ah!' Matthew nodded. 'Is that what they say?' For a moment he wondered if the good people of Onswick believed him to be a French spy. 'If I see any Frenchmen, I will be sure to let you know.'

'Is that what you were looking for on the Black Corbie?

Frenchmen?' Grover was grinning as he pointed to Matthew's case. Matthew shook his head. 'No, not Frenchmen.' He was not yet ready to divulge his interest in the Black Corbie. As Grover lifted a hand in salutation to men on the stantage, the area of common land squeezed between the beach and the Heights, Matthew sought a distraction from the ever more pressing questions.

'Mr Grover, can you hear a bell ringing? Not the church bell surely, not on a Saturday.'

Grover halted his explanation of the social habits of the ant in mid-sentence. He cocked his head to one side. 'No, that's not the church bell. We'll have to hurry, Mr Pryde. That's Her Ladyship's warning bell. We'll have to get indoors quickly.' Grover seemed quite agitated as he grabbed Matthew's arm and guided him over the last few yards of the beach and into the village.

'Why?' Matthew shook off Grover's hand. 'Why indoors?'

'Into the Mermaid now, and hurry. Her Ladyship does not like to be kept waiting.'

About to argue, Matthew realized that the streets were emptying of people. Fisherwomen abandoned their creels and bait; fishermen left their nets; old men who had been gathered to gossip at the pier head and even children were hurrying to get indoors as the ugly clamour of the bell echoed through the village.

Billy Anderson stood at the door of the inn ushering people inside. He nodded to Matthew, checked to ensure that the street was clear and slammed shut the door. 'Glad to see you are here, sir,' he said, 'for it's not wise to cross Her Ladyship.'

'Cross Her Ladyship? I don't follow?' Matthew moved to the window, just as Anderson closed the shutters.

'Best not look, sir, just in case.'

The sound of the bell increased, then faded away, and Matthew realized that the bellman was patrolling the streets. He asked Anderson what was happening.

'I believe that I warned you about Her young Ladyship's bell, sir,' Anderson reminded. 'She likes to bathe in the sea, so sends the bellman to warn the village. It's just her little

31

whim. When the bell rings, we all retire indoors until she's finished. I did warn you about the cove.'

Matthew stared. 'So we're all to do nothing while Her Ladyship takes a bath?' He shook his head in wonderment.

'Indeed no, sir, Miss Grace Fenwick, Her Ladyship's daughter, is not taking a bath. She's swimming, I believe, although I've never seen her.'

'Good God!' About to laugh, Matthew realized that nobody else in the inn was amused. 'Miss Fenwick must be very important then?'

Anderson looked at Grover before nodding. 'Her Ladyship owns the village, sir –' he spoke slowly – 'and if Miss Fenwick wishes to swim in private, then we will respect her wishes.'

'And if I don't? If I choose to walk outdoors just now?'

'I'm afraid we could not let that happen, sir.' Anderson placed a hand on the handle of the door. 'Best to stay inside, Mr Pryde.' Although he spoke softly, there was no mistaking his determination.

The room was suddenly very quiet. Weather-beaten fishermen and their capable wives mingled with coal-smeared seamen from the collier brig and more enigmatic mariners who wore brass rings in their left ear. All were watching him, some with fear in their eyes, others with surprise, but all with suspicion.

Matthew placed his case on the ground and forced a smile. He might need the help of these men in the near future. 'In that case, Mr Anderson, would you and your friends care to join me in a drink?' He was almost overwhelmed with the sudden goodwill from the clientele of the Mermaid.

The church of St Cuthbert looked as if it was an organic extension of the rocky mound on which it was built. Square, with a squat tower and a round-headed doorway complete with worn carvings of strange animals, it sat a hundred yards from the harbour in a tiny churchyard in which gravestones fought for space. Matthew spent a few minutes reading the inscriptions on the stones as he watched the congregation gather.

'Jacob Charleton, fisherman.'

'Simon Charleton, fisherman.'
'William Wharton, mariner.'
'Mary Wharton, weaver.'
'Sarah Megstone, beloved mother and wife.'
'William Anderson, mariner, and his wife, Mary.'

Four surnames predominated – Anderson, Wharton, Charleton and Megstone – and Matthew guessed that the families were closely interrelated. The dates crept back for centuries, with each generation sharing similar Christian names and professions.

Some stones were decorated with carved vessels with single masts and billowing sails, and one with three masts and the splendid inscription 'Walter Megstone, Master Mariner, sailing to the arms of the Lord'. Then there were the memorials on which the names were unreadable, weathered through time so that only a fragment of grey stone protruded through the harsh soil. Most poignant of all was the large stone in the darkest corner of the churchyard, shaded by a yew tree from whose branches rain water wept on to the sad spring grass.

'Known only to the Lord', it read, 'cast up by the sea and buried in this place'. A vivid carving of a ship in distress surmounted the inscription.

Matthew paused for a moment at this stone, and would have knelt in prayer had he not been so aware of the lively conversation of the villagers who filed into the church. Although they were all dressed in their Sunday best, with women limping in unfamiliar shoes and men in broadcloth or homespun that only escaped from the closet one day a week, the people of Onswick did not look particularly solemn.

Rooks competed with seagulls to make more noise than the chattering congregation, while the church bell clattered in the tower overhead. Waiting until the last of the stragglers sauntered into the church, Matthew entered, nodding to the beadle as he searched for a pew. There were none vacant, so he squeezed against the bare stone wall at the rear and waited for the conversations to subside and the sermon to begin.

Matthew was not a particularly religious man, but had

been trained to attend church on Sundays, and did so as a matter of routine rather than in search for salvation. On the few occasions that he missed the Sunday service, he felt uneasy, and then would pray in earnest for forgiveness, so he found that it was better to conform to his old habits and obtain peace of mind. Now he watched the congregation chatter cheerfully together.

There were young men exchanging meaningful glances with girls who lowered their eyelids in feigned shyness, and children who restrained their exuberance until their parents' attention was elsewhere. There were the devout, who took the opportunity to pray, and the guilty, who clutched their Bibles and hoped for a deliverance that they did not believe they deserved. Matthew felt mild surprise when Charles Grover, in his wig and neat grey clothes, mounted the pulpit and raised his hand for the vestry prayers.

The sermon was longer than Matthew expected, and impressed him with its power and eloquence. He watched as the sexton, a small, nervous man with a face of innocence that surely did not belong in Onswick, read from a huge prayer book, running his finger along each line to ensure his own accuracy. The sermon was followed by hymns with which he was unfamiliar, but which the fishermen in the congregation sang powerfully. Before Matthew could relax there was a christening that ended in comedy as the baby put forth a podgy hand and grabbed Grover's wig. After an initial undignified tussle, Grover relinquished control and continued his service with his cropped grey hair exposed to public scrutiny. The unrestrained laughter of his flock subsided as he held up his hand for the final benediction.

'O God, grant your protection to ships at sea, but if it be thy inscrutable will, O Lord, in this season of inclement weather, to inflict the doom of total loss, let thy mercy direct them to the shore of this kindly and deserving place.'

The 'Amen' that followed was uttered with genuine enthusiasm.

As the congregation filed out, buzzing with conversation, the Reverend Grover shook each by the hand and enquired after their health or family. As he came to Matthew he adjusted the wig that the newly baptised baby had at last released. 'Well, Mr Pryde, I hope that you gained something from the service?'

Matthew grasped the hand. 'Indeed I did, Reverend, but you may not need the last portion of it for much longer.'

'And why not, pray?' Grover asked.

'Because I am here to aid the Lord in protecting ships at sea. I hope to ascertain the possibility of building a lighthouse on the Black Corbie.'

Matthew did not expect the sudden hush that followed his announcement, or the single muttered comment, 'Her Ladyship will hear about this.'

Three

Black Corbie, March 1804

They set off with the morning tide, just as dawn cracked the eastern dark. Waves like oil hushed along the wall of the harbour or broke in shining phosphorescence against the hull of the coble and splashed over the low gunwales. Huddled on his thwart, Matthew could only admire the skill of Robert Megstone as he eased through the narrow channel between the pillars at the entrance of the harbour and into the North Sea beyond. At once the bows rose to higher, white-crested waves and a host of seagulls gathered overhead, circling hopefully for food.

Matthew had never seen a northern dawn before and admired the pink flush that spread along the horizon, surmounted by a delicate translucent grey that edged into the surrounding black. He knew the bitter dawn of London, with the stink of 100,000 houses poured into the streets, and he knew the soft southern light of Sussex and Kent, but there was more spectacle here. He could taste the salt of the sea, hear the calling gulls and the bubble of the water beneath the bow of the boat, and breathed deeply of air so brittle that it burned in his lungs, until he realized that Megstone was looking directly at him.

When their eyes met it was Matthew who dropped his gaze and Megstone pulled at his bushy side-whiskers before touching the silver ring in his left ear, either out of habit or for luck. Like most of the Onswick fishermen, he was shorter than Matthew, but powerfully built, with forearms that were all muscle and great fists that wrapped around the tiller. His wide-bottomed trousers and short blue jacket were far more practical that Matthew's knee breeches and grey cloak, but his sea boots looked clumsy. From his position in the stern Megstone worked the single lugsail with casual skill. 'The Reverend said that you were going to build a lighthouse?'

'Not quite.' Matthew ducked as Megstone tacked and the boom swung over his head. 'I'm here to see if it is possible to build one.'

'Oh aye.' Megstone produced a hunk of tobacco and, when Matthew refused his offer, bit off a mouthful and began to chew. 'Where?'

'Somewhere on or around the Black Corbie. To warn shipping to keep clear. There have been a lot of losses there, as you'll know.'

'Aye, I know that.' Megstone glanced upward to check the weather, adjusted the set of the sail and sat back, chewing slowly.

About to explain further, Matthew glanced at Megstone's sardonic face and remained silent. He had not endured the painful process of being raised as a gentleman so that he could discuss his business with a common fisherman. Instead he opened his case, shielding the contents from Megstone as he extracted the spyglass and focussed on where he knew the Corbie Rock to be.

'You won't see much in this light.' There may have been satisfaction in Megstone's voice. 'And once you see the Corbie, you'll wish yourself back safe on land.'

'Perhaps so,' Matthew retorted, 'which is precisely why a lighthouse should be built there.'

The creeping sun had turned the sea a misty grey, with a horizon upon which leaping waves could faintly be seen. Lights from passing vessels probed through the mist, gradually fading as daylight grew. Not a single ship ventured close, for the Black Corbie cast its wicked spell in a wide arc. Seen from the sea, the group of islands and rocks appeared quieter, even smaller, with only a few areas of white froth to mark their danger.

'Tide's high,' Megstone explained, 'so there's less of the Corbie exposed. Most is under water now.'

'How much water?' Matthew asked quickly.

Megstone sucked and spat a brown stream of tobacco juice

37

over the side. 'Depends,' he said at length. 'A fathom in some places, less in others, much more where the rock is low. That's the danger, you see. Ships cannot see beneath their keels, and do not know how much clearance they have.'

Visibility had improved by the time they reached the Corbie, so Matthew could see the extent of the island on which he had asked to land. Mostly bare rock, with pools of dark water and areas of glistening seaweed, it looked more hostile than anywhere Matthew had ever imagined. Hauling down the sail, Megstone used a pair of long oars to keep the boat from touching the rock. 'You're sure that you want to go ashore?'

Matthew nodded, very aware of the tight knot in his stomach. 'I am.'

'I can't wait for you. Tide's falling.' Megstone ejected more tobacco juice. 'I'll leave you here and return before next high water – about eight hours' time.'

Seaweed and slime made landing on the island difficult, and Matthew swore as he slithered into a rock pool. As he scrambled to the higher and drier parts of the island, Megstone had already hoisted the sail and was heading back to Onswick. Matthew realized that he was alone on this desolate scrap of rock for the next eight hours, like Robinson Crusoe except with a bitter Northumberland wind and nowhere to shelter.

When he had inspected the island with his spyglass two days previously, Matthew had located what seemed like a level area on which a lighthouse might have been built. Now he realized that the ground was pitted with deep pools and seamed with sharp ridges. It also sloped steeply to the north. The crash of waves and the suck of receding water surrounded him, mingling with the unending scream of seagulls to create a cacophony of sound that besieged his concentration as he opened his case and extracted the various pieces of his theodolite. After his long journey from London and the excitement of an attempted robbery, it was finally time to start work.

Matthew struggled to assemble the tripod where he judged the centre of the island to be, ducked as a gape-mouthed gull rustled overhead and clutched at his head as the wind threatened to remove his tricorne hat. Grunting as he splashed through pools in which seaweed curled cold and slippery around his ankles, he used a spirit level to determine the area with the least slope. Ignoring the seabirds that squabbled raucously as they searched for crabs and other scuttling creatures, he pulled a lead-weighted plumb line from his case to ascertain his vertical axis. He had been taught to have it 'as accurate as a cow's thumb', and although that was not possible in these conditions, he would compensate as best he could.

A gust of wind upset the tripod and Matthew cursed again as he fitted the tribrach or centring plate on which were the adjusting thumbscrews. Only when he was certain that everything was secure did he lift the theodolite itself, holding it with great care. Consisting of a telescope mounted within two perpendicular axes, one horizontal, the other vertical, this instrument had cost him a Flanders fortune. On this surface the axes were not perpendicular, so he measured the deviation and noted the difference in a small notebook under the heading of 'horizontal axis error'.

Matthew glanced up, surprised how far the tide had receded during the time he had been working. The dawn mist had lifted, and pale sunshine glittered from the rock pools that surrounded him. He could see movement nearby as a red-backed crab scuttled from shelter, its pincers waving menacingly. Matthew stepped aside, unsure if the creature was about to attack him, then returned to his work when it moved in the opposite direction. Something long and smooth rolled with the tide, and Matthew realized that it was a spar from some unfortunate ship, trapped amongst the seaweed. Now he could see other fragments of broken ships, a reminder that seamen's lives could depend on how accurately he worked.

Matthew intended to create as precise a map of this group of islets as possible, and was aware that he had not much time in which to work. Eight hours had sounded like an age, but every movement seemed to take twice as long in the adverse conditions. Wind-driven rain constantly smeared the lenses of the microscope through which he peered, so he had to stop, cover the instrument and carefully clean it with a cloth.

By noon, Matthew realized that he would never complete the task in one day. Instead he concentrated on the main island and then quickly sketched the outlying rocks and small islets, paying attention to the sea passages and assessing the tidal races. He measured the distance between each rock and, using the extending rod and marked line that he carried in his case, checked the depth of water around the main island when the tide was at its lowest, and did the same every hour as it rose.

Every time he made a measurement or calculation, he added it to the list in his small book, dipping his quill in the ink and taking great care to shield the pages from the intermittent showers. He frowned at the occasional blot that spoiled the appearance of neatness.

On its most easterly side, the island rose to the tall, bird-like formation that gave the place its name of Corbie Rock. There was a rounded head, from which a pointed peak projected seaward, and what an imaginative person might think of as wings that extended from each side. For a minute Matthew contemplated climbing to the summit, but the rock seemed so smooth that he turned away. He had never been keen on heights and with the sea a sucking menace below, such an ascent would test his nerves to the utmost. Instead he sat on a handy knot of rock and chewed on the hunk of bread and cheese that he had brought with him. He had long given up hope of retaining his hat, so had placed it inside his case and allowed the wind to whip the ribbon around his club pigtail.

There were a dozen sails in sight, from the tan lugsails of the local fishing boats to pyramids of light canvas that marked the passage of large trading vessels. Extending the spyglass, Matthew focussed on each in turn, picking out details as he wondered where they were heading and how they felt about the Corbie Rock. There were strange sounds out here, the whine of the wind, the harsh squalling of seabirds and a hoarse barking sound that he could not recognize but which raised the small hairs on the back of his neck. Matthew felt for the pistol that he had placed inside his cloak and allowed himself to ponder his situation.

He had been warned that civilization ended just north of London so had not expected such a prosperous little village as Onswick. He had been prepared for squalor and deprivation, not neat cottages with yellow brick walls; and rather than hosts of beggars and religious zealots he had found independently minded fishermen and a cheerful, insect-catching vicar. Nothing here was as he imagined . . . and there was Her Young Ladyship's bell again, carried to him by the offshore wind.

Shifting his stance, Matthew bit off more bread and extended his spyglass, focussing on the village where it crouched beneath the cliff. The cottages leaped into view, with the square tower of St Cuthbert's prominent above the haze of pale blue smoke. Matthew thanked the luck that had led to a beached naval officer pawning his expensive spyglass, enabling him to purchase it relatively cheaply.

There was a small knot of people marching in what appeared to be gaudy yellow and red uniforms. One carried the bell, ringing it two handed, and the others were burly men with staves. He watched them parade through the village, clearing the population before them, and then he swept the spyglass along the coast beyond Onswick, searching for the cause of all the upset. Low cliffs, a scattering of cattle, a building that might have been a mill, and then Matthew saw a lone horsewoman cantering toward the coast. She rode astride, vanished into a dip and reappeared beside a two-storeyed tower.

The tower was built of dressed stone, with glazed windows overlooking the sea. It perched above a fissure in the cliffs, with a narrow path descending to a small cove with yellow sand and a wall that seemed to completely enclose a section of the sea. It was a sea bath, or a grotto, a sheltered spot for bathing. Intrigued, Matthew watched the rider smoothly dismount before freeing her horse in a walled paddock. She looked toward the village for a moment, lifted her skirt above her ankles and entered the tower.

So this was Miss Grace Fenwick, the daughter of Her Ladyship, the woman who wielded so much power that one sound of her bell sent grown men running to cower indoors.

41

Amused that he had unconsciously managed to circumvent all her precautions, Matthew watched as smoke began to rise from a tall central chimney, and then started as Her Ladyship emerged from a hitherto unseen doorway.

She was tall and slender, with subtle curves and blonde hair that flowed free to her shoulders. For a full minute she stood at the cleft in the cliffs, legs apart and arms akimbo as she surveyed the view. As she stretched her arms aloft, she seemed to glance in his direction, but then began to descend the path. Matthew watched her reach the beach, walk confidently across to the enclosed grotto and, without a pause, stride into the water. Her mouth opened as she plunged in, and then she began to swim, a long, smooth stroke that carried her to the wall at the far side in a matter of seconds. It was only then that Matthew jerked away the spyglass as he realized that he was acting as no gentleman should. He was more like a peeping Tom, for Miss Grace was entirely naked.

No wonder she sent the bellman to warn away the villagers. Matthew felt the colour burning his cheeks as he turned to face the sea. He was suddenly ashamed of himself, disgusted that he had behaved in such a manner. He had been educated at one of the best schools in England and here he was, no better than the village roughs with whom his companions had brawled, and whom he had been taught to treat with contempt.

All the same, he admitted, she had been worth watching, and nobody would know if he had another look . . . Succumbing to temptation, Matthew raised the spyglass again and shook his head in admiration. Miss Grace was surely hardy to go swimming in the North Sea this early in the year, either naked or fully clothed. He had never known a woman to act so. Indeed, he had never heard the like.

He had been so intent on the view that Matthew had not noticed that the wind had changed direction and the horizon was hazing over. Fighting the desire to have a last glance at Miss Grace, Matthew realized that there was a sea mist creeping toward him so he could only see those sails that were closest to the island. Even the sounds were becoming muffled. Packing the theodolite into his case, he closed the spyglass and tucked it into the correct compartment, then swore as a wave swept over the buckle of his shoe.

The tide was rising fast, so his island was beginning to shrink. Checking the silver watch that he carried at his breast, Matthew saw that it was past two, so more time than he thought had elapsed since he began to watch the antics of Miss Grace. He began to retreat from the advancing water to the higher parts of the island, only now wondering if Megstone would indeed return for him. Each wave ate a few more inches from the island, each wave pushed him a step further back, and all the time the white mist crept closer.

By three in the afternoon Matthew was even more worried. He could no longer see the land, which meant that Megstone would be unable to see him. Perhaps the Onswick fisherman would not care to venture out in these conditions; he might not risk the danger to pick up a stranger. Matthew wondered if he had been foolhardy to venture on to this island, knowing how perilous it was and how many ships had foundered here. He began to listen for Megstone's boat, occasionally shouting, only for the mist to throw back his voice.

Replacing his hat on his head, Matthew huddled deeper into his cloak as the chill began to bite. He withdrew a few more paces, hearing strange scuttling sounds that could only be marine animals, and a soft coughing that he could not explain at all. He began to worry in earnest as the mist rolled right over the island, cold, clammy and clinging. He checked his watch; it was nearing four o'clock and already the light was fading. He had forgotten that the days were shorter in the north. Peering toward the land, he flapped his hand in front of his face in a futile gesture to clear the mist.

The sea was much closer now, each wave breaking with a sinister hush and a deluge of cold water that lapped the rock near to his feet and occasionally splashed him with spindrift. He looked landward again, shouting uselessly, and backed to the edge of the Corbie. The rock was cold to his touch, slippery with sea slime and studded with limpets. He had not dared climb it in full light, but now there seemed little choice but to get as far from the sea as he could.

More used to the gentle Downs of the south, he climbed slowly, checking each handhold before trusting it with his weight. Twice he winced as he rasped soft flesh against sharp limpets; he waited for the pain to abate before moving upward, with the surge of the sea sounding below. Even if he had had the use of both hands, climbing the Corbie would have been hard, but he also had his case to carry. He had pawned his future to the instruments inside: with them he was a skilled man able to command a position of respect; without them he was nothing.

'God in heaven!' Matthew's boot slipped on seaweed and he slammed against the rock, clinging by one hand and a precarious foothold. He swore, feeling the sweat start from him as he hugged the Corbie, very aware of the twenty-foot drop to curling waves and unforgiving rock below him. Suddenly the case seemed less precious, but he recovered and continued, feeling the aching strain in fingertips and wrist. A rising flight of gulls nearly unbalanced him as he reached the rounded head that marked the summit, and he sat down, clutching the rock with damp hands as he held his case close by his side. He waited for his breathing to recover and his heart to reduce its ragged pounding.

The strange sounds that he had heard were louder now, with that eerie, coughing bark predominating. Matthew suppressed the tales of monsters that he had heard in the dark dormitories at school. He remembered how he had shivered with delicious fear when he had been safe in the company of his fellows, but there was nothing to enjoy now, when that grunting cough sounded so close in the mist and something splashed below him. There was a slithering, scraping sound as well, as if something was creeping up the Corbie.

Matthew had not thought of ghosts and hobgoblins for many years, but out here, stuck on this rock on which so many ships had foundered and so many men had died, he was unsure. All the logic of mathematics mattered nothing compared to the irrational fear that lifted the small hairs on the back of his neck. He knew that there were no sea monsters and that ghosts belonged to the world of romantic poets, but when a long moan dragged out from the rock beneath him, he gasped and pulled himself even further along the head of the Corbie. Nothing living could make a noise like that.

'Get back!' Matthew had bought the pistol in case of highwaymen, but this unknown sound seemed a much more terrifying danger. Holding the smooth walnut butt in his right hand, he pulled back the hammer with his left. 'Get back, I say!'

The coughing increased, and now there was a smell, of salt and damp and musk. It was no trick of the mist; there was something large moving beneath him. He could see the shape through the shifting white moisture and hear the scraping of a body against the rock. No ghost then, but some sea monster, perhaps the mermaid that the inn had been named after. Levelling the pistol, he prepared to fire, when suddenly another sound bellowed through the mist. Loud and harsh, it seemed to echo for ever, clashing against the rock beneath him before slowly fading. Matthew fired, feeling the recoil of the shot jerk his arm into the air. He slipped on the rock, nearly falling off his perch.

'Hey! Careful there!'

Matthew nearly sobbed when the voice roared through the mist. 'Megstone! Is that you?'

'Of course it's me! Who else is stupid enough to sail in this weather? Come off that bloody rock and get inboard, damn you!'

Four

Onswick, March 1804

Matthew leaned back in the hair-bottomed chair in the parlour of the Mermaid, stretched out his feet to the fire and sipped at the tankard of ale that a grinning Anderson had brought for him. He listened as Megstone related his story to the laughing crowd and wondered at his own foolishness.

'Huddled up on the rock, he was, cuddling that case of his and trying to scare away the seals with a pocket pistol.' Megstone's laugh might have been intended to hurt, but Matthew acknowledged its justice.

'You have my gratitude for rescuing me from those sea monsters.' He decided that it was best to accept the ridicule rather than retreat behind the shell of gentlemanly disdain. Since Megstone had witnessed him trembling in fear, he could hardly pretend to have been otherwise. 'I know now that it was seals that were barking and coughing, but I still do not know what caused that other sound.'

Most of the men present joined in Megstone's laugh. 'The sound like this?' Pursing his lips, Megstone gave a good imitation of the low, penetrating rasp that had caused Matthew so much concern. 'That was my foghorn.' He leaned closer. 'We use conch shells here, brought back from the Indies – it's a sound that travels and we know exactly what it is.'

'So will I, next time,' Matthew agreed ruefully. He knew what a conch shell was, but had not expected that knowledge to be shared by these northern fishermen. 'I don't mind admitting that it scared me half to death.'

'Scared of the seals, were you?' The speaker was long and lean and ugly, with a straight scar that cut through part of his nose and curled his upper lip into a permanent sneer. He smelled of tar and salt and smoke. 'Well, Mr London, there are worse things at sea than seals.'

Matthew nodded. 'I can believe that, sir, but with Mr Megstone to rescue me, I have no cause to fear.' Nodding to Billy Anderson, he ordered another round of drinks. He knew that he was depleting his meagre purse, but after that day's adventures, money was not at the forefront of his mind.

'I said I would be back for you,' Megstone told him, 'so I don't know why you climbed to the top of the Corbie's head.' He shook his head, smiling. 'You should have known that I could not come direct in this weather. With an offshore wind I had to come around the rock, for the tide race in the Gut would have capsized me.'

'The Gut?'

Dipping his forefinger in his tankard, Megstone drew a rapid map of the islands on top of the table. He stabbed downward. 'This is the main island, on which you landed, and this is the collection of rocks and small islands to the lee of the Corbie. We call them the Raven's Brood, and the channel in between is the Gut.'

Matthew glanced at the map on the table, mentally comparing it with the official chart that he had bought in London and the measurements that he had taken himself. 'Could you draw me a map of the islands? A proper one, on paper?'

'No, he can't.' The scarred man smoothed a hand across the top of the table, obscuring the map. 'He's told you enough.' As he sat down beside Matthew, his jacket flapped open, revealing the barrel of a pistol thrust in his waistband.

Other men crowded close, some acknowledging Matthew with a lift of their tankards. He knew that they were watching to see his reaction. He was being tested. 'Perhaps you could help me then, Mr . . . ?' Matthew held out his hand.

Ignoring the hand, the scarred man stirred the coal in the fire with a booted foot. 'Maybe it would be best if you left Onswick now, Mr London. You've seen the Corbie and come back safely. There's many a poor sailor man that can't make that claim. Maybe it's best if you leave it at that.'

Only the crackle of the fire disturbed the sudden silence of the parlour. The scarred man stared directly into Matthew's face. 'Maybe it would be best if you returned to London.'

Aware that everybody in the Mermaid was watching him, Matthew took a long pull at his tankard and put it down carefully on the table. He hoped that they could not hear the frantic beating of his heart. 'Thank you for your advice, Mister whatever-your-name-is, but I will not return until I have finished my work here.'

The scarred man nodded slowly. 'You may find your work finished quicker than you wished.' He put a hand deliberately to his ear. 'Is that a seal I hear? No, it's a crow, best shoot it, Mister London, or get yourself measured for your coffin.'

'Is that a threat? Are you threatening me, sir?' Matthew had been taught how to act with gentlemen, but while in the company of these fishermen and foremast-hands, he had to resort to the behaviour of his early childhood: meet bullying with bluster and glowers with assumed anger. 'How dare you, sir!'

'Oh, I dare,' the scarred man lowered his voice, 'but there are others who will more than dare. As I said, there are worse things at sea than seals.'

Matthew forced himself to stand. He could not remember if he had reloaded his pistol after firing at the seal. 'My work will be completed only when I say it is complete.' The eyes of the scarred man held a flat contempt that was hard to meet. 'And you, sir, would be better to mind your tongue.'

The scarred man was around the same height as Matthew, but he had a wiriness about his frame that told of explosive strength and a face that held a lifetime's experience of violence. Suddenly Matthew felt very alone and far from home, but he had spent much of his life trying to prove himself, and this encounter was just another episode. There was so much about these northern parts that he did not understand. As well as the independence of the yokels, so different from the docile clumpertons of the south, there was casual mention of voyages to the Indies and now threats to a gentleman. Such a thing would never happen in Kent.

'Good evening, good evening!' The cheerful tones of Reverend Grover broke the tension. 'Having a discussion? Excellent!' Grover forced himself between the two men and thrust his hands out to the fire. 'My, but it's nippy out there! Winter lingers in the lap of spring, so they say, and by George it's lingering tonight. Time for some hot rum, I say, don't you agree, Billy? Hot rum sweetened with sugar for me!'

'Coming right up, Reverend!' Billy Anderson had been as interested a spectator as any in the inn, but now he hurried to do Grover's bidding as conversation resumed around the fire.

'Settling in, are you?' Turning around, Grover lifted his coat-tails to toast his backside at the fire. 'Good! Excellent news. And how is the lighthouse coming along? All built and ready yet?' He sniggered at his own joke, adjusted his wig before it fell backward into the flames and accepted his rum with a broad grin. 'Capital, Billy. Mr Anderson here is the best rum-and-sugar maker in Northumberland. Aren't you, Billy? I think so, anyway. Never think to go elsewhere for it!' Allowing his coat-tails to flap down, Grover sipped his drink noisily. 'Well now, what were you talking about?'

Matthew realized that the scarred man had retreated to a seat far from the fire and now sat in sullen isolation. 'I was telling everybody about my adventures today. Mr Megstone was good enough to take me out to the Corbie, and he rescued me from a score of wild seals just seconds before they devoured me.'

'Good gracious! You were lucky.' Grover finished his rum, accepted another with alacrity and shook his head. 'Wild seals are the worst kind, so they tell me. I'm always hearing about their ferocity. Did you achieve your objective out there, though?'

'I did.' With the tension broken, Matthew was glad to talk. 'Now I hope to compare my findings with the chart I bought in London, and with anybody willing to share his local knowledge. I had hoped that Mr Megstone might oblige?' He pitched the question toward Megstone, but it was Grover who replied.

'I am sure Mr Megstone would be delighted to help.'

Grover finished his second rum-and-sugar with a single swallow, burped gently and handed the empty glass to Anderson. 'But first, take a walk with me. Mr Anderson will take your case up to your room. It will be safe there, believe me.'

For a second Matthew hesitated, and then held out his hand to Megstone. 'Thank you again, Mr Megstone. I really thought that those wild seals would have me.'

Glancing at Grover, Megstone accepted the hand in a grip that seemed forged of iron. 'You were safe enough on the island.'

'You had better go home, Clem Wharton,' Grover spoke quietly to the scarred man. 'I think that you have had enough to drink for one night.'

The mist had rolled inland so Onswick sat in the light of a half-moon, silent save for the never-ending suck and surge of the surf and the sound of waves booming against the Corbie. Most houses were in darkness, with only the occasional gleam from a window probing the night. Reaching up, Grover unhooked the lantern that swung above the door and beneath the sign of the Mermaid. He held it in his right hand so the light bounced along the painted walls and reflected from the water as he walked slowly beside the harbour.

'So you survived your trip to the Corbie, Mr Pryde.'

Matthew acknowledged the fact.

'And did you find it useful?'

Matthew nodded. 'I was able to see for myself what conditions were like, and to start a rough survey of the island.'

Grover nodded, stepping wide of a pile of mussel shells. He directed the lantern light downward to help Matthew negotiate the obstacle. 'I see. Are you sure that this is your first visit to these parts?'

'It is. I've never knowingly been north of London before.' Matthew looked out to sea, where not a single light broke the darkness. He shivered and pulled his cloak closer, glad that he was no longer on the island. In his imagination he could still hear the barking cough of the seals and feel the chill of the creeping mist.

'Just so. Indulge me, Mr Pryde, as I take you around our little village.'

With Grover's lantern shining a circle of yellow light ahead of them, they slowly walked the narrow streets of Onswick.

'Forgive the jumble-gut lanes, but it's an old place,' Grover explained, tactfully lighting up a deep puddle of some substance more noxious than mussel shells. 'The name is Norse, from Odin's Wick – Odin's Bay.' He waited for Matthew's exclamation of interest before continuing. 'Odin was a Norse god, as you know, so the Vikings probably founded this village.'

'Is that so?' Matthew listened politely as Grover spoke about the Vikings' love of the sea, their long dragon ships that crossed from Norway and their eventual conversion to Christianity.

'So this has always been a seafaring community, Mr Pryde. Fishing, trading, that sort of thing. Seamen tend to drink rather a lot when they are on shore, so forgive Mr Wharton's words. He was a trifle jug-bitten.'

'I see.' Matthew nodded. Drunken clods did not interest him much, and no harm had been done.

They had stopped outside a long row of cottages, and Grover allowed the lantern to illuminate the curious yellow bricks that Matthew had already noted.

'Onswick has long established trading connections with the continent, you know. The village imported French and Spanish wine and all sorts of goods from Rotterdam. Not any more though, what with this war. Bonaparte has closed off many of the ports of Europe and Onswick vessels no longer trade abroad.'

'I see,' Matthew repeated, and wondered to what Grover was leading.

'Yet, Mr Pryde, do you notice anything about Onswick? Anything that helps it to stand out from other coastal villages?'

'Indeed I do, Mr Grover. Onswick has all the appearance of prosperity.' Matthew knew the docks of London and had helped survey some of the fishing harbours of the south coast. He had seen the broken men discharged from the Royal Navy

51

and the atmosphere of anxiety over falling trade, privateers and the Press Gang.

'And why should that be, Mr Pryde, do you imagine?'

'I really could not say, Mr Grover. A benevolent proprietor, perhaps? Or good fishing grounds off shore?'

'Neither, Mr Pryde. We do send the occasional cargo of fish to Newcastle, but in exchange we import coal. No. Much of our prosperity is due to the Black Corbie.'

The thunder of surf directed Matthew's attention to the rock in question; phosphorescence gleamed suddenly through the night. 'I don't see how, Mr Grover.'

'Did you not hear my sermon? I asked that if the good Lord chose to send ships to their doom, he should send them to the Corbie.'

Matthew frowned. He had dismissed the words as an appeal to some sardonic northern humour. 'I was listening, but you can't have meant it seriously.'

The lantern cast Grover's face into deep shadow. 'The people of this parish are my flock, Mr Pryde. If their bodily comforts are secure, they will have more time to concentrate on their spiritual well-being.'

'But you're a man of the cloth!' Once again Matthew heard the sinister boom of a wave breaking on the Corbie. 'There were two ships lost on that rock only last winter,' he said, 'and three more on this coast as they tried to avoid the rock. Scores of poor seamen drowned, the shipowner lost money, and think of the widows and orphans!'

'I do, Mr Pryde, but I do not question the will of the Lord. If He should choose to end the earthly existence of men, then why should we not benefit from such a calamity?' Grover allowed his lantern to play along the line of the wall. 'These bricks came from the wreck of a Dutch emigrant ship bound north-about to the West Indies. Her supplies kept the village alive through a long winter. Other ships have provided these fine clay pantiles that you admired, and lengths of timber for building, ropes and cordage, and good warm clothing against the cold.' Grover shone his lantern directly into Matthew's eyes. 'The Black Corbie is an asset to this village, Mr Pryde, not a danger, for no local vessel has foundered here for a century and more. You will be hard pressed to find a family in the village that has not benefited from that rock.'

They were walking again, with Grover allowing the light from his lantern to flit from house to house. He rested the yellow pool on a carved doorway. 'The captain of a Prussian snow once used that door, while that window,' he shifted the light to the next cottage, 'came from the stern cabin of a Frisian barque.' Grover moved on, highlighting a ship's mizzenmast that was now used as the ridge of a roof; a line of washing that was far too exotic for the north of England; a water butt inscribed with unfamiliar Russian letters. 'Do you understand what I am trying to say, Mr Pryde?'

Matthew nodded. 'I believe so. You want me to see the advantages that the Black Corbie brings to Onswick.'

'Good,' Grover's voice sounded from the dark.

'Which means,' Matthew followed a logical course of thought, 'that you wish me to return to London and report that it would be impractical to build a lighthouse here.' They had halted outside a small cottage with an upturned coble for a roof.

Grover adjusted his wig, which was again sliding down his face. 'That might be best for the village,' he agreed.

'I am afraid that I cannot do that. The Association of Shipmasters of Newcastle intends to petition the government for a bill to build a lighthouse on the Corbie. The Shipmasters hope to reduce the number of wrecks and make the coast safer for mariners of all ports, not only Onswick.'

'Most commendable,' Grover said. 'And no doubt the Association of Shipmasters of Newcastle would be the major beneficiary?'

'Everybody would benefit.' Matthew could not quite understand Grover's objections. Building a lighthouse was a commonsense step to creating a safer coast. 'A lighthouse on the Corbie would encourage trade for all, help the village and create employment.'

'And bring the attention of the Royal Navy,' Grover added quietly. 'The Corbie has guarded this village for centuries, ever since the Norse named it. They called it Raven's Rock in honour of their sacred bird. In time the name changed to a more common black bird, the corbie, or crow, but the protection remained. Any lighthouse would ease the hazards of navigation and expose Onswick to far worse dangers.'

Matthew frowned. He was accustomed to guarding his words and actions, but he had not expected any objections to what seemed only rational. 'Surely as a man of God, you must approve of anything that helps save life? A lighthouse would do just that.'

'As I said before, my priority is to my flock.' Grover's smile was benign. 'But of course I approve of preserving life, Mr Pryde. I am only voicing the opinion of my parishioners. Many of them may not wish a lighthouse built here.'

Matthew calmed down at once. 'My apologies, Reverend. Naturally you must work in the best interests of your parishioners, as I must for those who sponsor me.' He lowered his voice. 'Between you and me, Mr Grover, your parishioners may well have their wish. My task is to make the initial survey, which I have done, and present my findings to Lord Chevington, the local Member of Parliament, in the hope that he brings a bill to the House of Commons. That is what the Association of Shipmasters expects, but there is no guarantee that Lord Chevington will agree.'

Grover smiled and began to walk again, with the lantern swinging in time with each step. 'Lord Chevington is not your problem, Mr Pryde. Her Ladyship is. But come with me. I can show you something that may be of interest.'

Grover led him around a corner and through a lynch gate into the churchyard. The lantern cast weird shadows around jumbled gravestones as Grover walked straight in, past the tall memorial to the unknown mariners, and stopped at the furthest corner, where a miniature mausoleum hunched beneath a small copse of stunted silver birch trees. Matthew ducked as a bat fluttered past his head. Branches were silhouetted starkly against a rising moon.

'Before you do anything else, Mr Pryde, you may wish to have a look inside there.' He produced a large key from inside his cloak and unlocked the iron gate, which opened with only the hint of a creak. Thirteen stone steps led down to a paved interior where, instead of coffins, the figureheads of ships mingled with other nautical impedimenta. 'We try to keep some reminder of every ship claimed by the Corbie,' Grover explained, 'in gratitude of the Lord's blessing.' He allowed the light to play on the nearest figurehead, a representation of a dolphin, then slowly shifted along the stone wall of the interior. Fragments of ships' names, complete or broken figureheads lay neatly beside splintered stumps of spars and a selection of seamen's chests.

It was like another graveyard, with memories of dead ships and lost crews. Matthew could nearly hear the suffering of the men as the sea smashed them against the harsh rocks, could visualize the death of each vessel in the terrible surf around the Black Corbie.

'I say a prayer here every night,' Grover said quietly, 'to keep the souls of these unfortunate men at peace. Would you care to join me?'

Matthew knelt beside the Reverend on the cold stone floor. The prayer was short and sincere, a request for mercy for each man lost on the Black Corbie, followed by a grateful thanks for the munificence of the Lord in thus supplying Onswick with such help, especially at this time of great suffering. Strangely, Matthew found the experience intensely moving and choked back his tears as Grover ended with a memorized list of the ships that had been lost. He spoke slowly, ensuring that each name was clearly transmitted to the Lord, and ending with, 'And we especially ask that you care for the crew of the whaling ship that was cast ashore here in September 1777.'

As Matthew's eyes opened Grover allowed the light of his lantern to shine on a black painted harpoon that rested against the furthest wall of the mausoleum. When Matthew looked up, Grover had vanished, and only the lantern remained, its light illuminating the ship's name engraved on the shaft of the harpoon. As Matthew traced the letters, sharp agony stabbed inside his soul: *Pride of Matthew*.

Five

Maidhouse College, Kent, 1789–1793

'What's your name?'
'Where do you come from?'
'Who is your father?'

The questions seemed endless as young Matthew stood in terrified isolation inside the gates of Maidhouse College. A few moments ago the driver of the stagecoach had dumped him and his meagre luggage with a terse 'Good luck, youngster'. Now he looked at the circle of inquisitive boys that surrounded him, each one resplendent in black tails, high collar and white top hat as they demanded to know every detail of his life, ancestry and experience.

'My name is Matthew Pryde,' he began, and flushed at the howls of laughter that this simple admission brought forth. 'And I come from London.'

'London? What part of London? Where is your house?'

The accents were strange to Matthew's ears. His memory only extended to the chill tones of the masters and the sharp, thin cockney of his fellow orphans in the foundling hospital that he had attended until the previous day. He had been summonsed to a master's study, given a new suit of clothing and deposited inside these stone-pillared gates with a short note of introduction and a small purse of gold. Somehow he knew that his world had changed for ever.

These boys were different to any that he had known before. Their voices were more rounded, their faces were better washed and their clothes made of thicker cloth, yet their behaviour was utterly feral. They surrounded him, poking, pinching, questioning until he could no longer bear the noise and pushed them away as he fought the tears that seeped from his eyes.

'He's blubbing! Hasn't been here for ten minutes and he's blubbing!'

'Somebody fetch Nursie! Little Matthew's crying!'

'Crying for his mama! Just wait until tonight, and then he'll have something to cry about!'

'Matthew Pryde from London is a crybaby!'

The advent of the Rector in flapping black gown cleared the crowd, and Matthew was conveyed to a comfortable room with a cheerful fire, shelves of books and a broad cupboard fastened with a large key. The Rector was tall, jovial and corpulent as he instructed Matthew in the basics of life at Maidhouse College.

'This is an ancient establishment, Pryde,' the Rector, who introduced himself at Dr Trueman, explained, 'and we have educated gentlemen since the sixteenth century. The Cheapside Foundling Hospital sent you to us, so I know that you are not a gentleman, Mr Pryde, but by the time we have finished with you, you will act like one, think like one and believe that you *are* one. I have put you in the lower form. In time you will progress.'

Dr Trueman stood with his thumbs in his waistcoat and his black gown wrapped around his shoulders. He beamed down on Matthew. 'When you stand in the great hall, Pryde, you will see a large door at the north side. That door is the entrance to progress. All our Maidhousians who succeed will leave by that door. It is a sign of honour, the sign of a true Maidhouse gentleman. Work hard and obey, and you will be happy here, Pryde, and in time, some years hence, you too will leave by the Door of Honour.'

'Yes, sir.' Matthew stared up at this benevolent man who seemed so sure of himself. If Dr Trueman was an example of what a gentleman was, then Matthew wanted desperately to be like him. He wanted to leave by the Door of Honour. He wanted to be a true Maidhouse gentleman. When he walked out of the study he was filled with hope for his future.

Despite his work and obedience, Matthew found happiness hard to obtain at Maidhouse. A knowing youth introduced him to the long dormitory that he shared with the fifty boys of the lower form and left him to become acquainted

57

with the two rows of iron beds and the permanently open windows, the tall ceiling and bare floorboards of his new home. Matthew had hardly unpacked his things when a bell rang and a horde of immaculately accented savages descended upon the room. They threw off their clothes in seconds, drew on long nightshirts and only then circled around Matthew, speaking in an argot with which he was totally unfamiliar.

'There he is! There's Matthew Pryde, who blubs at the gate!'

'Blanket him!'

'You're in the basket now, Pryde!'

'Look at him, all airs and graces and not a feather to fly with!'

'Let's see if he's got a gaper!'

They ran at him, laughing, and despite his struggles stripped him stark naked and bundled him on to a blanket held by four stalwart boys.

'Now answer the questions, Pryde, and no cutting shams or it'll be the worse for you!'

The four boys lifted the blanket and began to toss him, gently at first, while all the boys screamed questions.

'Name?'

'Matthew Pryde!' And the blanket heaved, throwing him halfway to the high ceiling. He gasped at the sick feeling before the descent, and yelled in fear in case he was not caught. The boys laughed at their sport.

'From?'

'London!' And the blanket heaved again, and this time he thumped painfully against the cobwebbed ceiling, hanging there for another heart-stopping second before the long descent.

'Your father's name?'

The staff at the foundling hospital had taught Matthew to be honest, but life was tough for an orphan and he had learned to disguise his past.

'Matthew Pryde!' Again came the heave, the trip to the ceiling, again the sickening wait and the descent.

The interrogation continued, with Matthew becoming more involved in the false life that he had created for himself, manufacturing a distinguished lineage of gentlemen with large houses and vast acreages of land, and with each answer obtaining a retort of 'Bouncer!' or 'Farradiddle!' from the jeering boys. At last the tossing stopped and the four boys callously tipped him out of the blanket. Matthew lay dazed on the bare wooden floorboards as the circle of boys stared at him. The largest stepped forward.

'Matthew Pryde, you have presented us with a bag of moonshine. You have lied to us.' His voice rose. 'You have lied to me! That's just too smoky by half, Pryde – if that is your name.'

About sixteen years old and clad in a long nightshirt, the boy leaned over Matthew. 'I am Nicholas Elmstead, captain of the lower house. You will learn to tell the truth and you will be my fag.' He pushed Matthew with his foot. 'The gauntlet, I think, gentlemen, then a nice warm bath.' Cruel laughter followed his decision.

Unsure what was about to happen, Matthew tried to struggle as Elmstead lifted him upright, holding him firm as the boys formed themselves into two lines that stretched the length of the dormitory. Behind them, candles flickered from their holders along the wall, their yellow light casting shadows that highlighted predatory faces and malicious eyes.

Much older and stronger, Elmstead twisted Matthew's arms behind his back and forced his head forward.

'Bow, Pryde! Bow to your superiors.'

Matthew's kicks were useless as Elmstead dragged Matthew to one end of the double row of boys and ordered one of the others to tie his ankles together.

'Not too close – he has to be able to hobble.' Elmstead was grinning as a slender boy passed a thin cord around Matthew's ankles, leaving a length of six inches slack between them. Other boys yelled their advice as Matthew hoped desperately for Dr Trueman to appear, but he was to learn that the masters left their charges horribly alone at night. Believing that their job was only to teach, neither Dr Trueman nor any other master would venture into the boys' dormitories, leaving Elmstead free rein in the lower house.

Only when he was hobbled did Elmstead release Matthew's arms.

'Now walk the gauntlet, Matthew Pryde!'

Elmstead began the torture with a hefty kick that sent Matthew staggering forward.

'Corker! Right on the breech!'

Matthew glanced along the double line of boys, of all ages from eight to sixteen, some grinning, some taunting, some looking faintly guilty but all holding a belt or a stick, a knotted cord or some other instrument with which they commenced to pummel him as he stumbled along. His attempts at self-defence were in vain, with so many boys striking him simultaneously, and when he tried to hurry, he fell, which allowed more time for the boys to thrash downward, jeering as he wriggled and yelled and cried.

'Harder! Hit the shamming bachelor's son harder!' Elmstead encouraged his peers, leading by example as Matthew crawled forward, shielding himself with hands and arms that were already bruised and wealed. Twice he stopped, pleading for mercy, but there was none so he forced himself forward, wriggling under a score of blows, until he reached the end of the gauntlet and the torment stopped. He could hear his own whimpering even above the gasping of boys who had performed their task so well.

Elmstead bent over him.

'He's still blubbing.'

The other boys laughed.

'Look! His face is all dirty!' Elmstead lifted Matthew's face with one hand, brushing away a tear with a hard thumb. 'Would you like Nursie to give you a nice warm bath?'

The other boys laughed again. Matthew struggled weakly as Elmstead lifted him to his feet, but the older boy subdued him with a few stinging slaps to his head as he pulled him outside the dormitory. There was a flight of stone stairs that led to a quadrangle enclosed with blank windows, and Elmstead dumped Matthew beside a stone trough. Water dripped slowly from a wooden-handled pump.

'In you get!' Elmstead ordered, kicking Matthew to encourage him to clamber inside the trough.

'Can I untie my ankles?' Matthew spoke through his sobs, but there was neither sympathy nor help as he struggled inside the trough.

'Lie on your back,' Elmstead instructed, still grinning, and Matthew did so, watching in terror as the older boy climbed on to the sides of the trough, one foot on each side. The other boys crowded close, baying their laughter as Elmstead lifted his nightshirt and directed a stream of urine on to Matthew.

'Wash his face, Elms! Wash out his mouth!'

Now Matthew could not restrain his howls of horror and disgust, but willing hands held him down as, one after the other, the boys took Elmstead's place until Matthew lay in a warm bath of urine. They left him there, crying, and it was not until the early hours of the morning that Matthew pulled himself out of the trough and crawled to the door of the dormitory.

Nobody looked up as he entered.

After that initiation to Maidhouse, Matthew realized that he was entirely alone. Controlled by a thousand rules, he learned to obey instantly. Life at Maidhouse was about conformity, and a boy who was different in any way was marked down and castigated. He had to look the same, speak the same, act the same and think the same as every one of his fellows. The alternative was unthinkable. Somehow, the boys learned from where Matthew had come, so he worked twice as hard to fit in, suppressing his own personality as he adopted that of the community.

Fagging for Elmstead, Matthew found himself in a position of slavery, with perfection the sole option. Any deviation earned him a savage beating, where only the pain exceeded the ritual humiliation. He quickly learned that weeping brought further blows, that nobody would heed his pleas for help and that a gentleman never complained. Stoicism was the only acceptable behaviour, no matter what the provocation, and as he slowly and painfully ascended the ladder of seniority in Maidhouse, he adapted to the role of a young gentleman.

However bad life was, Matthew was acutely aware that it

was worse for others. He was fortunate that he was unprepossessing in build and not particularly handsome in appearance, for the slender, good-looking youths were the most likely to be targeted by the predators who stalked the dark dormitory. Homosexuality was one of the cardinal sins of Maidhouse, but night after night Matthew would pull the single blanket over his head to stifle the terrified squeals of the youngsters who were being sodomized. On the one occasion that Matthew had attempted to interfere, Elmstead had beaten him to a bloody pulp, with the warning words: 'One gentleman does not interfere with the pleasures of another.'

Matthew had learned. He befriended one of the victims, hoping to offer sympathy, if not help, but when another boy misunderstood and crept into his bed a few nights later, Matthew threw him out and withdrew into his own world of misery. When the boy was found in the cold corridor a few mornings later, hanging by a cord from the beams above, Matthew laughed with his peers, for to sympathize was to show weakness. It was much easier to conform, hiding the horror beneath a callous façade.

Dr Trueman held a service for the unfortunate victim, in which he reminded the boys that suicide was a sin and a sure way of entering hell. Gentlemen were too manly to commit such crimes. Matthew learned not to listen to the sounds in the night and to ensure that his armour of stoicism had no chink through which vulnerability could show. However, there was one annual ritual that always reduced him to bitter tears.

On the final day of every school year Beggs, the burly porter-cum-janitor, opened the great Door of Honour for the successful Maidhousians to troop through. Matthew admired that marvellously carved door, set in its marble surround, and he watched eagerly as it opened and daylight flooded into the ancient hall. Then the school would intone the school song as the leavers walked free for the last time in their lives:
'Splendeas spledeas in aeternum
Alma Mater atquae amabolis,
Vivas Schola Maidhouses
Vivas Schola Maidhouses
Vivas, Vivas, Schola Maidhouses.'

As the Latin words echoed from the ancient beams, Matthew watched in envy, wishing that he was among those boys, men now, who were leaving, but always aware that he was one year closer to his goal, and aware that he had another ordeal ahead.

After the leaving ceremony, the Rector always summonsed Matthew to his study. Dr Trueman sat behind his vast desk of polished oak, his face a mask of benevolence and his hands curled into fists in front of him.

'Matthew Pryde,' the Rector said in a formula that did not vary from year to year, 'you are here by an act of philanthropic charity.'

'Yes, sir,' Matthew agreed, standing stiff-faced and terrified. He had seen the Rector's benevolent mask drop more than once, when he had turned the key in that sinister cupboard in the corner of the room. Matthew had no desire to again feel the bite of the birch that hung inside.

'You are not a gentleman by birth, Pryde, but only by compassion. Are we training you well, Pryde?' Then the Rector would repeat the question in Latin, to which Matthew would reply in the same language.

'Are you becoming a gentleman, Pryde?'

'I am, sir.'

'And are you grateful for that honour, Pryde?'

'I am grateful for that honour, sir.'

'Then sing to me, Pryde.'

Opening his mouth, Matthew would sing all five verses of the school song. He always wavered at the same line, whereupon the Rector would reach across and slap him hard with the palm of his hand. When Matthew had finished the song, the Rector produced a letter.

'This has come for you, Pryde.' Breaking the seal, the Rector unfolded the paper, ensuring that Matthew could not see the contents. 'It thanks Maidhouse College for its many kindnesses in caring for you and asks me to continue with your education. The writer adds that you are to be rigorously schooled in the behaviour and practices of a gentleman, and requests that I ensure you do not backslide.'

Dr Trueman always leaned forward at that point and smiled

coldly into Matthew's face. 'The boys believe that you are a bachelor's son, Matthew Pryde, and perhaps you are, but I will train you as a proper gentleman, despite that.'

On the first occasion that Matthew had been summoned to the Rector's study, he had hoped that the letter writer would release him from his purgatory, but by his fourteenth birthday he was aware of the advantages that a gentleman enjoyed. If he could only endure the torture of his youth, he would have the chance of a better life. He had survived Elmstead's regime, and cheered silently when his tormentor, then the captain of both the upper house and the school, left. Rumour claimed that he was sailing to his plantation in the Indies, but Matthew did not care. Now he had only to survive the torments of Dr Trueman and hope that his unknown bene- factor continued to pay for his education. Sometimes, less often now than formerly, Matthew wondered why he was there, and who in this world cared for him.

'Please, sir,' greatly daring, Matthew posed the question, 'may I ask who sent the letter?'

'No, Pryde, you may not ask.' The Rector rose slightly in his seat, and Matthew fought the tremble that would have brought instant retribution.

He recalled the first occasion he had witnessed what lay beneath the Rector's mask of benevolence. 'A gentleman does not flinch,' the Rector had told him during the first of his end of term visits, and had promptly provided more than adequate reason for nervousness. Sending a fag to fetch Elmstead, he pointed to the cupboard in the corner of his study. 'Open the cupboard, Mr Pryde.'

Unsure what was about to happen, Matthew turned the key, hearing the well-oiled snick of the lock. He pulled open the door and felt sickening terror as he beheld a heavy wooden birching bench and a four-foot long birch.

'Don't stare, Mr Pryde. Bring the bench into the middle of the room.'

Dr Trueman hummed the school song as he quietly ordered, 'Lower his clothing, Mr Elmstead!'

Matthew had never forgotten the horror of that first flog- ging, when Elmstead had slowly stripped him from the waist, and held him face down across the bench while the Rector had plied the birch. His whimpers of fear had quickly changed to screams of genuine pain, but Elmstead had held him all the tighter as the Rector continued.

Matthew had learned that a gentleman did not flinch.

There had been other punishments from the Rector and occasionally from the other masters, but more often from Elmstead, who held the power of the cane over his underlings.

As his fag, Matthew was responsible for keeping Elmstead's study spotless, despite the many boozy parties that were held there. He was also responsible for cleaning Elmstead's clothes and shoes, keeping his books in order and waiting on his every whim. He dreaded the sharp call of 'Fag!' from that end study, with its almost invariable demand for impossible tasks and the inevitable humiliation that would follow.

'I would like to let you off, Pryde,' Elmstead would say, 'but there are one or two obstacles that prevent me. You see, I must try and turn you into a gentleman, and I insist on perfection, therefore . . .'

Elmstead was inventive in his amusements, sometimes demanding that Matthew stand on his head all night, or chalk Latin insults on the door of the Rector's study. One favourite was to have Matthew hang by his fingers on the outside of his study window, with a thirty-foot drop sucking at his heels. Another was to have him approach a senior boy with an insult that he had learned by rote, and Elmstead would watch the ensuing slaughter. In time, Matthew learned to subdue his feelings, accept that life was nothing but a burden and wish for death. Suicide beckoned on a daily basis, a golden escape that hovered constantly at the back of his mind. He created deadlines for himself – survive another day, another hour, another ten minutes – and cowered under the burden of life.

Only time eased the horror, and Matthew continued his slow progression up the school, constantly facing reminders that he was not a real gentleman while being instructed to act as if he was. Humbled and castigated, he aped his betters, imbibing the minimum of classics but finding that his genuine talent for mathematics made him popular with at least one master. He could soothe away the worst of the days by solving complex problems in spherical trigonometry or creating new algebraic formulae. By fourteen he was devouring the mathematical textbooks intended for the most senior boys and even, greatly daring, asking the mathematics master for extra work.

It was the search for more advanced material that some years later encouraged Matthew to leave the grounds of the school for the first time since he had arrived. Only the senior boys were permitted outside the high stone walls of Maidhouse, so Matthew moved with care. He knew of a beech tree whose branches stretched over a neighbouring field, climbed slowly to avoid damaging his clothes and lowered himself to the grass below. As a permanent boarder, Matthew had lived the last four years inside the school perimeter, passing the holidays in the echoing corridors and shadowed dormitories. Now he felt an unaccountable excitement, mingled with fearful guilt as he walked away from the walls toward the town whose spires punctured the horizon. Despite the chill, for this autumn was one of the coldest that he had ever experienced, he felt new warmth as he approached this new place.

For a moment he recalled the tattered orphan of the foundling hospital, the boy who had quarrelled with his peers. That Matthew Pryde was long gone now, but today something of the memory returned, a ghost of happier times, when he was not afraid to break the rules. He was himself again, flouting Dr Truman, thumbing his nose at authority, doing something that he wanted to do, rather than something that he had to do.

'I am Matthew Pryde!' he shouted to the frost-hard field, and leaned back to watch a long skein of geese wing their way inland.

'I am Matthew Pryde!' he told the trees, whose branches held only remnants of dead leaves.

'I am Matthew Pryde!' he told himself, but he knew that he was lying, for he did not know his real name. Perhaps his benefactor knew, but that person was another mystery. Yet today it did not matter, for adventure lay across the fields and he was outside the jurisdiction of authority.

He had heard the other boys speak of Ashbourne, but had never before visited the town. Now he wandered the narrow streets in delight, staring at the shop windows and the mass of bustling people, quite forgetting the mission that had brought him here. There were confectioners' with more sweets than he had dreamed existed; a shop whose multi-paned window was packed with brass and crystal lamps; another that sold china and silk, painted fans and silver watches. There were even pedlars who walked the street proclaiming the desirability of 'fresh eels', 'spiced wine' or 'juicy oranges and lemons', while other men, more disreputable in appearance, offered to 'sharpen your knives and scissors' or 'mend any brass pots'.

There were rough looking carters who swore with an abandoned freedom that thrilled Matthew. There were farm labourers in elaborate smocks, who spoke with a soft burr he had never heard before. There were gentlemen on horseback, some of whom looked down in disdain at the crowds, others who joked happily in a manner that Matthew found scandalous, for Maidhouse had taught him that a gentleman only spoke to the lower classes when giving an order. There were brewers and churchmen, workmen of a dozen trades, a small body of scarlet-coated soldiers who kept in a tight, unsmiling group, and a lady in a closed carriage.

Feeling distinctly out of place in his Maidhouse tails and top hat, Matthew knew that he was the object of a hundred stares as he weaved through the streets, open-mouthed and absorbing everything. It was only when he came to the bookshop that he recalled why he had come, and he gathered his courage and walked in. 'Charles Denton', the sign proclaimed in faded gold lettering, 'Purveyor of New and Second-Hand Books'.

The school library was an imposing place, with high, arched ceilings, an open fire and tall cases crammed with leather-bound volumes of Tacitus and Homer, Latin grammar and Greek philosophy. This shop was far different, a place

67

that smelled of dust and mustiness, where half a dozen people pored over shelves of decidedly battered books, some of which had vivid titles that tingled the imagination of a boy long starved of stimulation. There was a pair of well-worn chairs beside a circular table, on which reposed a small pile of periodicals, while the faint smell of pease pottage wakened the taste buds on Matthew's tongue.

For long minutes he could only stand, and then he nerved himself to reach forward and pull a book from the nearest shelf. It had a long title, purporting to be the adventures of a mariner named Robinson Crusoe, and he scanned the text before replacing it. He was not interested in mariners or adventures, only in the clear logic of mathematics.

The next book fell open at a ridiculous illustration of a man surrounded by tiny people who had tied him to the ground, and the third was a volume of poetry, with words in some strange dialect that he did not understand.

'You like Burns?'

'Burns?' Matthew had never heard the name. He felt the colour rush to his face when he faced the young lady who was speaking to him. For the past four years he had only seen one female, and she was the terrible creature who acted as school matron. He dropped the book with a clatter that drew quick tuts from the other customers. One old man glowered over his pince-nez spectacles and looked away in disapproval.

'Obviously not,' the young lady said.

'Oh, Robert Burns!' As he retrieved the book, Matthew read the author's name. 'Of course I do. Do you?'

The lady shook her head. She was perhaps sixteen, with bright eyes that dominated a face whose features seemed to have been arranged by God to disturb the equanimity of pubescent boys. The hem of her blue and yellow dress lifted from the ground as she stretched to the highest shelf for a book, revealing low-heeled black boots. 'No. I try to deny any Scottish blood in me.' Her giggle attracted the attention of the gentleman with the pince-nez, who raised bushy eyebrows and smiled indulgently as he bowed to her.

'Oh.' Normally reticent, Matthew could think of nothing

to say. He could feel the perspiration starting on his face and hoped that this girl would go away, nearly as much as he wished her to stay.

'Are you going to at least look at the book then? Or are you trying to weigh it?' The girl was laughing at him, her mouth open and her tongue delightfully pink against her teeth. Matthew gazed at those teeth; they were very white but slightly crooked, which, strangely, made them even more attractive. Indeed, Matthew thought, all teeth should be shaped like that.

'You're staring at me,' the girl pointed out. 'Put the book back, for goodness' sake. You're obviously not interested in it.'

The snap in her voice shocked Matthew and he tried to replace the book, fumbled, nearly dropped it a second time and eventually succeeded in sliding it back on to the shelf. 'No,' he took a deep breath to control his nerves, 'I don't really like poetry.'

'No?' When the girl half turned away, as if to leave, Matthew was not sure whether to be relieved or to drag her back. 'You don't like poetry, and I saw the look on your face when you picked up *Robinson Crusoe* and *Gulliver's Travels*, so you don't like adventure. And with that Friday face on you, you don't like talking to me, either. You don't like much, do you?'

Matthew could only stare after her as she walked slowly out of the shop, straight backed and with her head held high, but the man with the pince-nez prodded him with a thick finger. 'Go after her then, boy! Don't just stand there like a stranded fish.'

'What?' Matthew felt himself colour up again.

'I said, go after her.' The gentleman gave him a gentle push. 'Don't let her get away.'

Luckily, the girl had dallied to look in the multi-paned window of the lamp shop, enabling Matthew to catch her. 'I like mathematics,' he blurted out, to the amusement of a passing middle-aged woman. 'I was looking for a book on mathematics.'

'Well, you won't find one out here, will you?' the girl told him. 'This shop only sells lamps.' Her sudden smile took him by surprise. 'They will help you read your book in the dark, though.' This time he smiled back.

'Come on then,' she said, 'let's go inside and we can look for a book on mathematics.'

Her name was Kate, she told him, and she had loved books all her life. She knew her way around the shop, taking him on a guided tour of the humanities, travel stories, biographies, literature and finally ending at a short shelf of technical volumes, which he lifted with reverence and perused with awe. He had never seen such complex equations or imagined the depth of knowledge that was available. One book in particular called to him, and he scanned the pages with a fascination that made him forget the time, and even, for a while, the young woman who smiled so patiently at his side.

'I've never seen an engineering book before,' he said, when she gently took it from him and returned it to its place on the shelf.

'Maybe you should buy this one,' she told him, 'then you can read it when you are alone, and not neglect the companion who is trying to talk to you.'

It was a gentle rebuke that immediately returned him to the blushing boy of half an hour previously. 'Yes, of course. I do apologize.'

'So tell me about yourself,' Kate asked, and Matthew lost his tongue.

'Nothing much to tell,' he said at last, and Kate nodded. The bonnet she wore rocked when she moved her head, which fascinated Matthew nearly as much as the rebellious ringlet of brown hair that curled under her left ear.

'I did not think there was,' she said. 'Boys are usually boring.' Her eyes were light with mischief as she teased him. 'No doubt you know all about shooting and hunting and horse-riding?'

'No.' Matthew had always felt excluded when the other boys discussed such things. Even after four years at Maidhouse he was an outsider, with neither an estate nor anecdotes of hounds or wild fowling of which to boast.

'No? My, you are a serious-minded fellow, are you not?' Kate waited for a minute, while flicking idly through a book that was obviously of no interest to her at all. 'So what do you like, Matthew?' She had squeezed his name from him. 'Apart from mathematics, that is?'

'I don't know.' Matthew realized that he had been so busy surviving in Maidhouse College that he had never cultivated any interests.

'Well then, you'll just have to ask about me, won't you?' Kate's prompting at last brought a response.

'Of course.'

Kate's laughter made one of the other customers shake her head. 'Look! You *can* smile! I was beginning to wonder.'

Unsure whether he was being taunted or not, Matthew blushed again. 'So tell me about yourself, Kate. Are you a lady?' As soon as the words were out, Matthew regretted them. Four years of Maidhouse had taught him to view everybody only in terms of social status. Now Kate's expression altered, the light faded from her eyes and she took a definite pace backward.

'You're from the college, aren't you?' The tone of her voice had also changed.

'I am,' Matthew said, and for the first time in his life he felt proud of the fact.

'I didn't know that boys from the college were allowed into town,' Kate said. 'Won't you get into trouble?'

'Trouble?' Matthew spoke as if such matters were of small concern to him. Then he glanced at the clock that overlooked the shelves of books. The hands indicated that he was long past call over; his absence would have been noted and he was indeed in trouble. 'I'd better get back.'

'Yes, you had better,' Kate agreed. 'Maybe they can teach you some manners there.'

Even as he bared his buttocks across the birching block, Matthew thought of those bright eyes of Kate. By leaving Maidhouse College for a few free hours he felt he had regained a small part of himself. Kate had kindled feelings

71

that he had not realized existed; he knew now that he could survive another two years of this purgatory. Maidhouse might fashion him into a gentleman, but somewhere inside he would still be Matthew Pryde.

Six

Kent, 1793–1795

'You again?' The gentleman with the pince-nez spectacles raised bushy eyebrows as Matthew entered. He stood behind the small counter on which he performed the business of the shop and carefully closed the wooden door that separated the retail section from the living quarters. The smell of cooking was familiar, although on this occasion the dish was Salamangundy. 'I thought that we had seen the last of you.' Weary blue eyes ran down Matthew's body. 'Maidhouse College informed me that you had been, as they euphemistically put it, "properly dealt with".'

Matthew tried not to blush. 'I'm sorry, sir, I did not know that you worked here.'

Pince-nez nodded. 'I own these premises and you are breaking the rules of your school.'

'Yes, sir,' Matthew agreed. 'Do you still have that engineering book, sir?'

'I suggest that you look on the shelf.' Pince-nez indicated the direction. 'I have quite a number of engineering books. Choose whichever you wish.'

There were seven books on engineering, all of which Matthew examined with great care before selecting the title that had originally captured his interest. As he paid for it with the savings of his entire half-term, he gathered his courage to ask the question that had been on his mind for two weeks. 'There was a girl here the last time . . .' he faltered as the man removed his pince-nez and looked directly at him. His eyes were surprisingly clear.

'I remember,' the man said.

Only the slow ticking clock disturbed the silence inside

73

the shop. The sound of carriage wheels from the street outside was very loud. 'Yes, sir. Her name was Kate.'

'Kate?' The man placed his pince-nez carefully on to the counter behind which he sat. He nodded, repeating the name. 'Kate. Quite a common name. Do you think it a common name, Mr . . . ?'

'Pryde, sir. Matthew Pryde.' Matthew took a deep breath. 'I think that it is a wonderful name, sir.'

'Ah.' The man nodded solemnly. 'But perhaps too common to be used by a lady?'

This time Matthew could not control the blood that rushed to his face. 'You heard our conversation.'

'I heard *about* it,' the man corrected him. 'So tell me, Mr Pryde, why you are asking about this girl called Kate who may not be a lady?' He was quite a large man, above forty years of age, with a fat, florid face and a suit of clothes that had been in fashion about ten years previously.

Matthew took a deep breath. 'I would like to meet her again, sir, and I wondered if you might know where I could find her. She did tell me that she spent a lot of time in this shop.'

'Indeed?' The man raised his eyebrows again. 'And if you do find this girl called Kate, Mr Pryde, and you do speak to her again, may I ask what you might say?'

For the third time that day, Matthew felt himself blush. 'I'd rather not divulge that, sir.'

'I see.' The man nodded his understanding. 'Well, if I meet Kate again, shall I tell her of your visit, and say that you wish to speak to her about some matter that must remain secret between the two of you?'

Matthew looked away. 'I would like that, sir,' he began, then, realizing that he might never have the opportunity of returning to this shop for weeks, if indeed he could ever sneak out of school again, he blurted out, 'Please, sir, tell her that I would like to apologize. I certainly meant no offence and I am sure that she is a real lady, and even if she is not, I do not care, because I like her and would like . . .' Matthew tailed off as he saw that Kate had emerged from the door behind the man.

'You would like?' Although her voice was taunting, the eyes were as bright as Matthew had remembered and there was no cruelty in her smile.

'To see you again,' Matthew finished.

'Even though I might not be a lady?' Kate tilted her head to one side as she waited for his answer.

Although Matthew had been preparing for this meeting for two weeks, the power of speech deserted him and he could only stutter as Kate and the bookshop proprietor looked at him. 'I am sure that you are a lady,' was the best that he could manage.

'But I am not,' Kate was not prepared to let him off so easily. 'At least, not in the sense of the word that you mean.'

Inspiration at last came to Matthew's aid. 'A lady in the best sense of the word,' he said, and tried to ignore the raised eyebrows of the proprietor. 'Kind, generous, cultured . . .' His words failed again as he attempted to dream up compliments.

'I see that you stop short of beautiful, wonderful, charming, intelligent and educated, sir.' The frown sat badly on Kate's face as Matthew stepped back in terrible confusion. All at once he knew that he should never have returned; he would have been far better to live on the memory rather than attempting another meeting. Now all he wanted was to turn and run from this mocking, angry woman who could turn him from ecstasy to torment with such ease.

The bookshop proprietor balanced his pince-nez on his nose and lifted the book that Matthew had purchased. 'Mr Pryde has bought this engineering book, Kate,' he said slowly. 'I do not think you should tease one of our customers.'

The words sunk only slowly into Matthew's consciousness. 'Our customers? Do you work here, ma'am?'

'I see that I have been relegated from Kate to ma'am,' Kate said acidly. 'Does that mean that I am so much less than a lady that you cannot use my given name?'

'Of course not,' Matthew began, and then he saw that the frown had dissipated and Kate was trying hard not to laugh. For four years Matthew had been trained to stoicism, to control all his emotions, from fear to desire to compassion, but now his natural self came to the fore. 'Madam Kate,' he

75

said, with his voice rising with every word, 'I am trying my best to speak honourably and decently with you, but I find your taunting attitude too much to bear! I suspect that you know full well that I intended no insult, but you persist in twisting my words. Very well then, if you find my company so amusing, then I shall leave. I bid you good day, Madam Kate.'

Then he realized that Kate was openly laughing, with a hand extended in apologetic friendship, and that the proprietor had lifted the flap of the counter.

'Matthew, I was wrong to torment you,' Kate said, between her laughter, 'but I much prefer you when you are angrily honest and talking fustian nonsense than when you pose as a prig. Pray forgive me, for I am sure that we can be friends.'

'Come inside, sir, do,' the proprietor invited, 'and you can speak in more comfort. I assure you that I will correct my daughter's manners later.'

'Your daughter?' Matthew was stuttering again. 'I truly intended no insult, sir, I'm sure.'

'Oh, come in, man, and stop postulating! If she did not like you she would never have spoken in the first place.'

It was only then that Matthew remembered to remove his hat, and Kate looked away, smiling. 'Oh, there's no need to be so polite, Mr Pryde, when we have already seen your true character.'

'Leave the boy alone, Kate,' her father said, but quietly she reached across and placed the hat back on Matthew's head.

'How tall are you, Matthew? About a head taller than me, and that white lid makes you soar even more. I wonder that you can fit inside our humble house.'

'I wonder that your father allows me,' Matthew said honestly. He did not see the look that passed between father and daughter.

'I hope that you like Salamangundy,' Kate said, 'for I set a place for you as soon as I heard your voice.' Her eyes were as bright as any star in Matthew's heaven. 'You know Salamangundy, of course? Or is Maidhouse College too grand for herring and salad?'

'I have never smelled anything so delicious,' he told her truthfully, which increased her smile.

'And do you like beetroot pancakes too? Out of season, I'm afraid, so not at their best, but fresh from somewhere or other, the barrow boy assures me.'

Matthew looked in awe at the carefully prepared food and the white linen cloth that had been spread over the mahogany table. White porcelain china sat between steel cutlery, with the Salamangundy salad as centre piece and roast beef waiting to be eaten. 'I'll like your beetroot pancakes,' he assured her, and again she smiled to her father.

'We don't usually eat this well,' she excused the ostentatious display, 'but we're celebrating. It's Father's birthday.' Kate poured melted butter sauce over the meat and tried not to see Matthew's discomfort as he ate.

For the first time that he could ever remember, Matthew was welcomed into a family. He sat at a well-set table and ate wholesome food in the company of people who laughed with him, teased him gently and listened to what he had to say. After Maidhouse, he found it impossible to drop his guard for long, but when he did he relished the experience. Matthew learned that Mr Denton had been a widower for some years; that Kate had worked in the bookshop since she could walk and read; and that both were better educated than he was. They could lace their speech with quotes from Latin and Greek scholars, Kate spoke fluent French and they could discuss natural history or current affairs with a depth of knowledge that left him ashamed of his own ignorance.

'You must remember to return in time, today, Matthew,' Mr Denton said quietly, as Kate's face fell slightly. About to speak, she closed her mouth and looked away and for once Matthew blessed her tact. He certainly did not wish to discuss his unwelcome school experiences with any young lady. In this setting the memory, so normal within the gates of Maidhouse College, made him squirm with embarrassment.

'Yes, Mr Denton,' was all that Matthew could say. He opened his new book to hide his feelings, and read the inscription on the flyleaf.

To William, it read, *may this volume lead him on the path to success.*

'Is that not strange?' Matthew said, in an attempt to forget the horrors of Maidhouse. 'This engineering book was given to a man named William, and your last name is Denton.'

'Strange? Pray, Matthew, tell me in what manner is this strange?' Kate spoke with a piece of buttered toast halfway to her mouth, and popped it in with a delicate grace that fascinated Matthew almost as much as the movement of her chin and lips as she chewed.

'Strange in the merging of names. You see, William Denton is one of the most famous engineers in the country.'

'Yes.' Kate swallowed and nodded simultaneously. 'Cousin William gifted these books to the shop.'

'Cousin William? You are the cousin of William Denton?'

That charming ringlet of hair escaped again as Kate nodded. 'Yes, of course. Did you not know that?'

'How could he know, Kate?' Mr Denton asked. 'We have only just met the boy.'

'I'll introduce you, if you wish, but he's rather a bore,' Kate said, adding slyly, 'a bit like yourself really, in that all he talks about are bridges and roads and gradients.'

'Kate!' Mr Denton's attempt to sound stern failed miserably. 'I'd be obliged if you were more polite to our guest.'

'Guest?' There was something aside from mischief in Kate's eyes. 'I thought that he was a friend.' She paused for a second as her father gathered himself for his next assault. 'And one must always be honest to one's friends. Even if they do not believe that I am a lady.'

By now Matthew was more used to Kate's manner. He ducked his head as if in shame, and muttered, 'Having met your father, Miss Denton, I am in no doubt that you were raised a lady.' He waited for a moment as Kate began to preen herself, then added, 'Even though you do not always act like one.'

Charles Denton's laughter echoed around the room as Kate stared at him before she reached across the table to touch Matthew's arm with a small hand. 'Well said, Matthew Pryde.'

Seven

Kent and London, Autumn 1795

Matthew stood in front of Dr Trueman's desk once more, listening to the heart-stirring tones of the blackbird outside as he wondered what was in the letter that lay unopened on the Rector's desk. It seemed like a lifetime since his first visit, when he had been a terrified boy of twelve, and now he was eighteen, taller than the Rector who had once towered over him, but still slim. The deficiencies of diet through the early years of his life would always be with him, ensuring a slender build and rather gaunt face. He scanned the books that filled the shelves on the Rector's wall, read the Latin titles with ease but no interest, and looked down on the arrogant man who had made his life so miserable while keeping his promise of a gentleman's classical education.

'Well, Mr Pryde.' Dr Trueman's wig fitted snugly to his head, and as he spoke a little shower of white powder landed on his shoulders. 'This will be your last visit to my study.'

Six years had taught Matthew instant obedience. 'Yes, sir,' he agreed. He stood at attention, aware of the starch in his broad collar and the crease in the sleeves of his long-tailed coat. He held his topper in the crook of his left elbow.

'I have tried to make you a gentleman, Mr Pryde. Starting from unprepossessing beginnings, I have taught you manners and speech. I have given you a classical education and more than the rudiments of geography, grammar, mathematics and history, but more importantly, I have installed character in you.'

'Yes, sir.' Matthew remained at attention. That blackbird was still singing, a song of freedom within the confines of an establishment whose memories would fester for years. How many tens of thousands of men must look back at their alma mater with a similar mixture of horror and disbelief?

'Most of my boys return to their homes, Mr Pryde, or enter the clergy, Army or Navy. Unfortunately, you do not have the requisite wherewithal to do any of these.' Dr Trueman looked smug at the reminder. 'I suggest that you enter the Honourable East India Company, where you may make a career for yourself.'

'Yes, sir,' Matthew said once more. He remained at attention.

'However, that choice may not be yours to make. As you are aware, a charitable benefactor has financed your education, and perhaps will advise you on a choice of career.'

It had been a number of years since Matthew had asked the identity of his mysterious sponsor, and he now refused to be drawn into a situation where Dr Trueman could snub him. He remained silent, wishing that he were anywhere but here.

'Your benefactor has instructed me to hand you the fare to London on your last day at Maidhouse College, Mr Pryde.' Opening a drawer in his desk, Dr Trueman produced a small metal box, from which he extracted two silver coins. 'Five shillings is the fare.' He slid the money across the desk. 'Your benefactor also instructed me to give you this letter, Mr Pryde, and so I shall.' With a flamboyant gesture that seemed out of character, Dr Trueman stood up and bowed forward as he presented the letter. Even before Matthew opened it the Rector had returned to his seat and pulled the first of a pile of documents toward him. 'That will be all, Mr Pryde. Please leave my school.'

'Sir, the door?' Ever since his first day at the school, Matthew had lived for the day he walked through the Door of Honour. Now he was being denied that ceremony. Rather than be accepted as a success by Maidhouse, he was being shown out like a common beggar. It was one final insult to add to six bad years.

'Please leave now, Pryde.' Reaching forward, Dr Trueman rang the brass bell that sat on his desk. 'Beggs will accompany you.'

Still holding the letter, Matthew nodded and left the Rector's study. Beggs, the porter, was a large ex-prizefighter who was also employed to quieten any boy who became too rowdy. He shook his head sympathetically as he escorted Matthew outside the gate, along with the single leather portmanteau that contained his entire worldly goods.

'There we go, sir. There'll be a coach along in an hour or so, depending on the driver's mood and the state of the road.' Beggs lowered his voice. 'Bit of a rum do this, though, Mr Pryde. Here.' Delving into the side pocket of his breeches, he produced a silver coin. 'You've always been decent to me, sir, not like some of the others.' Matthew knew about the various tricks that were habitually played on Beggs, from nailing shut his door to blocking his chimney with turf so smoke from the fire drove him outside. 'I haven't got much, but I wish you all the best.'

Without a single penny to his name apart from his fare to London, Matthew overcame his pride and accepted the shilling. 'I'll pay this back, Mr Beggs, as soon as I can.'

'Don't you worry your head about that, sir. You just get along now, and forget this place.' Beggs's shiver betrayed his own feelings about Maidhouse College.

While he waited for the coach, Matthew controlled the trembling of his fingers and felt for the seal of the letter. It was already broken; Dr Trueman the gentleman had acted in the most ungentlemanly manner possible by reading private mail. Matthew shook his head, dismissing this final act as unimportant, for at last he would know the identity of his benefactor. He might know his destiny, find out from where he came and what was expected of him.

Unfolding the stiff parchment, he read the single paragraph of text: 'Pray attend the following address at your earliest convenience. Request the attention of Timothy Flintock.'

The address read: 'Number One, Blackstock Square, by St John Street, London.'

There was no signature, and the seal was plain, with no coat of arms. Matthew held the letter tight, turning it over in his hands. Was this unknown Timothy Flintock his benefactor?

81

The thought was exciting, yet also strangely unsettling. However, Blackstock Square sounded promising, so Matthew fought his excitement until the stagecoach eventually rumbled up. Tumbling his bag into the boot of the coach he hoisted himself on to one of the cheaper outside seats and braced himself for the jerk as the driver cracked his whip.

Returning to London after an absence of six years, Matthew resisted the temptation to revisit the haunts he remembered from his childhood and requested directions for Blackstock Square. The city was different from his memory, just as large, just as dirty, but even more noisy, less friendly and crowded with characters that he now regarded as unsavoury. Avoiding the beggars that he had once befriended, he walked the dusty streets, rubbing shoulders with flower girls and watermen, sailors and porters, gentlemen and a score of different types of tradesmen. Men from a rope work laughed as an Irish beauty hurried past, shoulders bowed and shawl pulled high to cover her bruised eyes. Matthew ignored both the workmen and the woman, for a true gentleman did not dwell on the misfortunes of others.

He found St John Street with no difficulty, but spent quite some time searching for Blackstock Square.

'Round that way, sir,' the one-eyed barrel boy told him. He offered some hot-spiced ginger wine and swore when Matthew refused to buy.

Expecting to find a square as grand as Berkeley with its thirty maple trees, or Bloomsbury with its famous book vendors, Matthew was disappointed when he squeezed through the alley that led into a tiny space stinking of human ordure. There was glass in only half the windows that glowered from the overlooking houses, and the ragged youths that stared at him had predatory, slum-thin faces. Guessing that Number One was the first door he came to, Matthew ascended the circular stairs, which led to a low door that boasted a sign so dirty it could hardly be read: 'Bell and Flintock: Attorneys at Law'.

Matthew sighed, realizing that the mysterious Timothy Flintock was a lawyer and not his benefactor. Taking a deep breath, and ensuring that none of the youths had followed him to pick his pocket or worse, he rapped smartly and waited for the door to open. He heard an outburst of swearing from below, and a squeal that could only have come from a pig, but then the door opened and a small man peered out. His skullcap hinted at Jewish ancestry, but his accent was pure London as he asked what Matthew's business might be.

'I am looking for Timothy Flintock.'

'That door.' The small man gestured with a thumb whose nail was long and horny, then retired to an obscure cubbyhole from which came the smell of food, which made Matthew suddenly hungry, despite his rising excitement. He stepped into a small, square passage from which four more doors opened, on one of which hung a board bearing the name Flintock. There was no answer to Matthew's knock, so he pushed open the door and stepped inside.

'And you are?' Flintock was so tall that he had to stoop under the low ceiling, but his grip was powerful and his eyes level.

'Matthew Pryde,' Matthew said, and some devil inside him made him add, 'I think.'

When Flintock smiled, his eyes narrowed in a mass of creases. Matthew could not guess his age, but put him somewhere between thirty and fifty, and knew by the quality of his clothes that he was not a poor man. Maidhouse College had taught him more than he realized. 'I know something of your situation, young man. After all, I have been acting as your solicitor these last fifteen years.'

Matthew swallowed. 'Yes, sir.' He hesitated, bracing himself for the final revelation. 'May I ask on whose behalf you have been acting?'

'I am afraid you may not.' Flintock shook his head, still smiling. 'I am not at liberty to release that information.'

Maidhouse had taught Matthew how to suppress his sick disappointment. 'I understand, sir. I have a letter instructing me to come to you.' He produced the letter, which Mr Flintock glanced at and handed back.

'I sent it,' he said, 'for I have a little information for you.' Flintock sighed and sat down, inviting Matthew to occupy the only other seat. The type of candle known as a long lady

83

flickered in the uncertain atmosphere, its wax dribbling down the shaft to form a small pool in the saucer in which it stood. The illumination was necessary as piled-up papers nearly covered the tiny window that was the only other source of light.

Hardly able to control his trembling, Matthew sat down. He waited with rising impatience as Flintock produced a key and opened a drawer in his desk before extracting a bundle of papers tied with a linen cord. He sighed again as he unpicked the knot and selected one of the enclosed documents.

'So you have finished school then, Mr Pryde?' Flintock spoke with maddening slowness, but Matthew forced himself to reply politely.

'Indeed, yes sir.'

'And did you enjoy your time at Maidhouse?'

'I learned a lot, sir,' Matthew said carefully.

Flintock looked at him, his smile gentle. 'Of course,' he said at length. 'Dr Trueman would take pains to instruct you.' Still slowly, he unfolded the chosen document and laid it on the desk in front of him. He read for a full five minutes, tracing the words with his finger as Matthew's impatience grew stronger. 'Well now, you are a bit of a mystery man, are you not?'

'Am I, sir?' Matthew leaned forward expectantly. 'What can you tell me?'

'I am instructed to tell you this,' Flintock looked up, 'you are an orphan, Mr Pryde. When you were very young, you survived a shipwreck. A lady rescued you and brought you up for the first three years of your life.'

Matthew closed his eyes, digging deep inside him for any memories. He had a vague recollection of a small house of darkness, the sound of the wind and a woman's face smiling into his own. He had long thought that the image had been of his mother. Now he knew that it was a memory of his rescuer. That knowledge was a disappointment in itself.

'Does that document say who I am, sir? Or who was that lady?'

Ignoring the questions, Flintock continued. 'Then you were sent to a foundling's hospital in London.' He raised his eyebrows as Matthew nodded.

He had many memories of that time. He remembered a long uncomfortable journey and the shock of arrival cushioned by friendship from the other orphans. He remembered the basic food but also the laughter, the scanty clothing and hard work as he was farmed out to a factory for an eternity of hours a day. He remembered the comradeship of his peers and the many small acts of kindness, the constant gnawing hunger and the sound of rats scurrying at night. 'Why was I sent there?'

'That I cannot tell you.' Flintock shook his head and leaned closer. 'I don't know, Mr Pryde. I only work with the information that I am given.'

Matthew remembered the bewilderment of a young boy in London, the thought that he was not wanted, the lack of support in an alien environment. After six years in which he had learned to control his emotions, he had to fight the tears that threatened to mar his expressionless face. 'Maybe the lady died?'

'I cannot say.' Flintock waited for a few minutes as Matthew regained his composure. 'When you were twelve years old, I was given instructions to enrol you in Maidhouse College. I was given funds to pay your fees for term times, and to cover your boarding arrangements when the school was closed. Sometimes the moneys varied, but there was always enough to cover your clothing and other essentials.' He looked up, one finger resting on a line of the document in front of him. 'And now that you are no longer a scholar, I have further instructions.'

'Yes, sir?'

'I can now offer you a paid voyage to Hindustan, with a place as a clerk with the Honourable East India Company.'

Matthew noted that somebody else was trying to send him to Hindustan. It seemed that nobody wished him to be in England, but the stubborn rebellious streak that had forced him out of the school to meet Kate Denton again surfaced. 'Thank you, sir, but I must decline.'

'*You must decline?*' Flintock looked up, obviously not used to young men rejecting good advice from their mentors. 'Mr Pryde, I am offering you a chance to better yourself. Many young men sail to Hindustan as virtual paupers and return as nabobs, able to buy a country property and a good address in town. The Honourable Company is the making of them, as it could be of you.' He shook his head, unable to comprehend such ingratitude. 'Your benefactor has perhaps planned this very move for years, to give you a good start in life.'

'Or to get rid of me.' Matthew could hear the unaccustomed edge in his own voice. 'No, Mr Flintock. I have chosen my own career, and it does not include sailing to the other side of the world, where fever kills those that survive the perils of the voyage. I thank you for your trouble, Mr Flintock, but my benefactor, whoever he is, has controlled my life for long enough. Now I must make my own way.'

Flintock's mouth opened in surprise. 'But Mr Pryde, this is an excellent opportunity. You could prosper; you could become a very wealthy man. Pray reconsider, for your benefactor has only your interests at heart.'

'Perhaps so,' Matthew leaned forward, 'but he would be better served in revealing himself, and in telling me who I am and from whence I come.'

There was a long silence in the room, spoiled only by the distant drift of a drunken song from outside and the scratching of a rat somewhere inside the building. Flintock shook his head in disbelief. 'Mr Pryde, may I remind you that you are not yet of age, so legally you cannot deny your benefactor's request.'

'I am afraid that I must, Mr Flintock.' Matthew took a deep breath as he finally declared his own destiny. 'I am set on becoming an engineer, sir. I have already arranged a seven year apprenticeship with Mr William Denton.'

This time the silence extended a full four minutes, with Flintock trying to subdue Matthew with an unremitting stare. When Matthew met his gaze, the solicitor lowered his head and began to shuffle the papers on his desk into some semblance of order. 'Then there is no more to be said. I will bid you farewell, Mr Pryde. If you reconsider your offer within the next three years, then pray call on me. If not, then it is unlikely that we will meet again.'

'I see, Mr Flintock.' Matthew rose slowly from the seat, wondering if he was making the right choice. 'Pray convey my gratitude to my benefactor for all his kindnesses, sir.'

'I will do that.'

The sudden knock on the door made Matthew jump, and for one ludicrous moment he thought that his benefactor was coming in person to persuade him to sail to the ends of the world. Instead it was the small man in the skullcap who poked his head into the room. 'Excuse my interruption, gentlemen, but I must ask Mr Flintock to come out for a moment. There is a piece of business that requires his urgent attention.'

Flintock continued to sort his papers. 'Just one minute, Mr Bell, that is all I ask.'

'And I cannot even allow you that, Mr Flintock. Please come this instant.'

Sighing, Flintock stood up and left the room. The sound of raised voices attracted Matthew's attention for only a few seconds before he realized the opportunity that lay before him. Leaning across the table, he peered at the documents on which Flintock had been working. He grunted in horror when he saw that the writing was in Latin, and focussed his mind to concentrate on the words, mentally translating as he read.

In the matter of the young gentleman, he read, *I desire that he is to enter the Honourable East India Company, there to seek his fortune. I have already asked Dr Trueblood to prepare him for this career. I will fund his endeavours to the tune of £500 a year, for no more than three years, after which he should be sufficiently established not to need further financial assistance.*

Five hundred pounds a year! It was a sum far beyond Matthew's expectations, although well beneath that of a landed gentleman. With such ample finance, and a career with the Honourable Company, Matthew knew that his future would lie in his own hands. There was no limit to the possibilities, provided he agreed to leave England and followed the instructions. He read on.

However, should the young gentleman ever discover about Ederford . . .

'Mr Pryde!' Mr Flintock's voice was sharp as he moved quickly from the door to his desk and covered the papers with an open hand. 'These documents are confidential, and must remain so. You cannot read them, or know any more of their contents than I permit.' His voice dropped. 'I am sorry to deny your natural desire for enlightenment, but I am acting on the instructions of my client, and in your own best interests.'

Matthew stepped back and made a small, polite bow. 'My apologies, Mr Flintock. I confess that my curiosity did get the better of my manners.' He forced a smile. 'Unfortunately, you returned before that curiosity was in the least bit satisfied. My Latin was always poor and I got no further than East India Company.'

'As well, Mr Pryde.' Flintock's anger dissipated as quickly as it had risen. 'So we shall say no more about it. Can I ask you one last time to reconsider your decision? You could have a glittering career in John Company, with rewards far greater than anything in England.'

'I believe that I could, Mr Flintock –' Matthew thought of a guaranteed £500 a year, a good position, advancement, servants and a return to England as a successful nabob – 'but I have no desire to ever leave England. I wish to be an engineer, to build canals and bridges, and to design new harbours to advance the trade of the country.'

Flintock shook his head. 'A capital notion, Mr Pryde. All progress is admirable, but in this case it is admirably foolish! After all the trouble taken to raise you as a gentleman, you are discarding your patron's generosity.'

'I am grateful for all that he has done,' Matthew said, 'but I cannot alter what I am.'

Flintock conceded defeat with a sigh that must have sounded dramatically through many a courtroom. 'As you will, Mr Pryde, as you will.'

Matthew hesitated. 'I have one last favour to ask, Mr Flintock. Pray tell me at least the name of the vessel whose wreck I survived.' He already knew that it was Ederford, but wanted to hear that confirmed.

Flintock seemed to consider for a long time before reaching his decision. 'I can see no harm in that, Mr Pryde. She was named *Pride of Matthew*, and it was from her that you gained your name.'

Eight

Onswick, March–April 1804

Matthew ran his hand along the shaft of the harpoon, feeling the name that had been stamped into the smooth iron. *Pride of Matthew*. Harpoons came only from whaling ships, so his father had been a Greenlandman. That was one clue to his past. He looked around to ask Grover a question, but the vicar had disappeared, leaving his lantern behind. Still holding the harpoon, Matthew sunk down on to the cold floor of the crypt as he tried to make some sense of this new revelation.

He had been little more than a baby when he was cast ashore here, so presumably his mother had also been on board. Although women were not permitted on whaling ships, he knew that some shipmasters brought their wives, which meant that his father had been master of *Pride of Matthew*. To trace his father, he would have to discover from which port *Pride of Matthew* had sailed, and then ask who the shipmaster had been. The thought made him suddenly weak. He would find his real name, perhaps be able to trace a blood relative or even find a family who would welcome him back like the prodigal son.

The prospect was exhilarating but also frightening, and for a minute Matthew felt the blood pounding inside his head. The temptation to rush away and indulge in his private business was overwhelming, but duty must come first. Matthew called on his training in self-discipline. His entire career could depend on the success or otherwise of this commission, so logic dictated that anything else must be subordinate. Yet his own feelings betrayed him.

Pride of Matthew had foundered here, on the very Black

90

Corbie that his light would make safe. The irony was so inescapable that Matthew wondered if he were the victim of some divine practical joke. What sardonic providence had sent him here, where his parents had died and his life had taken the first of its many twists? He laid the cold shaft of the harpoon across his thighs, wondering if his father had wielded this weapon in some dramatic encounter with the whales. Matthew discarded the image as romantic fustian; only hard facts mattered.

Gathering his thoughts, he concentrated on the next piece of the puzzle. Surely he could now make progress with the name Ederford. Was that the name of his benefactor, or of the lady who had cared for him? Perhaps they were one and the same person? For one wonderful second Matthew imagined that Ederford was his own name, but he forced away the fantasy, wishing that there were somebody whom he could ask.

He was aware that the villagers would tell him nothing, even if he chose to pose the question. They were uneducated, ignorant, probably superstitious; certainly not the type of people that he would take into his confidence. Mr Grover was the only exception, for the vicar certainly knew more than he was saying. Matthew sighed and shook his head. He was not sure what to do; but until he decided, he would work on the plans for the lighthouse. The Black Corbie must be tamed.

Retreating to his room, Matthew blocked out his personal worries as he concentrated on creating an accurate map of the Corbie. Using the chart he had purchased in London as a guide, he worked with hardly a break. First he copied his own measurements, checked them against the published chart, and then drew a rough plan. Only when he was satisfied with his own accuracy did he begin to transfer his work on to high quality paper.

He worked meticulously, dipping his quill into the inkpot, using the sunlight when he could and lighting candles when the light faded, until the steady rhythm of mental work soothed away his worries. Intent on the map, he neglected the food that Billy Anderson or Ruth, his cheerful wife, brought up to him, and snatched only a few minutes of rest in the chair. He neither shaved nor undressed, but continued to work until he could see the outline of the island, with the Black Corbie a menacing presence on the north-eastern side.

'Are you all right, sir?' Ruth asked when she appeared, but Matthew was too busy to do more than grunt an impolite reply. He said nothing when she removed his untouched food, opened the window and smoothed down the coverlet of his unused bed. 'You'll do yourself a mischief, sir, unless you take better care of yourself.'

He enjoyed this part of his job, watching his calculations take shape on a map, forming the shape of the island and the innumerable rocks and islets on either side. This was real creation, unlike the romantic nonsense of Wordsworth that Kate had liked so much. How could people be so deluded as to enjoy such a bag of mawkish moonshine?

Twice Matthew contemplated descending to the taproom and asking the local fishermen for their advice, but he knew that such muttonheads would be unable to match their knowledge with an abstract drawing. When he had completed the map, Matthew drew another sheet of paper toward him and made a copy, forcing himself to take just as much care. He worked around the clock so that he looked up in surprise when daylight crawled across his page and he had to snuff what remained of the candle.

Matthew decided that he would pay Megstone to take him back around the island and mark in details of currents and tides, the safest passages and landing places and those it was best to avoid. Easing the muscles in his back, he dipped the finest of his quills into the pot of ink and scanned his creation. He could see the outline of the Black Corbie, with the passage known as the Gut and the mass of rocks that were the Raven's Brood. When he had started, he had thought of the islets as an amorphous mass of navigational hazards, but now they were plainly a continuation of the Hornshope Heights, a final hurrah before the range disappeared beneath the waves. He could see how the group secured the bay of Onswick, and how a north-easterly wind would drive shipping against the

Corbie. The rocks both shielded the harbour from the wind, and acted as a giant trap for shipping.

While high tide submerged the island, only the Corbie protruded. The appearance of clear water tempted ships to try the gap between the Corbie and the mainland, not realizing that there was no depth of water for their keel. Perhaps that was how his father's ship ran aground. Matthew shivered and covered his face with his hands. Now that the map was complete he was suddenly tired. The thought of the bed was even more tempting than the prospect of eating that last tray of cold ham that Ruth had provided.

No wonder this bay had attracted the Norse. Once they understood the winds and currents, it would be a safe haven, sheltered from the worst of the weather and nearly hidden from the land. What more would sea raiders need? He could imagine the Vikings worshipping Odin beneath these cliffs, the great bearded men with their horned helmets raising their voices in praise as they sacrificed slaves. Did the Vikings sacrifice slaves? He neither knew nor cared, but the fact that he was even thinking along these lines proved his fatigue. With sleep suddenly a priority, Matthew quickly folded away one copy of his map, changed rapidly into his nightshirt and tumbled into bed.

He must have slept the whole day through, for when the sudden hammering of booted feet woke him, it was once again night outside.

'What? Who's there?'

The group of dark-clothed men swore loudly as they stumbled over furniture. 'Get the bastard!'

Matthew heard the swish of the stick and jerked aside. Something hard and heavy thudded against his pillow, but there was sudden pain as a second blow caught him full on the mouth, splitting his lips, and a third cracked against his knee. He yelled, spitting blood, and raised a hand to his mouth.

Another blow landed high on his chest and he tried to kick back, but the bedclothes clung to his legs and the effort was wasted. Somebody swore, then laughed, and Mathew protected his face with his arms, rolling into a foetal ball to ride the storm of pain.

'Cowards!' Matthew resorted to the language of Maidhouse, where night attacks had been common and the insults predictable. 'Fight fair!'

When somebody smashed a cudgel into his kidneys he roared and punched wildly. He felt quick satisfaction at the splinter and sudden wetness of a nose breaking beneath his fist, but his retaliation had left him open. He curled in agony as somebody thrust shrewdly to his groin, rolled off his bed and lay whimpering in a tangle of blankets.

The noise must have shaken the whole house, but the cudgels kept rising and falling, supplemented by kicks and a barrage of foul language. He gasped as a boot crashed into his stomach, yelped as somebody stamped on his bare feet, grunted as a cudgel thumped against his hip.

Another boot hammered on to his neck, and another slammed into his ribs, so he rolled away, hoping to take shelter beneath the table, but there were too many men, too many boots lashing into him.

'Got it!' The gasping voice seemed to come from far away.

'Give him a few more. Teach the bastard a lesson!'

Then there was a woman's voice, high pitched, screaming. The men scrambled away, one colliding with Ruth in the doorway, knocking her backward. He dropped something that landed with another crash. The man scrabbled for whatever he had dropped but somebody snapped a crisp 'Leave it!' and they were gone, leaving Matthew dazed and groaning on the ground.

'Oh, you rogues! You vile creatures!' Ruth was bending over him. 'Oh, Mr Pryde, sir, are you all right? Oh, what a terrible thing to happen, and you such a polite gentleman, too! Oh, sir, I am sorry.'

She had a candle lit in a moment and was guiding him to the chair, all the while making sympathetic noises. 'There, sir, you have a nice sit down while I tidy up the room. See, they've tried to take your case away, and dropped all your things on the floor.'

Matthew nodded, more intent on nursing his injuries than on the condition of his case. He recalled the night-time visit of the thief in Foulmire Cross and wondered if all northern inns were so dangerous, then sat down carefully and stifled another groan. A gentleman did not give in to pain, especially not in the presence of a lady.

'My case.' Matthew carefully raised himself from the chair and stooped to recover his instruments. Without them, he could not work, and he was unlikely to find replacements outside of London. Fighting the pain, he began to check his instruments for damage.

'Oh, sir, you're all bleeding!' Ruth shook her head. 'I've never seen the like. Now you go back in your chair there while I fetch a basin of water.' She swept away, leaving Matthew to replace his instruments. Save for a few scuff marks, they appeared undamaged. There was a slight scratch on the lens of his spyglass, but nothing major.

'Now, sir, let me see you.' Ruth had been quick with warm water. She settled Matthew back on the chair and began to gently sponge his face and head. 'Oh, sir, they have hurt you so. Your poor mouth, and your eye! Such a bruise you'll have there in the morning!'

Strangely, Matthew found her ministrations quite soothing, and allowed her to bathe his face and hands, but objected when she asked him to remove his nightshirt.

'No, madam, I am quite capable of washing myself.'

'It's all right, sir,' Ruth sounded quite amused by his reticence. 'I only want to tend your bruises. You've nothing I haven't seen before. I've three brothers and a husband.'

'No doubt, but I'm not one of them. I will take care of myself now, but thank you for your help.' Matthew held his nightshirt firmly in place.

'As you wish, sir.' It was only when Ruth reluctantly withdrew that Matthew realized that the copy of his map was missing. He remembered one of his attackers saying 'got it', which suggested that the map had been the men's primary object, with the assault perhaps an attempt to scare him away. Matthew winced, shifted uncomfortably in his chair and put a hand to his split lip. Maidhouse had inured him to pain, but the theft only hardened his resolve to continue. He would do everything in his power to ensure the Black Corbie had a lighthouse, partly to honour the memory of his parents, partly because it was his duty, and now, partly to spite whoever had attacked him.

'I came as soon as I heard! That's a terrible thing to happen!' Cloakless, with his wig aslant and his waistcoat incorrectly buttoned, Reverend Grover stood in the doorway. 'Are you badly hurt?'

Matthew tested each limb and rib in turn. 'I'm not too bad, Reverend, but lots of cuts and bruises. They seemed to want to hurt, rather than damage me.'

'God will strike the guilty,' Grover assured him, bustling around the room, lighting the candles, tidying Matthew's papers on the table and poking at his scientific instruments. 'Be assured of that, Mr Pryde, the Lord will avenge the injustice.'

'No doubt, Reverend.' Matthew felt his split lip reopen when he replied. 'They knew what they were doing, Mr Grover. Two attacked me while the third rifled my papers and tried to steal my case.' A glance around the room confirmed his suspicions. 'Look, there's my watch untouched on the table, and my money is safe in my pocketbook.'

Grover crouched down at Matthew's side. 'Here, let me.' He helped Matthew remove his shirt, took a sympathetic breath and began to minister to the various contusions. 'Just an attack on your person, then.'

'And they stole my map,' Matthew said. He did not mention the copy.

'Your map? Can you make another?' Grover was nobody's fool.

'Not as good as that one,' Matthew said truthfully.

There were a few minutes' silence as Grover peered at the spreading bruises that covered Matthew's ribs. 'It's the lighthouse, Mr Pryde. Change frightens people.'

'So does the Black Corbie.' Matthew gasped as Grover pressed the damp cloth on to a tender area.

When Grover had completed bathing his wounds, he helped Matthew dress and they sat at the table, with the candles casting pools of yellow light that only highlighted the dark shadows beyond. A rising wind rattled the pantiles and whined around the corners of the inn.

'Now you are here, Reverend, you can tell me about *Pride of Matthew*. I think that you know more than you are saying.'

'I know a little, Matthew, but not all.'

Matthew nodded. 'Every little helps, Reverend. Pray tell me all that you can.'

'As you will.' Grover rearranged his wig so it sat square on his head. '*Pride of Matthew* was a whaling ship. That much you know. I believe that she was returning from a voyage to the Greenland Sea when a sudden storm blew her against the Black Corbie.' Grover listened to the wind for a second. 'Round here, they call the north-east wind "Lady Fenwick's wind" because it blows ships on to the rock. That's a northeaster now.' He shook his head. 'Her Ladyship gets the blame for many things outwith her responsibility,' he said. 'I would ask you to remember that.'

'I will,' Matthew promised. 'But the wreck?'

'Of course.' Grover nodded. 'There was great surprise when you were found alive, for the Corbie and the Raven's Brood usually claim all that are cast upon them.'

'I was the sole survivor? My parents?'

Grover shook his head slowly. 'As I said, it is unusual for anybody to survive the Corbie. The local fishermen do not even attempt to rescue those who are stranded until the storm blows itself out. There have been too many deaths.'

'I see.' Matthew closed his eyes. For as long as he remembered, he had hoped that his parents were alive, that he had been separated from them by chance. His childhood had been punctuated by daydreams of an ethereal mother whisking him home, or of a beaming father greeting him in the street. His parents would rescue him from the torment of his existence and carry him to a better life. He had persuaded himself that the life he led was only temporary, that things would improve tomorrow, next week, sometime. Although such fantasies were in the past, there was always a faint flicker of hope. Now it seemed that even that tiny light was doused. 'So my parents died?'

'Without doubt.' Grover's eyes were sympathetic. 'They are in the hands of the Lord.'

Matthew smoothed a hand down his face. The name on

the harpoon had shocked him, but now he felt numb. The physical aches from the recent assault were irrelevant compared to the chronic mental anguish that was his constant companion in life, but both had disappeared in the face of an immense weariness. His parents were dead; there was no doubt that he was alone in the world.

There were so many questions that required answers, but experience had taught him that to reveal weakness was to invite exploitation. He wanted to know his real name, who rescued him from the wreck, what happened in the first few years of his life, why he was sent to London and who had paid for his education and organized his life. There was so much he did not know.

'And me?' Matthew asked. 'How did I survive?'

'You were carried ashore, I believe,' Grover's voice was gentle in his ear. 'Some freak of the current, or perhaps the hand of the Lord.'

'The same Lord who killed my parents?' Matthew could not keep the bitterness from his voice.

'The Lord's ways are mysterious, but He knows best.' Grover allowed Matthew a few minutes to recover. 'One of the local women found you. She cared for you.'

'Who? Who was she? Was her name Ederford? Where is she now? Can I talk to her?'

Grover slowly shook his head. 'So many unanswered questions! I said that I know some things, but not all. I cannot tell you what I do not know. I was not in this parish then.'

'So who will know?' Matthew stood up, gasping as his battered body complained about this unwanted movement.

'Probably most of the village, Mr Pryde, but I do not think that they will talk of it.' Adjusting his wig, Grover prepared to leave. 'Perhaps you would find out more if you decided not to build a lighthouse. People might be more open, then.' As he reached the door, he held out a hand. 'These are not bad people, Mr Pryde, only scared that you might take away their livelihood. If you assure them that you will not, I believe that they will attempt to answer all your questions.'

'Thank you.' Matthew took the hand. 'Before anything is decided, I must speak to the Member of Parliament.'

Grover nodded. 'Lord Chevington. Once you have seen him, things may be clearer.'

Left with only the soft glow of the candles for company, Matthew stared out of the window. Lady Fenwick's wind blew ragged clouds from the east, partially obscuring the spreading light of dawn. Stark in the middle distance, he could see the silver-white streak that marked the Black Corbie, and he could hear the rising growl of breakers. So that was where his parents had died, and this was where he had spent some of his life . . . There was a sound from below as Ruth began her preparations for the day's work, and somewhere outside a seagull screamed.

Grover could not have been clearer: if he reported that building a lighthouse was impractical, the villagers would tell him more. He could find out who Ederford was, and perhaps other details of his past, but he would have betrayed the trust of Mr Denton. As he stared out of the window until dawn stretched across the entire horizon Matthew struggled between temptation and duty.

'Who am I?' he asked. 'And why am I here?'

There was no answer, just as there was no decision to make. He had ascertained that it was possible to build a lighthouse, and now he had to obtain the consent of Lord Chevington.

Matthew stood with a groan; his bruises had stiffened, with his face swollen, one eye closed and much of his body too tender to touch. Refusing to allow his attackers any satisfaction, he went down to breakfast at his normal time, accepted Billy Anderson's explanation that he had been fishing, and limped around the village with the aid of a stick. He carried his pistol hopefully, but he did not meet anyone with a newly broken nose. The attack was just another mystery of Onswick.

It was three days before he felt able to ride, and even then he sat gingerly in the saddle. Grover had given him directions to find Chevington Hall, and he followed the road inland for just over a mile before he reached a copse of wind-tortured hawthorn which screened a road that headed due north.

Fringed by juniper bushes, the road rose over a ridge, then dipped and narrowed through heather moorland. The lonely cry of a curlew disturbed the silence as a rabbit bounded frantically from cover, and Matthew jammed his hat down, bowing his shoulders against a blustery shower. The heather eased into rough grassland, with strips of farmland surrounding weary farmhouses. He passed through a small village of solid stone houses, where a gaggle of brown and white geese gossiped around a central green and rangy, dark-headed men watched him suspiciously. Outside the village was a belt of mixed woodland – beech, laurel, silver fir and spruce – through which yellowhammers yammered.

The road stretched ahead, bright between the showers, but Matthew stopped at a set of iron gates that stood between two high stone pillars. An unmistakable carved stone duck topped the pillar on the left, while the right sported a bird that Matthew did not recognize. An ornate lodge house squatted outside the gates, with tall chimneys from which issued blue smoke.

Dismounting, Matthew knocked at the door of the lodge and requested that the gates be opened.

'Is His Lordship expecting you?' The gatekeeper was squat and ugly, with a nose that had been broken many years ago.

'No,' Matthew said. 'Open the gates, there's a good fellow.'

'His Lordship won't be pleased.'

'That is hardly your business.' Matthew adopted his most imperious Maidhouse expression.

The gatekeeper's look was venomous, but the gates opened smoothly and Matthew rode through. 'Watch for the mantraps,' the gatekeeper said as he closed the gates. 'His Lordship won't be pleased if you set them off.' He retreated inside his lodge before Matthew had time to reply.

After the moorland and modest cottages, he was pleased to see manicured lawns and new plantations of trees, although he did not venture from the road in case Lord Chevington had indeed laid mantraps. Young partridge scampered before him as he rode on, but he stopped in surprise at his first view of Chevington Hall.

Matthew had expected antiquity, either romantically

Jacobean or a grim tower of impenetrable stone, but Chevington House was built in the most modern style imaginable, as good as anything he had seen in the south. Doric pillars soared around tall, classically proportioned windows set in three storeys of dressed stonework.

Gravel crunched beneath Sally's hooves as he approached the staircase that swept to an impressive front entrance. Matthew dismounted, throwing the reins to a waiting servant whose ornate red and yellow livery contrasted with his black skin. 'Pray tell your master that Matthew Pryde is here to see him.'

'Your card, sir?' After a few moments' fumbling, Matthew produced one of his few visiting cards and dropped it on to the silver tray that another servant proffered. 'Pray wait inside, sir.' The servant bowed low and ghosted away.

An arched entrance led into a cool and airy hall enhanced by Greek vases set into niches on either side. Light reflected from the crystal chandelier that hung from a chain which appeared to be pure silver.

'This way sir, if you please.' Another liveried servant led Matthew into a room where a long mahogany table was laden with a selection of bottles. Another chandelier hung from an elaborate ceiling rose, its candles casting bright light into every corner. In one corner a large, colourful bird chattered noisily from its tall cage.

'Matthew Pryde! Now there's a name I know well!'

The voice was loud and fruity, and the hand extended in friendship as Matthew found himself staring into the deep brown eyes of Nicholas Elmstead.

Nine

Northumberland, April 1804

For an instant Matthew felt genuine fear. Elmstead's face was one that still appeared to him in nightmares, and one that he had hoped never to see again in his life.

'A fellow Maidhousian up here, by God!' Elmstead seemed genuinely pleased to see him as he pumped his hand. 'What brings you here, old boy? Come to see an old friend, eh? Talk over happy memories?'

Matthew forced a smile. His memories were anything but happy. 'I did not realize that you were Lord Chevington, Elmstead.'

'No?' Elmstead raised his eyebrows, then laughed again. 'Not surprising, old boy, for the title is as new as the money. Fruits of the Indies, Pryde!' His laugh was much as Matthew remembered, but this was not the Elmstead of old. Rather than a sadistic bully, this man treated him as a friend and an equal, taking him by the arm to guide him to the long table and pour a generous brandy. Matthew remembered Elmstead as a bit of a dandy, but now he was dressed quite casually, with faded buckskin breeches that displayed his powerful legs, an open-necked white shirt and a waistcoat from which dangled a watch chain and a lorgnette.

Holding his glass to the chandelier, Elmstead allowed the light to diffuse through the liquid and sparkle from the deep cuts in the crystal. 'Here we go then, Pryde. Probably smuggled, but who cares, eh? Confusion to Boney!'

Matthew joined in the toast. 'Confusion to Boney. And you're a Member of Parliament too?'

'That's right, my boy. Lord of the manor, Member of Parliament, rich as Midas and monarch of Chevington.'

Elmstead poured another brandy for them both. 'So tell me about yourself. You were a bit backward when we first met, but Maidhouse soon straightened you out, eh?'

Matthew nodded. 'Maidhouse made a gentleman of me,' he admitted, and swallowed hard. He needed the help of this man. 'With your assistance.'

'Well said, young Pryde!' Elmstead clapped Matthew on the back. Always tall, he overtopped Matthew by a good three inches and was broader in the shoulder and chest. His face and hands were deeply tanned by the sun so that his hair, always fair, seemed almost a bleached white in comparison. 'And what are you about now? Married into money, did you?'

'No. I am an engineer.' Matthew stepped back slightly, expecting the ridicule of which Elmstead had long proved himself a master.

'Well, that's different,' Elmstead said carefully. 'I don't think I've met one of them in England before. Met a couple in Jamaica, though. Useful fellows to have around.' His tone suggested that an engineer's usefulness mattered less than his low social standing. 'Building a navigation hereabouts, are you? The Great Newcastle to Carlisle Canal? You people like to add a "great" to all your works, don't you?'

'Not a canal,' Matthew said, 'a lighthouse.'

'Come to the wrong place, then,' Elmstead said at once. 'No need for lighthouses here. No ships, you see. No sea to put them on, you understand.' He laughed at his own joke. 'Come with me.' Ushering Matthew through the hall, he strode into a morning room where a small fire crackled in a neat marble fireplace. Throwing himself into one of the armed chairs, Elmstead clapped his hands to summon another servant, demanded more brandy from the broad-shouldered man with the tribal scars on his face that entered, and settled down. 'So tell me more about this light of yours. Not in my parish, obviously, so where?'

Elmstead nodded understandingly as Matthew explained about the dangers of the Black Corbie, of the number of ships that had been lost there, and of the request of the Newcastle Shipmasters for help.

103

'Fascinating stuff, young Pryde. But what has all this to do with me?'

'Quite a lot, Elmstead, my Lord. You see, a lighthouse cannot be built without an Act of Parliament, and that requires the local MP to present a bill.'

Elmstead took a deep breath. 'I see, but you can drop the "my Lord" stuff. We've known each other long enough not to be so formal, eh?'

The grin was friendlier than Matthew could have expected, and he wondered if perhaps he had been mistaken about Elmstead all these years. Maybe the bullying had been for Matthew's own good, after all.

Elmstead continued, 'Now I understand where I could be useful.' Signalling again to the servant, he demanded another drink, cursed the man when he brought brandy – 'I always have blue ruin for my fourth, you clod' – cursed him again when the glass was too light, and returned his attention to Matthew. 'I believe that the idea is excellent, Pryde, but is it practical? Is it possible to build a lighthouse in such a dangerous place?'

'Indeed.' Reaching for the case that he had brought with him, Matthew extracted the surviving copy of the map that he had made.

Elmstead seemed surprised. 'You have a chart too, eh? Very efficient.' For a second, his forehead creased, and then he signalled for Matthew to continue.

'As you see, the main island – Corbie island, if you will – is just over half a mile in length. However, parts of it are only above water for six hours at every tide, so there will be limited time for work.'

'I see.' However much of a hectoring bully he had been, Elmstead had never been stupid. He listened as Matthew explained the technical difficulties of building and asked about the proposed design.

'Because of the regular submergence by the sea, the lower courses of the lighthouse cannot be left to their own weight, however much aided by gravity –' both men smiled at Matthew's joke – 'they will have to be trenailed and wedged into position, much as Smeaton did at Eddystone.'

'I understand,' Elmstead caught on at once. 'And will it then be safe?'

'Safety at sea is always relative.' When Matthew spoke about a subject that he understood, his natural reticence and learned arrogance both disappeared and he became an articulate and confident man. 'We have to watch for the curve, where the base of the tower takes off from the platform of the rock. I intend to suggest a broader base than is normal in other lights. You see,' he smiled again as he quickly sketched an outline of his design, 'the sea is powerful against such an exposed place. My theory is that it would be better to minimize the action of the waves, rather than meeting force with some massy structure that would be expensive to build and clumsy in appearance. No, I want an elegant tower that deflects the force of the waves by a curved or angled base, rather than a perpendicular erection.'

Elmstead raised his eyebrows, but said nothing as Matthew continued. 'The actual building stones are to be dovetailed; one hooking laterally into the other so there is a vertical bond of connection.'

'That way there is no single join for the sea to attack, no straight point of weakness!' Elmstead immediately understood the design and smiled as Matthew nodded eagerly.

'Exactly, but we still depend on gravity to provide the main strength of the structure.'

'I can see some difficulties with that,' Elmstead shook his head. 'I hate to pour cold water on a hot idea, but if you have so little time to work before the tide comes in, how could you shape the stones?'

'On land,' Matthew replied promptly. 'We'll create a mould so that each building stone is exact, and have expert stonemasons hew the stone to the required shape and dimensions. We'll perform this part of the work on shore, possibly on the stantage next to Onswick harbour. I've yet to draw up the design for that, but once the stones are completed, we'll lay one course at a time on an exact replica of the site. Only then will they be shipped out to the island and placed in the required position.'

'Even if correctly shaped, would the stones not be porous?

105

Would not the sea eventually force its way through the cracks, however ingenuously dovetailed?' Elmstead poked an elegant finger at Matthew's sketch.

'That is easily remedied, Elmstead,' Matthew said. 'Have you heard of Mr Parker's Roman Cement?'

'Can't recall that ever coming up in Latin classes,' Elmstead grinned. 'Not that I listened much anyway. I always used to crib my answers.'

Matthew smiled at the frank admission. 'It's a modern invention, or maybe I would be more accurate to say that it is a rediscovery of an old invention. Mr Parker of London patented Roman Cement, which is a very quick-setting mixture that can be used for the lower courses. It's an ugly brown colour, and comes from calcined nodules . . .' Matthew paused, aware that he was lecturing to the man who had made his life a misery for years, but Elmstead appeared to be listening.

'Go on, Pryde. Calcined nodules, you were saying.'

'Yes. Or argillaceous limestone, which will have to be shipped up from the south coast.'

'That will cost,' Elmstead said.

'Yes. But we should not need great quantities. We will mostly use a mixture made from Welsh lime, Sicilian pozzolana and simple Northumberland sand.'

'An international lighthouse, this one.' Elmstead was sitting back in his chair. He nodded his approval. 'You seem to have this all worked out, young Pryde.'

'Yes, but there's plenty more . . .'

Elmstead raised a hand to stop Matthew's eager discourse. 'I am sure there is, but I have heard enough to convince me.'

For a moment, Matthew felt a surge of affection for this man. 'Thank you, Elmstead, I appreciate that. Would you care to present a bill to parliament? A lighthouse on the Corbie Rock could save the lives of hundreds of men.'

'It might well do,' Elmstead agreed. Snapping his fingers to summon the scar-faced servant, he handed over his glass. 'But there may be one or two obstacles still in our path.'

Matthew felt his spirits sink. Elmstead had used these very words whenever he had dreamt up some particularly unpleasant form of torture for Matthew to undergo. Lifting his chin, he asked what the obstacles might be.

'The feelings of the villagers, Pryde, for one. How do the good people of Onswick feel about having a lighthouse imposed upon their bay? And secondly, there is the opinion of Her Ladyship to consider.' Standing up, he looked down on Matthew. 'By the appearance of your face, Pryde, you are not a popular man in Onswick. Unless you took an interest in some fellow's wife?' The grin invited Matthew to indulge in some intimate man-to-man conversation.

'No.' Matthew had almost forgotten the assault in his room. Now he felt the bruises begin to burn again. 'A group of men broke into my room and attacked me.'

'So I see. Did they say why?' For a second Elmstead reverted to his old sneering self. 'Or perhaps it was just your charming personality that irritated them?'

Matthew thought that he had outgrown the blush that spread over his face. 'I do not know who they were, and can only guess why they attacked me.'

'But perhaps something to do with the lighthouse, don't you think?' Elmstead allowed the question to hang uncomfortably for a full thirty seconds before laughing out loud. 'God, Pryde, you always were a serious minded fellow! I'm only joshing you! As if I care about the clods. Vacant drones, the peasantry, with no opinion save low superstition and no more imagination than the beasts they tend or the fish they butcher in their nets!'

Matthew did not know whether to feel relief at Elmstead's sudden volte-face or annoyance at his dismissal of the villagers. He decided to say nothing at all.

'They will lose their wrecking business, but that's of no account to me,' Elmstead said. 'They will simply have to work harder. The Navy will welcome them, I'm sure. I might even arrange a visit from the Press to avenge that black eye of yours.'

'No, not the Press Gang.' Matthew had seen the Impress Service operate in the south coast ports; he remembered the anguish of men being dragged from their families and the despair of the wives who were left behind.

'As you wish.' Elmstead dismissed the idea as casually as it had been introduced. 'But that leaves Her Ladyship. As you will no doubt have realized, nothing happens in this area without her consent.'

'But you're a Member of Parliament. You have the power to present a bill without asking the approval of anybody.'

'Ah,' Elmstead placed his empty glass on a walnut side table, deliberately avoiding the woven mat that had been placed there to absorb any drips, 'I'm afraid that things do not work quite like that.' His smile was a thing of beauty. 'It is true that I am the Member of Parliament for this constituency of Hornshope. However, it is what is known as a Pocket Borough; that is, a borough in the pocket of a local landowner.'

'And?' Everybody knew such commonplace facts. Matthew was not in the mood for a lecture on politics.

Elmstead continued, explaining as if to a child. 'There are only a very few people who actually possess the vote. By some quirk of fate, they are the owner of Harestone House, who is Her Ladyship, and her six chief tenants. Do you see the problem there?'

Matthew shook his head. He did not possess a vote and had not considered that he ever would, so did not really care about such matters. 'Not really.'

'Her Ladyship, naturally, does not use her vote. She is, after all, a woman. However, she does control this constituency. I have to do exactly as she wishes, or lose my seat, with all its privileges and power.' Elmstead was busy with another brandy. 'It's not the ideal situation, but there you have it.'

Matthew sighed. 'So I should approach Her Ladyship first, and if she agrees to the lighthouse, she will tell you to approach the Commons with the bill?'

'Eureka! At last you see!' Elmstead snapped his fingers as if an idea had just occurred to him. 'Tell you what, Pryde, I'm a sporting man, so why not make a game of it? We can race for the honour of approaching Her Ladyship. If I win, why, then you shall approach her yourself, and if you win, then I shall have the task. She may not listen to you, but she may at least grant me an audience!'

Matthew remembered Elmstead's games all too well. They usually involved extreme physical discomfort for everybody except Elmstead himself. 'Why don't I just approach Her Ladyship myself?'

'What? Giving up before we even begin? Still no backbone, Pryde?'

The sneer was an echo of his youth. Matthew took a deep breath; Elmstead had not changed, he had only learned how to cover his bullying with a façade of comradeship. 'I'll race you, Elmstead,' he said, 'with pleasure.'

'Carriages then,' Elmstead decided. 'You have yours with you?' The sneer was more pronounced than ever.

'I have no carriage,' Matthew replied.

'Then I shall supply both,' Elmstead said. 'No time like the present, don't you think?' Snapping his fingers, he gave orders to the scar-faced servant. 'Ready the racing curricles, boy!' As the man bowed and hurried away, Elmstead hooked his arm through Matthew's and dragged him out of the room, stopping only to rattle the bars of the bird cage so its occupant emitted a high pitched screech and lunged at him with its wickedly curved beak. Elmstead laughed. 'Come this way, Pryde.'

A hundred yards from the main house, a high wall contained the stable block and coach house. There was a gated doorway, flanked by high columns that again were adorned with stone birds, to which Elmstead pointed with pride.

'I had them both sculpted specially. That one is a duck, for wild fowling is meat and drink to me, and the other is a parrot, which is a reminder of the Indies. I brought one back with me, as you saw. Can't get the damned thing to speak.' He sauntered into the neatly cobbled courtyard.

Both the stables and the coach house were newly built in the same classical style as the house, with wide, arched entrances beneath a loft. The dressed stone façades seemed very grand for such functional buildings.

'I got Henry Holland to design them,' Elmstead said, mentioning the royal architect as casually as if he were discussing a new shirt. 'He looked at me a bit cutty-eyed at first, but money talks.'

Matthew tried not to look impressed as what seemed like a vast number of black servants bustled around two nearly identical two-wheeled curricles. He had never driven such a contraption before, but knew that it would be pointless to admit as much to Elmstead. Instead he tried to look knowledgeable as he walked around the nearest machine.

Light and open, curricles were among the fastest vehicles on the road, often selected by young men to impress the world in general and the female population in particular. They seated two people, side by side, while their pair of horses gave them more speed than a gig and made them more manoeuvrable than a post-chaise or a mail-coach. Wealthy men might own one curricle, but Matthew had never conceived that a man might possess two. Such extravagance was overwhelming.

He looked over to Elmstead, who was watching him, smiling.

'Beautiful equipage,' Matthew allowed.

'Glad you approve,' Elmstead acknowledged with a wave. 'Take your choice.'

Both pairs of geldings also matched, with their bay coats well groomed and their eyes clear and bright. They nuzzled Elmstead with obvious affection.

Matthew leaned over the curved trunk of the nearest curricle, admiring the leather cushions on each seat and the gloss of polish on the splashing-board. Set against a background of dark green, the coat of arms on the door boasted a parrot beside a Negro's head, with the St George's Cross of England and a full-sailed ship beneath.

'The arms are not approved yet,' Elmstead admitted, 'but I like them!' His smile was a token of broken rules and daring exploits, a hint of piracy in the mould of Drake and Hawkins. Matthew felt small and weak in such company, as so often before.

There was a lamp on either side of the trunk, and the silver moulding had been polished until it glittered. Matthew ran his hand over the ironwork, hoping to find some sign of rust, but everything was in perfect order.

'Does it come up to your high standards, Pryde?' Elmstead

asked mockingly. 'See, it even has Obadiah Elliot's new elliptical springs fitted!'

Invented only the previous year, elliptical steel springs were a great advance towards making carriages more stable. They also made it possible to discard the perch, the lower framework of the coach, so Elmwood's curricles were low and light, but every bit as safe as the older models. Checking quickly to ensure that all the springs had been fitted correctly, Matthew admired this new advance in engineering technology: safety.

'Are you satisfied yet, Pryde?' Elmwood was frowning as the servants backed the horses between the shafts.

Matthew had never owned a horse, but he had enough knowledge to tell a bad animal from a good, and Elmstead's were top quality driving animals. Blowing into the nostrils of the nearest, Matthew fondled his ears and peered into his eyes, which showed little of the white of temper. The neck was perhaps slightly long, but his shape was fine, so the nose neither thrust directly in front nor sniffed the clouds above.

'Come along, Pryde!' Elmstead was already in his seat, bunching the ribbons in his left hand and tutting with ill-concealed impatience. 'Are you going to race, or make love to my horses?' One of the servants grinned at that, but Matthew said nothing. He knew the importance of making friends with the team before he began to drive any equipage.

As Elmstead began to whistle in exasperation, Matthew made haste to finish his inspection, brushing over the straight back and long quarters as, disdaining the use of the hinged door, he vaulted inside the body of the curricle.

'Oh, at last!' Elmstead's temper, never known for its longevity, had worn away. Lifting his whip, he cracked it loudly with a fine disregard for horses and servants. The lash whistled past the head of a girl who rode into the courtyard at just the wrong moment.

'Careful, Nicky!' Her complaint was lost in the echoes of the whip's crack.

'Where are we going?' Matthew tried to remember all that he had been taught as he balanced inside the body of the curricle. Keeping his arms around fourteen inches apart, he grasped the whip with his right hand and the reins with his left. When he noticed that the girl was watching him, he touched his hat and bowed stiffly before sitting down, feeling the carriage rock under his weight and the nearest horse give a little shiver of anticipation. These beasts were thorough-breds then, and not the usual plodders used to pull a carriage.

'Just keep to the road, Pryde, and it will take you around a small part of my estate and back here!' The voice was so fruity and confident that Matthew felt himself hating its owner all over again. Suddenly he wanted to win this race, and glared at the broad back of Elmstead with more venom than he had ever allowed himself at Maidhouse. 'You won't get lost, Pryde,' Elmstead taunted, 'if you keep in my dust!'

Elmstead's whip cracked again, the horses jerked forward and the curricle was rolling across the gravel, picking up speed so the wheel spokes became a blur of yellow. Barking excitedly, a pair of black and white Dalmatians bounded from the stables and took their place at Elmstead's rear wheels. He glanced back, shouted something unintelligible and transferred all his concentration to his driving.

Holding the whip just above the collar, Matthew cracked it above the ear of the offside horse, nearly unbalanced as the pair pulled forward and bent his hand to control the reins. He had to be quick to manoeuvre between the pillars. He feather-edged around the curve of the road and then relaxed into a straight that stretched toward an obviously newly planted copse of trees. Although he knew how to drive, Matthew had never before taken part in a race, so repeated the rules as he chased after Elmstead.

'Keep the driving hand level with the breastbone,' he muttered. 'Point the knuckles forward and square the forearm with the upper arm.' Easy in theory, it was next to impos-sible with the curricle buzzing beneath him and Elmstead's Dalmatians dodging around his wheels.

He saw at once that his nearside gelding had a high, showy action that was poor for a carriage horse, while the offside animal was better, with a short, quick step. The difference in stride would make the driving even more difficult, so he had to call on all the theoretical knowledge that he had. A glance in front revealed that Elmstead's horses were better matched, or, as he suspected, His Lordship kept them better together.

Elmstead's curricle was well ahead, the wheels purring musically and Elmstead's laugh taunting. He eased into the next bend, around a large oak to the fringe of a swathe of parkland. Plump deer scattered before them, their white rumps bouncing merrily. By the time Matthew passed they had settled a good hundred yards back from the road. They neither looked up when his curricle whirred past, nor moved when Elmstead's Dalmatians barked in their direction.

The sound of Elmstead's team altered as he applied the whip, the hooves hitting the ground more often, their speed increasing to a gallop. Standing up and balancing against the sway of the carriage, Matthew followed, shouting to his horses and flailing the whip. He could see another bend ahead, but knew that he could not allow Elmstead to get too far in front. Splashes of mud showered him from Elmstead's equipage as he yelled encouragement to his team.

'Come on there! Move now!'

There was a group of men beside the road, watching as he passed. One raised a hand in greeting, then they were behind him and he was at the bend, a vicious left-hand curve that passed so close to a copse of elms that he had to duck beneath the lowest branches. Rooks scrambled above his head, somebody was shouting and then the road dipped before rising steeply in front of him, narrowing at the top where it squeezed through an ornate gateway.

Elmstead was already there, his whip cracking, voice sounding loud as his curricle vanished into a series of tight bends, the wheels spinning so rapidly that the spokes appeared to be running backward. Matthew swore and plied his whip, shouting in complete abandon now as he urged his team to greater efforts. Forgetting about the lighthouse and Her Ladyship, he wanted to win this race purely to spite Elmstead. Memories of years of bullying returned, memories of a solitary boy cowering in fear, memories of passive misery and active terror.

'Get along, there!' Disregarding the danger, he stood erect,

113

cracking his whip above the ears of the frantic horses, watching the boot of Elmstead's curricle leap as he hit a dip in the road. He heard Elmstead's curse and laid his lash along the flank of the nearside horse so it jerked forward urgently. 'Come on, you beauty! Pull for me, you daughter of Satan! Move, you bone-setting birds of paradise!'

He hardly noticed when his hat blew free, but he was aware that somebody was riding alongside. It was the girl from the courtyard, with her hair flying loose and her legs shockingly astride the horse. She was laughing, her mouth open with joy. 'Go on, make a race of it!'

Intent on controlling his team, Matthew could barely spare her a glance, but he saw enough to convince him that she was a rare beauty.

They were moving uphill now, through manicured park-land. Even the edgings were trimmed to perfection, except for the clods of turf thrown up by the laughing horsewoman, who seemed determined to gallop between the two curricles, scattering a handful of servants as she offered advice and criticism.

'Go on, Nicholas! Show him whose land this is!'

'Come on, Mr Visitor! Make a race of it, make him work for victory!'

'Too slow, Nicholas, he's catching up! Use the whip, man, don't just tickle them!'

The hill eased into a level ridge of rougher grass that stretched for a full half mile, dotted with wind-twisted thorn trees. A dog rose sat in the lee of a drystone wall, displaying a single white blossom that had miraculously survived the winter. As she passed, the girl leaned over the neck of the horse, plucked the rose and held it in her gloved hands. It was a display of riding skill that Matthew had seldom seen equalled, but he had no time to voice his admiration.

When the road widened ahead, Matthew whipped up the horses to a full gallop, ignoring the drop slithering to a fast-running stream on his right. He could hear the girl screaming in delight, could hear Elmstead roaring on his team, and rose in his seat to shout in his turn. Now he had a chance

114

to overtake, to pass Elmstead on this broad stretch, to take some revenge for all these hideous years at Maidhouse.

'Come on, boys! Run for your father!' Matthew's whip cracked loudly as he leaned forward over the swingletree and the bouncing rumps of the horses. 'Pull, damn your black hearts!'

Matthew saw the girl overtake him and run alongside Elmstead's curricle. She shouted something to him, and in replying he momentarily relaxed his concentration so his equipage slowed a fraction.

'Now, boys!' Matthew cracked his whip again. 'Now's your time!' He felt his horses give an extra ounce of effort and laughed, just as Elmstead looked over his shoulder.

With his long hair blowing in the wind, Elmstead shouted something incomprehensible to the girl, then turned all his attention to his team. By then Matthew was level, allowing his offside wheels to leave the road in order to curve around the girl and overtake Elmstead. He felt the bump of a stone beneath the rim, the judder of soft ground, then he was level, with the girl falling back and his wheels buzzing alongside those of Elmstead, hubs almost touching as both teams strained at their harnesses. Matthew saw the great veins bulging in the horses' necks, saw the staring eyes, flat-laid ears, and knew that he had the advantage.

'On now, boys!' Giving Elmstead an ironic salute with the butt of his whip, he cracked the lash once more, pulling urgently ahead. The high laughter of the girl mocked them both.

'Well played, Pryde!' Elmstead met his salute, grinned, and then slashed sideways at Matthew's face with his whip.

Shocked, Matthew instinctively ducked and nearly dropped the reins as the lash whistled an inch above his head. He bobbed up at once, swearing, but already Elmstead was ahead, his horses galloping along the path with clods of earth and small stones pattering down on to Matthew's curricle. Gripping the ribbons tightly, Matthew retaliated, leaning forward to snap his whip to the side of Elmstead's pair in the hope of driving them off the road. But Elmstead had them well in hand and made the curricle sway from side to side, denying Matthew any possibility of overtaking.

'Chase him, stranger!' the girl encouraged him. 'He's not won yet!'

Elmstead's laugh was cruel as his curricle jerked forward, gaining a further nine feet. After a hundred yards the road again narrowed, passing between parallel drystone walls that would make overtaking impossible. Matthew swore as his anger took control. He reached forward, gripped the whip by the extremity of its butt to extend his reach, and lashed out, aiming at the back of Elmstead's head. Even with a five-foot-long stick of seasoned holly, and a lash twice that length, he failed to touch Elmstead, but did succeed in heightening the interest of the girl.

'Temper, temper!' Spurring level with Matthew, she leaned sideways to shout to him. 'My, what a wild man you are!' Her eyes were large and brown, her hair free and tangled, but she sat in her saddle like a centaur.

The road narrowed further as they approached Chevington Hall, and Elmstead was now well in front. The girl spurred to his side, yelling encouragement even as she glanced back toward Matthew.

In a last effort to draw level, Matthew cracked both ribbons and whip together, throwing the curricle forward with no regard for his safety. The girl pulled away as he jerked forward, but Elmstead eased through the gateway without pause and rolled up in front of the stable block, turning his equipage in a masterly display of skill that showered the waiting servants with gravel. He slithered to the ground, grinning as Matthew pulled his team to a halt.

'Well tried, Pryde–' the voice had lost some of its sneer – 'but you lost. For a second there I thought you might catch me!'

'You cheated!' Matthew jumped down from his seat, feeling his temper as hot as he had ever known. 'You tried to hit me!'

Elmstead widened his eyes in mock surprise. 'Of course I did. It was a man's race, not children at play. You'd be dicked in the nob if you thought that I'd do otherwise!' He

116

laughed and watched the girl dismount. 'Now don't raise a breeze, old man. It was a race and you lost. You could not beat me.'

'Nobody ever has; Nicolas is a top sawyer,' the girl said, pressed hard against Elmstead, then ducked away from his encircling arm. Matthew had never heard a voice so distinctive in his life. It seemed to flow like honey, but with a husky quality that made him desperate to hear her speak again. 'When you lost your temper like that, I nearly died, and now you're all ready to sport your canvas.'

'Pryde lost his temper?' Elmstead sounded amused. 'Little Matthew Pryde? My, my, you have changed, Pryde! Maybe you're becoming a man at last, gentle or not!'

The girl laughed at that, as Matthew fought the blush that so embarrassed him. She tapped him on the arm, her eyes quizzical as they scanned him from bare head to buckled shoes. 'You lost your fine hat as well as the race, Mr Temper, but here is a consolation prize for you.' Producing the rose that she had plucked, the girl did not have to stretch as she thrust the short stem through the top buttonhole of Matthew's waistcoat. 'There now.' She stepped back and patted the rose in place.

Matthew felt the heat increase in his face. 'Thank you,' he said, making a clumsy bow.

The girl smiled again. 'So introduce us then, Nicholas. Who is this man with the hot temper who blushes every time that I speak?' Her look was so bold that Matthew could not hold it, and looked down at the rose. Elmstead, displaying that lightning change of mood that Matthew had already noticed, clapped him on the shoulder in a demonstration of gentlemanly solidarity that he would have given anything for ten years previously.

'This is Matthew Pryde, a fellow Maidhousian. Indeed, he fagged for me, so we know each other well.'

The girl's smile broadened. 'You were at Maidhouse too? Did you enjoy it as much as Nicholas did?' At that moment, Matthew thought that she was the most appealing girl that he had ever seen, but he could not say why. She was certainly not of a classical beauty, with her nose slightly small and

117

her mouth slightly large, but something about her attracted him. There was a warmth, perhaps, or a sense of comradeship, almost as if she was a friend that he had known all his life. He found himself smiling.

Very aware that Elmstead was watching him with sardonic amusement, Matthew bowed to her. 'Ma'am, I found my time at Maidhouse . . .' he paused for a second, 'both instructive and interesting.'

The girl instinctively curtsied in reply to his bow. 'It is what you do not say that most arouses my interest, Mr Pryde.' Her voice had become huskier as her deep brown eyes continued to examine him with disturbingly frank curiosity. 'And as Nicky is obviously not going to introduce me, I shall take it upon myself to perform that irksome task.' A glove that had once been white but was now stained by the leather of the reins protected the hand that she held out. 'I am Grace Fenwick.'

Ten

Northumberland, April 1804

T he name jolted Matthew, so for an instant he could hardly
accept her hand and press it to his lips in a show of
courtesy that he had never before displayed. This girl was
Lady Fenwick's daughter, the young woman whose bellman
caused the entire population of Onswick to flee. This girl
was Grace Fenwick, who had a secret grotto for bathing in
the sea. For an instant the image of her long naked body
came to him, vivid in its detail, so he coloured anew. How
could he have acted the peeping Tom to such a lady?

'Miss Fenwick,' Matthew bowed again, making the most
elegant leg that he could and allowing his trailing hand to
flip backward, to the apparent great amusement of Grace
Fenwick.

'Oh la! Such elegance, such style, such a low bow, sir,
that I declare that you will scrape your nose on the ground!'
Grace Fenwick extended her hand and raised Matthew back
upright. 'On a formal occasion, Mr Pryde, I would expect
the civilities, as would anybody, but this meeting is hardly
formal.' There was mischief in her smile, and the tip of a
pink tongue flickered from the corner of her mouth.

Once again, Matthew felt the colour rush to his face, but
Grace's giggle was so infectious that he could not help but
grin in reply and soon they were standing laughing at each
other while Elmstead glowered from two feet away. 'I do
apologize, Miss Fenwick, for my behaviour. I did not know
who you were.' He could smell her perfume even through
the scent of horses and perspiration.

'And if you did, Mr Pryde,' her voice rippled over him,
seeming to enter every pore of his body and creep inside his

119

head so that he wanted to listen for ever, 'would you have run away and hid? Or perhaps just ignored me?'

Matthew stepped back, confused. 'No, ma'am, Miss Fenwick.' When he looked at her face she was smiling again, with that wide mouth so appealing that he wanted to hold her. 'No,' he said firmly. 'I believe that I would have acted exactly as I did.'

'And so would I, Matthew,' Grace said. The use of his Christian name was so natural that Matthew grinned, the feeling of familiarity regained.

'You are from the south, by your speech, Matthew,' Grace said, still smiling. 'So what brings you to the cold and barren north?'

For a moment, Matthew could not reply. Despite his best intentions, he could not help but think of that naked figure he had seen cavorting beside the sea. Miss Grace Fenwick appeared to be as wild as the heather, a regular out-and-outer, despite her position of privilege. He hesitated, not willing to damage a budding friendship with mention of the lighthouse. Elmstead came to his rescue.

'I neglected to remind you, Pryde, that you lost the race, so you shall carry your request to Her Ladyship.' Elmstead's voice was as acidic as the returning sneer. 'I may also have neglected to mention that Miss Grace and I have known each other since childhood, and are engaged to be married.'

'And an excellent match too, I'm sure.' Matthew collected his wits at the same time as he dropped his gaze from the soft brown eyes that seemed to entice him into some other world. 'Congratulations to you both.' This time some devilment made him linger over the kiss that he planted on Grace's gloved hand.

Matthew calculated that she was about his own age, or perhaps a year older, which made her five years younger than Elmstead, yet she acted like an unbroken puppy, dashing from one man to the other, yearning for affection or companionship, eager for fun. Matthew considered; if she had possessed a tail, he was sure that it would be constantly set a-wagging, and the thought made him smile anew, which caused Grace to giggle and deepened the frown that darkened Elmstead's forehead.

Elmstead looked from Grace to Matthew and back with a curious expression on his face, as if he was trying to work something out. Without smiling, he stepped forward, placing himself between the two, and remained there, immobile.

'So you are going to meet my mother?' Grace threw the reins of her horse to the nearest of the patient servants.

'He is.' Elmstead moved whenever Grace did, ensuring that she would not get close to Matthew. 'With some cock and bull idea about building a lighthouse or some such.'

For the first time in their short acquaintance, Grace looked serious. 'A lighthouse? I don't think that Mother will approve. She does not like change.'

'I'm sure that Her Ladyship will approve of a measure that helps mariners in distress and keeps the seas safer,' Matthew said as smoothly as he could.

Grace shook her head but said nothing.

'Pryde,' Elmstead held out his hand, 'you lost fair and square, and accepted defeat like a man – after your display of high dudgeon, of course.'

It was only after Matthew shook the hand that he realized Elmstead had not added the prefix 'gentle' to his description. He was sure that Grace caught the omission, and probably smiled behind those lively brown eyes. The only question was; did she smile with him, or at him?

As he sat in front of the fading fire in his room, with the wind rattling the pantiles and smearing rain over his window, Matthew hugged the cup of hot chocolate that Ruth had supplied and pondered over everything that had happened to him during the past few weeks. He had come to Onswick expecting to map out the dangerous rocks, create a rough draft for a lighthouse and persuade the local MP to back his plan. Now he felt that he was floundering in a morass of mingled motives. He was determined to complete his original task, but always his tangled past would drag him back.

He knew now that he had been a child on board a whaling ship named *Pride of Matthew*, a vessel that hailed from London. He knew that she had been wrecked on the Black Corbie, and he had been the only survivor. He also knew that an unknown woman had reared him for a few years, before sending him first to a foundling's hospital in London, then to Maidhouse College, where he had been educated as a gentleman. Could it only be coincidence that Elmstead, a local man and now Lord Chevington, had also attended the same school?

Matthew was not inclined to smoke, but the thought of drawing on a comforting pipe nearly tempted him to break the habit of a lifetime. Who was the mysterious woman whose hazy face was his earliest and most shadowy memory? Was she the same woman who had cared for him as a child, and who had paid for his education? If so, he owed her a major debt of gratitude. But, he also had his task to perform, for the sake of his professional pride and his future career. Who had attacked him, and why? Was it because of his connections with the village, or because of the lighthouse?

Matthew shook his head. He could not neglect his future for the sake of his past, but he knew that he must solve this mystery. He would fret himself to pieces until he found out from whence he came and who his patron had been. The fact that he had been sent to Maidhouse argued that his rescuer and benefactor was of some standing. She, if indeed it had been the woman whose face he remembered, may have been married to a merchant, but why look after a cast-ashore stranger? Merchants were in the business of making profit, not of making charitable gestures. Perhaps she had benefited from the wreck and had helped him as a gesture of gratitude?

Maidhouse had been purgatory, but Matthew was realist enough to know that it had prepared him for a far better life than he could have achieved as an orphan in Onswick. What would his future have been here? Unless a fishing family adopted him the fishing community would not have accepted him, so perhaps he would be a hand in a coasting vessel? He shuddered at the prospect, remembering the reputation of the Geordie bears who manned the great fleets of colliers that supplied London.

They were alleged to be among the finest seamen in England, which meant, of course, the finest in the world, but they were also the toughest, most obstinate, illiterate, uncouth

122

men anywhere. They existed in unbelievable hardship, used no gangways, but boarded their colliers by means of the anchor chains, slept on bare boards and used language so foul that even lobster-backed soldiers were shocked.

Hard experience had stripped Matthew of any self-delusion and he acknowledged that he was not fitted for such privation. Whoever his patron had been, he owed her a great deal, but he was no closer to solving the mystery.

Matthew shook his head, swallowed the last of his chocolate and placed the cup carefully by the now dying fire. He, who lived by scientific reasoning and mathematical logic, could make no sense of his own life. He closed his eyes, seeing again the tossing hair and darting tongue of Grace.

Tomorrow he would ride to Harestone House and seek an audience with Lady Fenwick. Tomorrow he must concentrate on the lighthouse and push aside the past that haunted everything that he did and coloured every word he uttered. His mathematical bent had directed him toward the life of an engineer, and in many ways he did not regret the decision, but sometimes he wondered if he had lost more than he had gained.

When he closed his eyes Matthew saw again the slim shape of Grace Fenwick poised above the cleft in the cliff. She was beckoning him toward her, but Lady Fenwick's wind blew him out to the Corbie, where the beat of surf sounded like his old school song.

'Ederford!' He jerked up in bed. 'The answer is Ederford!'

Eleven

Kent and London, 1795–1799

'So you are determined to be an engineer.' Mr Denton looked over the rim of his pince-nez spectacles and sighed. 'It is not an easy life, young Matthew, especially when you have the attributes and education of a gentleman.'

'I do realize that,' Matthew agreed. He had come directly from Flintock's chambers to the bookshop in Ashbourne and now perched uncomfortably on a chair in the back room. Kate sat nearby with a quill, pot of ink and a sales ledger. He knew that she was listening to every word, even though her head was bowed to her work and she appeared to be concentrating on the columns of figures that she balanced with such pleasing neatness and exactitude. 'But you must agree that engineering is a respectable profession.'

Mr Denton sighed. 'An engineer may be a highly respectable artisan, Matthew, but it is still lower down the social scale. You would not be accepted as an equal in the great houses of the land. Your compatriots in Maidhouse may not wish to invite you to their homes, unless as an employee. Do you also realize that?'

Kate's quill hesitated for a second. Matthew knew that she was forcing herself not to become involved in the conversation.

'I do. The question is, Mr Denton, would your cousin be willing to take me on as an apprentice?'

'Of that I am unsure. How old are you, Matthew?'

'Eighteen sir, I think. You know my background, so you know that I cannot be sure of my birth date.'

Mr Denton removed his glasses and began to slowly polish

them. 'You are uncommonly foolish, Matthew. An engineer's life is full of work and hard knocks, with little reward.'

'I understand that, sir, but it is the life on which I am set.' Matthew had not realized that he could be so stubborn.

Mr Denton nodded slowly and replaced the pince-nez on the bridge of his nose. 'If you are so inclined, Matthew, I will see what I can do, although I do believe that you would be better to take Mr Flintock's advice and accept a position with the Honourable East India Company. There are good careers, and much wealth, to be won in Hindustan.'

The quill faltered again, as Kate listened for Matthew's reply. She was indeed an inquisitive girl.

'My mind does not incline toward working a ledger, Mr Denton, nor to anything military. So I would be a poor merchant and a poorer soldier, while the very idea of sailing the briny deep quite makes me shudder!' Matthew's deliberately mincing tone brought a smile from Mr Denton, and Kate's quill resumed its scratching progress across the lined sheets of the book. Even with her hair severely tied back, that rebellious curl still managed to escape.

'As you wish, Matthew.' Mr Denton made his decision. 'I will contact William directly, and see if he agrees to accept you.'

With no money of his own, Matthew searched for some position where he could make a living while Mr William Denton pondered his request for an apprenticeship. Mr Charles Denton offered him a job as a bookseller, but Matthew knew that the shop barely brought in enough money to support two, let alone three, so declined with genuine regret. Instead he became the personal tutor to the two young sons of a respectable solicitor, taught them the rudiments of the Classics, mathematics, history and geography, endured their behaviour and accepted his meagre remuneration while he awaited a reply. Twice he had to avoid the attentions of a Press Gang, and once he was nearly inveigled into the arms of a scarlet-coated recruiting sergeant.

At last the acceptance came and he could turn his attention to things of a more practical nature.

'It's not too late to try John Company,' Kate said gravely,

looking up from a collection of books that her father had purchased, but Matthew did not listen. He had embraced a world that he understood and whose possibilities were exciting.

William Denton had been a friend of Smeaton, who designed the lighthouse at Eddystone, and, taking Matthew under his wing, taught by dint of experience, effort and theory. Matthew had fancied that his mathematics was equal to any challenge, but now he realized how much he had to learn.

'Pure mathematics is fascinating,' William Denton would tell him, again and again, 'but what matters is its practical application. We have to learn to make theory useful, or all learning is only vanity. We are entering an age of progress, Matthew, and we must learn to innovate.'

Matthew learned that William Denton was as good as his word. Before he unleashed Matthew on to the large-scale engineering programmes that he craved, he sent him to learn the intimate details that made things possible. For two months, Matthew worked in one of the watch-making workshops for which London was famous. After that he spent a further three months in the Mayfair works of Joseph Manton, the pistol maker, where strict attention to detail was a requisite skill. Only then did William Denton allow him to look at larger pieces, from the inch-by-inch ecstasy of map-making to the construction techniques of carving navigations through the countryside.

With no money save what he could earn by tutoring wayward children, Matthew worked every hour that he could. His visits to Mr Denton's bookshop became infrequent but all the more cherished. His initial fascination with Kate grew until he thought of her even while overcoming complex engineering problems. The longer the gap between their meetings, the more enchanting she seemed, and the more altered. She had grown an inch in height and slightly more around the hips and breasts, although a gentleman tried not to dwell on those areas when Kate's father was in close attendance.

In fact Charles Denton seemed so intent on monopolizing Matthew's company that he had very little time alone with Kate, which made him ever more determined to see her. Kate appeared to share his ideas, and more than once they slipped behind the aisles of books to talk in subdued whispers about the latest scandal to hit England or the course of the war or how Matthew's apprenticeship was progressing. Of course, the noise they made attracted Mr Denton, who broke up their enjoyment with a request for one or the other to attend on some small affair, and they parted, to seek further opportunities for conversation or just each other's company whenever they could.

It was in the spring of 1799, when Matthew was a deep two years into his apprenticeship and had assisted William Denton in planning a small navigation and an improved harbour for one of the south coast ports, that Charles Denton finally took him aside.

'Matthew,' Mr Denton was greyer about the temples, but his eyes were as amiable as ever and his pince-nez more precariously squeezed on a nose that seemed to grow more bulbous every month. 'I have a request to ask of you.'

'Yes, sir?' Matthew nearly leapt to attention. He would have done anything that would advance his cause with Kate's father, which in turn might make Kate look more favourably on him.

'I have occasion to send Kate into London, and I do not like the idea of her travelling alone, not with this war on and the presence of certain rough elements around the town.' William Denton paused to gaze doubtfully upon Matthew. 'I would like you to accompany my daughter.'

'Of course, sir,' Matthew agreed at once. The prospect of a day in London with Kate seemed like paradise, for much as he loved engineering, he would swap every complex equation in existence for a breath of her perfume, or one flicker of her bright, calm eyes.

'You have agreed without thought, Matthew!' Mr Charles Denton was testy for once, but immediately returned to his habitual amiability. 'I have made a formal request to cousin William, who has agreed to permit this absence from your duties.'

Matthew coloured as his dereliction of duty was revealed. 'Thank you, Mr Denton. Of course I would have sought permission.'

'Good.' Mr Denton nodded. 'If you are still willing, I wish you to catch the morning stage and return by the five o'clock flier, so you will be back around nine.'

Matthew pondered over his choice of clothes before deciding on his buff coloured knee breeches, with a long blue coat and the tricorne hat that sported a black cockade. He considered his only other coat too shabby for Kate's eyes, forgetting that she had purchased it for him, as she had bought both of his hats and his second pair of breeches. The ivory-topped cane that he carried was borrowed from William Denton, as were the pinchbeck-buckled shoes and the green waistcoat, from which hung the silver hunter watch that had been Mr Denton's unusually generous Christmas gift.

More sensibly attired in a hooded travelling cloak that afforded protection against the unpredictable April wind, Kate welcomed Matthew with a smile and allowed him to hand her inside the coach. He followed with his heart beating faster than normal. He had never travelled inside a coach before, with his previous journeys always on the cheaper outside seats, and hoped that he did not allow his lack of experience to show. Kate slid into the corner, patted the lined interior and indicated that he should sit opposite, so both could share the view from the window.

'Isn't this nice?' Kate smiled at him. 'Just the two of us alone in the coach.'

Their privacy did not last as more passengers boarded, cramming the interior with two fat women, a parson who sneezed incessantly and a country farm-wife who insisted on carrying her favourite hen in her arms. Rather than a haven where Matthew could exchange pleasantries with Kate, the coach became a place of bad odours, farmyard noises and raucous conversation as the women loudly discussed their quite disgusting ailments. Even worse, they asked for Kate's opinion, which she gave without any hesitation and a great deal more medical knowledge than Matthew would ever have given her credit for.

The views were little consolation for what Matthew considered the theft of Kate's company, with daffodils nodding welcome to spring and the country seats of the lords always impressive. The crowds and bustle of London, however, raised his spirits, and he watched eagerly as the coach pulled into Kent Street and passed the tall church of St George before entering the mad congestion of the Borough High Street and London Bridge.

Breaking into Kate's debate on the most effective remedy for piles, Matthew pointed beneath them as one of the small boats known as a light-horseman sculled madly to shoot the bridge.

'Oh, yes,' she said, 'I do hope that he makes it.' As she returned to her medical conversation, Matthew grappled desperately for something that would hold her attention.

When Kate greeted his descriptions of colliers, Indiamen and grain vessels with more politeness than interest, he spoke of the hundreds of thieves that swarmed around the river, from virtual pirates who worked from small boats to mudlarks who waited until low water before sneaking aboard an unwary ship.

'Oh really?' Kate feigned fascination but could not stifle her yawn. Matthew looked out of the window to conceal his frustration. He had been looking forward to showing her some of the sights of London.

As if she had read his mind, Kate leaned toward him. 'I am sorry to be such a dull dog, Matthew, but I find travelling so tiring.' He forgave her everything when she smiled and touched his shoulder with the ivory fan of which she was so proud. 'I promise you that I will be more amiable when we alight. Indeed, you might think me quite the gabster.'

'The fault is mine, Kate, for speaking such a bag of moonshine.' Matthew resolved to curb his enthusiasms in future. He should have realized that women would not share masculine interests. That was another lesson that she had taught him.

They alighted in Bishopsgate and headed toward Finsbury Square, one of the prime bookselling locations of the world, for Mr Charles Denton had asked Kate to obtain a selection of cheap travel books for a specific customer. She hurried Matthew through the streets, exclaiming at the number of woman street traders who yelled their wares in voices harsh

129

with the London smoke. Despite the earliness of the season, some proclaimed that they sold fresh vegetables, while others flouted their pails of milk or newly caught fish, although Matthew was more tempted by the aroma of meat pies. He had yet to meet a woman of Kent who could make pies to match those purchased on the London streets.

For somebody who had never before been to London, Kate seemed decidedly objective. She gave the fine architecture little more than a passing glance, shook her head at the mess that thousands of horses and other animals had made of the streets and completely ignored the admiration of passing men, gentle or otherwise. 'Take me to Finsbury Square, Matthew,' she instructed, and only then did Matthew understand that her curt attitude hid uneasiness. Rather than enjoying her visit to the capital, she was afraid. He had not thought that the sheer size of London could be overwhelming to a woman from a small country town. All at once he wanted to hug her, to pick her up in his arms and squeeze reassurance into her. For the first time in his experience, Kate was vulnerable. The knowledge changed Matthew from a loquacious youth into a considerate, overprotective man.

'This way, Kate,' he said. 'Keep close by me now,' he urged, aware of the new depth to his voice as he guided her through the streets, glaring at those men who dared to even glance at her and advising her to avoid the worst of the reeking filth on the roads that they crossed.

Only when they reached Finsbury Square did Kate show some approval. Rather than enter the first of the bookshops, she walked around the square, examining each shop critically before finally guiding Matthew into number thirty-two, the largest shop of all with its grandiloquent title of 'Temple of the Muses.' Kate looked up at the domed and shiny roof from which flew the shop's own flag.

'I have heard of this place,' she murmured, even the appearance of her small-town bounce evaporating when she faced the reality of London's pre-eminence in the book trade. Her bonnet, so correct in Kent, looked decidedly shabby as it swivelled from side to side when she peered around the interior.

'It is indeed large,' she allowed, 'but perhaps the books are not of the quality that I have come to expect.'

The assistant who glided up was dressed so elegantly in a tailed coat and powdered wig that he could nearly have passed for a gentleman in Ashbourne, but now he bowed his respects. 'We have a shop frontage of a hundred and forty feet, madam,' he informed her, 'and it is said that one could drive a coach and six around our counter, although I do not believe that theory has ever been put to the test.' He smiled at his own joke.

There were a score of customers examining the books that covered each wall, and a further two assistants worked behind the circular counter, under an internal shelter that Kate likened to a canopy from some Eastern fable. Her hands trembled when she handed a neatly written list to the assistant.

'I require these volumes,' she said, her imperious voice emphasizing her nervousness, 'but only if their quality is of the finest and their price is acceptable.'

The assistant bowed so low that the tails of his coat swept the floor. 'Madam, we cater for both quality and price.'

He led them up a flight of broad stairs to what he termed a 'lounging room', where he invited them to wait while he searched for Kate's books. While Matthew sank into one of the deep armchairs, Kate could not settle, but wandered through to the galleries beyond. Ignoring the copies of the *Spectator* that were on display, Matthew asked to view the latest engineering books, leaving Kate to explore the shop. He was still reading when she returned.

'This is an emporium of knowledge and romance, Matthew. Mr Lackington – he's the owner, don't you know – has it arranged with the books of most quality on the ground floor, and those of least on the top. He buys books that other shops cannot sell and displays them at a cheaper price.'

Matthew nodded. 'So I have heard.' He watched as Kate's face grew more animated.

'Father and I could emulate him, Matthew. We could open such an establishment in Ashbourne. Rather than travel all the way to town, people from Kent would come to our emporium.' There was no sign of nerves as Kate outlined her plans.

131

'You should have been a man, Kate,' Matthew teased, but Kate ignored the remark. She was quite composed when the assistant returned with every book that she had ordered, at a price that left her with money to jingle in her purse.

Ostentatiously checking his silver hunter, Matthew smiled at her. 'It is barely two in the afternoon,' he said, 'so we have three hours before the coach returns.'

'Indeed we have,' Kate agreed. 'Show me this London of yours.'

Seemingly intent to experience everything, Kate easily kept pace with Matthew's vigorous tour of the city. For the first time in his life, Matthew had the opportunity to show off. He took her to the summit of Highgate Hill, from where they gazed at the seemingly limitless squares and brick-built streets of Mary-le-bone and Bloomsbury, while enjoying the fresh spring air that made Kate burst into brief song, before she looked at Matthew, laughed and blushed.

They admired the thousands of masts that filled the Pool of London, despite the war that hindered trade, and still had time for a pleasant walk along Bond Street, where Kate stopped at every shop window and pointed out items for Matthew's attention. When she stopped, Matthew wondered if he had tired her out.

'Am I trotting you too hard, Kate?'

'Don't be a muttonhead!' Her smile was open as she tapped her fan against his shoulder. 'Show me more!'

They dodged some of the thousand lumbering hackney coaches that splashed and sped through the broader streets of the city, and made way, laughing, for a sedan chair whose carriers spoke in a mixture of Irish Gaelic and native Cockney. Kate giggled and theatrically covered her ears as watermen, exotically dressed in sheepskin hats and rug coats, cursed each other as they competed for trade on the river. They watched the shallops glide along the Thames, with wealthy passengers in the covered tilt that gave these vessels their alternative name of tilt-boats. When Kate commented on one particularly fancy shallop that was decorated with gilded carvings with what appeared to be a Persian carpet spread over the tilt, Matthew wondered if the owner was a returned nabob.

'That could have been you, Matthew, if you had joined John Company,' Kate said seriously, and he looked down at her face and knew that he could never have left her behind. It was then that the idea came to him.

It was so obvious that he wondered why he had not thought it before, but so daring that it caused him to feel nearly giddy with apprehension. Recalling his past life, he realized that he had only begun to know happiness the day that he had met Kate, and everything good in his life had flowed from that meeting.

'Let's go back to Bond Street,' Kate said, arbitrarily deciding their next move, and Matthew obliged her willingly, entranced by her pleasure. Together they watched the quality dismount from their carriages to enter the fashionable shops while colourfully dressed grooms held the horses in the street. From there they visited Mayfair, with Kate now marching ahead, exclaiming at the neatly paved streets which men with brooms swept clean of horse muck, at least in the immediate vicinity of the most elegant of the houses.

'Perhaps,' Kate said quietly as she enjoyed the atmosphere of wealth and opulence, 'if my improvements help Father's bookshop to become successful, we might live in such a place, one day.'

Matthew nodded. 'Perhaps,' he said. He was now more determined than ever to be a successful engineer, a man in the mould of Smeaton. He saw himself riding in a coach with four matched horses and a uniformed coachman. He saw himself promenading along Bond Street with a gold-topped cane and a wife at his side. He saw himself standing with his back to a fire, with Adam's elaborate plaster mouldings on the ceiling above and his children, all dressed in rustling silks and satin, being ushered to bed by a respectful nanny while his wife looked up from her sewing. That wife looked remarkably like Kate.

On an impulse, he linked his arm with hers and squeezed. Her responding giggle was encouraging, but he did not have the nerve to press further. Their arms dropped to their sides as they made fast progress toward their coach. It was nearly five o'clock and there was a long journey before them.

Light rain changed to a persistent downpour that soaked them long before the coach made its belated appearance. Dripping wet, they crammed into the interior, which reeked of the damp wool of a sturdy farmer and the even less salubrious aromas that his wife and three children emitted; yet still Kate seemed inclined to speak. She first outlined her plans for her father's bookshop, then examined them in detail, until Matthew thought he knew the position of every shelf and the name of every customer and publisher in England. All the while he smiled indulgently, happy with his own thoughts about the future.

Delayed by the muddy road, the coach jolted and slithered over every mile to Ashbourne, to arrive at such a hideously late hour that Mr Charles Denton was only one of half a dozen people who waited anxiously outside the inn.

Ignoring Matthew, he held Kate close for a comforting hug. 'You are safe and well?' he asked, as if she had returned from Africa rather than London.

'Very,' she responded, breaking free of his embrace. 'And Father, I have the most amazing ideas for our bookshop.' Without taking breath, she began a detailed account of her plans.

Mr Charles Denton smiled across to Matthew. 'I see that you looked after Kate well, Matthew, and for that I thank you. I also see that she found London stimulating.'

'Indeed, sir.' It was a short walk from the coaching inn to the bookshop and the rooms where Charles and Kate Denton lived. Ignoring the rain, Mr Denton listened to Kate's outpouring with a gentle smile, only stopping for an occasional exclamation of surprise and admiration, or to guide her around the deep puddles that had formed on the road.

Walking at their side, Matthew found it nearly impossible to keep silent. He knew that his idea far outshone Kate's in brilliance, yet it was difficult to voice, even if he could have found a gap in Kate's discourse. At length, when Mr Denton had opened the door of the bookshop and they stood inside, peeling off their sodden outer garments, Kate stopped talking and excused herself to attend to some private business. Matthew approached Mr Denton.

'May I speak with you, sir, man to man?'

Bending to build up the small fire, Mr Denton straightened. He adjusted his pince-nez spectacles. 'Since when did you need permission to speak to me, Matthew?' he asked amiably.

'This is an important matter, Mr Denton, and I wish your full attention.'

'And you have it, Matthew, but you had better be quick, for I fear that Kate will return soon, whereupon she will overpower us with her flow of chatter.' Charles Denton smiled to Matthew, two men acknowledging a shared secret.

'Mr Denton, I have known Kate, and yourself, for some time.' Now that the moment had come, Matthew found it difficult to frame the words. He felt the blood rush to his face.

'I already know that,' Mr Denton told him, with his face a picture of kindness. 'And we both value your company.'

'I have come to think of you as something of a father figure,' Matthew continued, ignoring the amusement with which Mr Denton raised his eyebrows. 'And Kate as more than a friend.'

'Pray continue, but hastily, for I hear your friend's footsteps approaching.'

'The thing is, Mr Denton . . .' Matthew began to stumble over his words and finished in a jumbled rush, 'I want to marry her, Mr Denton. I want Kate to be my wife.'

There was a minute's silence as Mr Denton beamed at him through the thick lenses of his pince-nez spectacles. 'My dear boy,' he said, 'my dear, dear boy,' and Matthew thought that he had never met a man who was more amiable than Mr Denton. He was a gentleman in the true sense of the word, in every aspect except land and fortune.

'Matthew, I am sure that you will make a kind and caring husband,' Mr Denton began, just as Matthew became aware that Kate was standing inside the room, listening to every word. The sound of the rain on the many-paned window was suddenly very loud. 'You are a man of honour and, I believe, integrity. Mr William Denton speaks highly of your dedication and hard work. But, my boy, you are a man without means. You might have made a gentleman, Matthew, you might have risen to great things in the Honourable Company, but you threw away that chance and lowered yourself to be a mere apprentice artisan.'

The now not so amiable head slowly shook. 'No, Matthew, I am afraid that I cannot and will not grant you permission to marry my daughter. Your income is yet too small to think of marriage, and you have neither a fortune nor an established career. I will not let my daughter marry into an uncertain future, my boy, and that is all that you are able to grant her at the moment.'

'And of equal importance,' there was a new light in Kate's eyes when she thrust herself between her father and Matthew, 'has anybody thought to ask *my* opinion about this?'

'You are in full agreement, surely?' Matthew stepped back from the fury in her face. 'You spoke of us living in Mayfair together.'

'I did *what?*' Kate stuttered as her anger robbed her of the ability to articulate. 'I said no such thing. I will say no such thing! I said that Father and I could live in Mayfair, not you and I!' Kate allowed full rein to her anger, ripping off her bonnet and tossing it against the nearest shelf of books.

'No, Matthew, I am not yet ready to contemplate marriage.' Perhaps she noticed the expression of dismay on Matthew's face, for she reached out a hand, as if in apology. 'When you were so intent on your own plans, Matthew, did you not spare a minute to listen to mine? Did you not hear my ideas for this shop?' She opened her arms wide. 'This is my life, Matthew, not eternal child-bearing and . . . and being an accessory.'

Matthew stared at her as his carefully constructed world collapsed. His plans for a wife, for a career in engineering, for the comfortable future that he had pictured, dissipated before the force of her words and the anger in her eyes. 'Hardly an accessory,' he defended himself weakly. 'I thought . . .'

'*You thought?* So you thought, did you?' Stooping, Kate lifted her bonnet from the floor and tapped it against her leg.

'You thought that as a woman I must jump at the chance of marriage to such a man as yourself.' She shook her head. 'Well, someday the world may well ring to your deeds, but did you, who thought so much, not *think* to ask me first?'

Charles Denton had been a silent observer to his daughter's fury. Now he put a restraining hand on her shoulder. He did not look at Matthew.

Blazing red with embarrassment, Matthew forced out the question. 'Kate, do you love me?'

'No,' Kate replied, 'not in that way.' She turned away, not meeting his eye. 'I do not love you and I will not marry you.'

Twelve

Northumberland, April–May 1804

As there was no mail delivery to Onswick, Matthew had to ride to the inn at Foulmire Cross. He placed no reliance in the innkeeper, so rather than entrust him with his letter, waited until the blare of the post horn warned of the arrival of the maroon and black Royal Mail coach. As the driver clambered from his seat and arranged for a change of horses, Matthew handed his letter directly to the guard.

'London, eh?' The man bounced down from his unsprung seat and glanced at the address. He opened the rear boot and placed the letter in a mailbag. 'Don't you worry, sir, the mail will get through.' He hefted his blunderbuss. 'There's not a highwayman will get past this, no, not even Captain Ellwood himself!'

Since he had been attacked, Matthew had habitually carried his pistol, and he touched the butt for reassurance before heading back toward Harestone House. The road was now as familiar as the sound of the skylarks overhead, or the wind that flattened the rough grass. Ignoring the rabbits that now swarmed in their scores around the road, Matthew patted Sally's neck and whispered brief encouragement.

He was not sure what to expect at Harestone House. If only half the tales were true, Lady Fenwick was a formidable presence, able to control even Nicholas Elmstead, who was a regular out-and-outer. Matthew swore as a hare broke cover in front of him and raced up the Heights, jinking and weaving in case of pursuit. Country sports had never interested him, but Matthew felt a momentary temptation to dig in his heels and chase the creature. He smiled, dismissed the notion and rode on.

Pulling to a halt at the point where the road branched off to Harestone House, Matthew rehearsed the words he had carefully written down the previous night. He would tell Her Ladyship of the terrible losses of ships and men. He would tell her of the request of the Newcastle Shipmasters, and of the need for the country to pull together. He would appeal to her patriotism at this time of national danger, when the French were gathering just over the Channel and every ship was needed to stem Bonaparte's armies. Save for one short lull, Britain had been at war since Matthew was sixteen years old, all his adult life, and there seemed no prospect of peace ever returning. He expected the war to last for ever, if Britain could only stave off this latest attempt at invasion, for while the French were rampant on land, Britain was triumphant at sea.

'Come along, Sally,' he guided her on to the Harestone road. 'This way.'

Matthew watched a buzzard slowly patrolling above the rough crest of the Heights. It called once, a clear bell of sound that smacked of freedom. For a fanciful moment, Matthew likened Britain to a buzzard protecting her own lands, but shook away the notion as romantic fustian so he could concentrate on matters in hand. If Her Ladyship disregarded his appeal to patriotism, then he would seek her softer side. He would remind her that the Black Corbie created widows and orphans with every ship it claimed. As a mother, surely Her Ladyship could not withstand such an image.

Matthew grunted as Sally stumbled. He leaned over to pat her neck and swore when she floundered a second time. Worried that she might have cast a shoe, he dismounted and checked each hoof, but everything was firmly in place. Sally nuzzled him as he fed her a lump of sugar.

'What's the matter, old girl? Don't you like this road?'

Matthew looked around. To his right, tangles of old brambles and hawthorn marked where a fast-flowing stream had carved a deep gulley down the Heights. Sally had stumbled where the road approached the ford that was the only conceivable crossing place. Matthew could see a number of low mounds from which grass and nettles waved, while weeds

139

glowered defiantly from the scattered stones that may once have marked a boundary wall.

Dismounting, he knelt beside the first mound and scuffed his riding boot into the grass. Stones and dirt, rotted wood and something else. He knelt down for a closer inspection and lifted first the stem of a clay pipe, then the bowl of a horn spoon. 'There was a house here once,' he told Sally, who was more interested in sampling the good grazing along the banks of the ford.

Checking each mound, Matthew found more small reminders of domesticity: pieces of clothing, fragments of broken property and the castor from a once-treasured chair. There had been a human tragedy there, the clearing of a village for some reason, and he shivered as a cold wind sliced from the Heights. This ford marked the centre of the gap, and from where he stood in the centre of what had been the village, he could see what must be the tallest tower of Harestone House. If there were anybody up there, he would be able to watch every movement along this track, and far north on the road to Scotland. For a second Matthew wished that he had brought his spyglass so that he could examine the house before approaching, then he sighed and whistled for Sally. The horse responded with a slight lift of her head, and Matthew took one step forward and stopped.

Mingled with the lark song, the plaintive call of a curlew haunted this desolation, but there was another sound; something so uncanny that Matthew felt the small hairs on the back of his neck prickle. He stood on the highest spot in what had once been the village, staring at that distant, suddenly sinister tower. The sound started low, grew in intensity and pitch and competed with the call of the moorland birds. Matthew shook his head, exorcising a distant memory, for he knew he had heard that ethereal wail before.

The past seemed to perch on his shoulder, an intensity of emotion to which he could not put a name. He saw the dim shadow of faces, sensed a whiff of wood smoke and the harsh laugh that had comforted him. He was no longer Matthew Pryde, pragmatic engineer, but somebody else, somebody vulnerable but protected; weak but safe.

'Damnit all!' Matthew reached inside his cloak and placed one hand over the butt of his pistol, but did not draw it free. He remembered his reaction to the call of the seals and had no wish to make a similar mistake, but there could be no seals out here, and this sound was thinner, even more primitive, and seemed to be emitting from the rough grass and heather of the hill itself.

Straightening until he nearly stood at attention, Matthew walked slowly back to Sally and prepared to mount. The sound faded away.

'You'll be leaving, then.' The voice was hoarse, as if the speaker was unused to talking, and Matthew tightened his grip on the smooth walnut butt of the pistol.

'Who's there?'

'I am.' Ferns clung to the man's tarred canvas jacket as he rose, and his moleskin trousers were stained and badly patched. He was of medium height, wiry rather than slim, with a clean-shaven face burned brown by wind and weather. 'Not many people take an interest in this place, save for the mad vicar. Why do you?'

'I just came across it.' Matthew noticed that the man was carrying what appeared to be a flute. 'Were you playing that just now?'

The man smiled, placed the instrument to his horn and blew. Once again the weird notes rose to the sky, but knowledge of their origin had removed all menace. 'It's a stock-and-horn pipe,' he explained, after he had removed the instrument. 'I've played it all my life. There used to be a tradition of pipe-playing here, until the village was removed.'

Torn between riding away from this strangely dressed rustic and satisfying his curiosity, Matthew hesitated, but accepted defeat. 'What happened? Why was the village removed?'

'On Her Ladyship's orders.' The man moved slightly closer. 'You're Matthew Pryde, are you not? The man from London who was at the Foulmire Inn?'

'Yes, I am. How the devil do you know that?' When the man said nothing, Matthew became more aware of the strong aroma of tar wafting from his jacket. He recognized the scent and saw the distinctive scuffmarks where his hand had once taken a firm grip. 'You're the man who broke into my room, aren't you?'

The man's smile displayed uneven white teeth. 'That was me. I had to find out who you were and why you were travelling to Onswick.' His eyes were vacant as he held Matthew's gaze.

'Why did you have to find that out?'

'I thought I might have known you,' the man said. His smile faltered. 'And here you are, full circle.'

Matthew shook his head, aware that there was another mystery here and unsure what question to ask next. 'How could you have known me? Wait – who are you, and what do you mean full circle, and why did Her Ladyship order this village removed?'

The man shrugged. 'Maybe she did not like the horn-playing, even though these are the Hornshope Heights and the Horns Hope is just over there.' He gestured vaguely with a black-nailed thumb.

'I see.' Matthew belatedly recognized that this man would talk in riddles, hiding what little information he had in an attempt to taunt the stranger. In Matthew's experience, country clods liked to flaunt their local knowledge to belittle outsiders. They had no other power. 'Well, I'll have to get along now. I have to meet Her Ladyship.'

'Of course.' The man had half withdrawn into his clump of ferns. 'I won't hold you back, Matthew Pryde.' He vanished with scarcely a sound, leaving Matthew staring at the place where he had been and even more apprehensive about meeting Her Ladyship.

The next village he passed was livelier, with a small green on which ducks wandered, and a straggle of stone-walled cottages that looked as enduring as their occupants. A blacksmith looked up from his anvil to wave a brief acknowledgement, while a woman walked gracefully from the well with a pitcher of water balanced on her head. Matthew felt that he was returning to normality after a visit to some dark place. He hurried on, wondering which of the two villages was typical of Her Ladyship's domain.

There was no high wall to mark the policies of Harestone, only a gradual appreciation that the land was becoming more cultivated, with small patches of flax mingled with barley and potatoes, and the presence of more people. The road curved to the north, past a collection of cottages from which came the clatter of looms and the chatter of children, then straightened into an untidy copse that looked as if it had been planted in the time of Adam. Beyond that was the house, which was unlike anything that Matthew had ever seen in his life.

The lawns could have belonged to any country seat in England, save that the sheep that occupied them were dark and ragged, and there was quite an extensive orchard that appeared well cared for. Outhouses had been planted wherever the whim of the builder dictated, with neither pattern nor sense, so that a coach house sat beside the gardener's shed, and the stable block overlooked what might have been an ornamental lake, save for the clinker-built boats that told of fishing parties and sport. Beyond the outbuildings, Harestone House reared up in a confusion of architectural styles that set Matthew's logical mind reeling.

There was a single central tower some five storeys high, topped with an empty flagpole and the expected beacon to warn of French invasion. Matthew had never seen a property built with undressed rubble mingled with great stone blocks, and he wondered that there was hardly a window for the lower thirty feet, as if intended for defence rather than habitation. Adjacent to the tower were Jacobean extensions, complete with twisting chimneys and windows whose ostentatious decoration seemed to apologize for the grimness of their neighbour. Outside again were extensive wings that would have been attractive in a different setting, and if they had matched, but the east wing was larger than the west, which seemed to possess the only entrance to the entire building.

There seemed to be an abnormal number of servants, few of whom showed any interest in the presence of a stranger or any inclination to do more than lounge about talking, but eventually one man sauntered over with his hands thrust inside the waistband of his breeches.

143

'You'll be the lighthouse man from London?' He jerked a thumb toward the entrance. 'Her Ladyship's expecting you. That's the main door there, but mind you touch the Hare Stone before you go in.' He reached for Sally's reins. 'I'll look after your horse.' He made it sound as if he were doing Matthew a favour.

'Touch the what?' Matthew asked.

'The Hare Stone! That big lump of rock at the door.' The man spoke as if to an idiot, then turned away, one hand caressing Sally's muzzle.

'Expecting me? How is Her Ladyship expecting me?'

When the servant ignored his words, Matthew straightened his shoulders and marched up a wide stairway toward the door. He had noticed the vertical boulder that stood in the shadow of the East Wing, but had discarded it as unimportant. Only when he got close did he realize that the Druids or some such ancient people must have erected it. Overtopping him by a good three feet, it was inscribed with carvings of strange creatures that looked like elephants or perhaps sea monsters. For a second he wondered what Kate would have made of such a stone, but dismissed the thought immediately as too painful.

There were two servants loafing in the doorway, but neither the tall, tanned washerwoman nor the stocky man dressed like a gamekeeper moved until he dutifully pressed his hand against the stone. It was cool to his touch.

'Good morning,' Matthew addressed the servants, who nodded back with a fine display of indifference. 'To whom should I speak to seek an audience with your mistress?'

'Is it Her Ladyship you want?' The man's accent was so thick that Matthew found it difficult to understand.

'Yes. Lady Fenwick.'

'Aye. This woman will help you.' The gamekeeper indicated the washerwoman, then sidled round-shouldered away, whistling.

'This way.' The washerwoman's accent was just as strong, but there was more than a hint of humour in her eyes as she led Matthew inside the house. 'You'll be the man from London come to speak about a lighthouse?'

By now Matthew had deduced that everybody knew about

144

him and his business. He nodded. 'That's correct. But I am here to speak with Her Ladyship.'

The washerwoman's shoes clicked on the black and white tiles of a surprisingly bright hall. She stopped at the oaken settle that was the only furniture, looked over her shoulder and considered him. 'So I hear. But will she want to speak with you?'

'I hope so,' Matthew said honestly. 'I have heard great things about Lady Fenwick.'

'Have you now?' Disdaining the use of the ornate banister, the washerwoman nearly ran up a curving flight of steps. She stopped at a landing that stretched the length of the wing. A double row of closed doors waited like soldiers on parade, or boys waiting for their victim to walk the gauntlet. 'Walk along to the end here, through the last door and on again. Don't stop until you come to the oldest part of the house. Lady Fenwick will greet you there.'

Matthew nodded his thanks and reached for a small coin. 'But should I not be announced?'

'Announced?' The notion seemed to amuse the washerwoman. 'No, we don't stand on ceremony. Besides, she already knows that you're here.' Without the briefest of curtseys, she vanished through a side door.

With his footsteps echoing loudly, Matthew marched along the polished wooden floor, very aware of the gaggle of children who had followed him. One, more daring than her friends, called out, 'There's the lighthouse man!' and ran away as Matthew contemplated whether his dignity allowed him to turn and chase them. The end door opened through a three-foot thick wall into the Stuart wing, with wood panelling and portraits of men whose grim faces belied their flamboyantly lacy collars and cuffs. The corridor continued, through yet another door that punctured an even thicker wall, into what at one time must have been the great hall of the original Harestone House.

The washerwoman was already there, standing at the head of a long table as she spoke with a tall, elegant woman who favoured Matthew with a long look before gliding away. Her skirt dragged smoothly over the floor.

'Your Ladyship?' Matthew addressed the retreating woman, who did not look back before ducking through a low doorway.

'Mr Pryde, I believe?' The washerwoman extended her hand, palm downward. Her accent remained the same, but there was something in her demeanour that warned Matthew exactly who she was.

'Lady Fenwick?' Bowing, Matthew kissed the hand. He felt immensely stupid and, as so often, embarrassed at his mistake.

Lady Fenwick took immediate charge of the situation. 'You have come to ask me about building a lighthouse, I hear. Well, Mr Pryde, you will have to work hard to convince me of the necessity.'

Matthew rose from his bow. 'So I believe, my Lady, but I will try my best.'

'No man can do more than that.' Sliding into a heavily carved chair at the head of the long table, Lady Fenwick invited Mathew to join her. He sat awkwardly, attempting to recall all his painfully learned lessons in deportment as Her Ladyship called for refreshments.

Dressed in what appeared to be cast-off rags, Lady Fenwick was somewhere between forty and fifty, with shaded green eyes that fluctuated between amusement and cynicism as she perused him. Her long fingers were as bereft of ornamentation as her neck was, but there was a definite air of authority that he cursed himself for having missed.

Despite the air of casualness that pervaded the house, the servant who brought a tray of drinks was quietly efficient, offering Matthew a choice between gin-and-water and brandy, while handing a small bottle and a glass to his mistress. Accepting the gin, Matthew waited for Lady Fenwick to drink, aware that she was scrutinizing everything that he did.

'Well now, Mr Pryde,' there was nothing about the washerwoman as Lady Fenwick took complete command. 'Tell me about this lighthouse idea of yours.'

Feeling the heat of his flushed face, Matthew did so. He spoke of the number of ships lost on the coast and of the desperate need of the country for trade. He spoke of the request by the Newcastle shipmasters for a lighthouse to mark that most dangerous part of the coast, and of the benefits to the local community, with jobs and increased trade. He spoke of the misery that shipwrecks caused, of the grief of widows and orphans and of the horrors of the Black Corbie.

Lady Fenwick listened quietly with an occasional nod of agreement or encouragement. She did not speak until Matthew was finished, then rose quietly from her chair. 'You argue most persuasively, Mr Pryde. I assure you that I am fully aware of the peril endured by mariners off this coast, as I am of the somewhat backhanded benefits that accrue to the villagers of Onswick. However, I believe that it is Lord Chevington who has the power to bring a bill to the Commons, not myself. I am only a poor widow woman, making her way through the world as best I can.'

'With your permission, Your Ladyship, but that is not quite correct.' Matthew was astonished at his own temerity in disagreeing with a Lady. 'I have approached Lord Chevington, and he, in common with everybody else in this part of the country, assures me that you are the real power here. With your agreement, this lighthouse could be built. Without it, neither Lord Chevington nor anybody else will approach the House and ships will continue to be lost on the Black Corbie.'

Lady Fenwick raised an amused eyebrow. 'My, my, what a burden of responsibility to lay on my poor widow woman's shoulders.' Her smile created a network of creases that made her eyes appear positively amiable. 'That is all nonsense, of course. I am as capable as any man of accepting responsibility and, dare I say it, seemingly more capable than Lord Chevington, despite his undoubted position as the elected Member of Parliament. However . . .' Lady Fenwick took a deep breath. 'Things are as they are. Give me but five minutes to change, Mr Pryde, and I will take a walk with you.' Rising swiftly, Lady Fenwick left the hall.

She returned within the allotted time, fully dressed in a sensible gown of some strong material, with a brown pelisse on top and a creamy bonnet keeping her hair under control. Unfashionably heavy boots completed her attire, while she carried a very manly cane in her right hand.

147

'Come, Mr Pryde.' She strode through the corridors of the house, attaching names to the various portraits at which she thrust her cane. 'That is the fourteenth Lord Fenwick, he was a drunken boor. Married three times and had a whole string of mistresses. Died in France, we believe, of some unspecified fever, but probably the curse of Venus.' She walked on, with servants and children scampering before her, until she came to a portrait of a young man in military uniform.

'This was the twentieth lord, who died at the capture of Gibraltar in 1704. He was a fool; never learned how to duck.' Turning abruptly, she crashed through a varnished door that led to a small room containing a four-poster bed. A dark painting of a man in armour adorned one wall.

'The sixth lord, died fighting the Scots, as did his father and grandfather.' She turned to Matthew with a small smile on her face. 'No Scottish blood in you, I hope?'

'Indeed no,' Matthew refuted any such suggestion immediately.

Lady Fenwick snorted. 'No? Are you sure?' She let the question hang for a second, then smiled, left the room and strode down a flight of steps that led to the hall where Matthew had first entered the house. She pushed open the outside door and stood at the carved stone. 'In case you had not realized, Mr Pryde, this is the Hare Stone from which the house takes its name.'

'It's very striking,' Matthew allowed.

'Indeed.' Lady Fenwick waited for Matthew to admire the carvings. 'The word "har" is Celtic for a boundary stone. This stone marked the edge of an old Celtic kingdom and the beginning of the English lands. Do you understand the implications, Mr Pryde?'

'It is indeed an old foundation.'

Lady Fenwick ran her right hand lovingly across the stone, caressing the carvings as if they were the face of her lover. 'Ancient. Harestone House and the Fenwick family are deeply intertwined with the very fabric of this realm. We have held the boundary of England for many hundreds of years. This was where the Scots were *stopped*.'

Matthew looked around, seeing the watching servants, the

copses of trees and the hills that rose on either side. He already knew that Harestone House was situated in the pass between the hills, a natural route south for any invader. It took little imagination to work out that Scottish raiding parties would have tried to force the pass.

'Hence the old tower with no windows and a view northward,' Matthew suggested. 'From this house you could see the Scots coming and bar their advance through the pass.'

'The Fenwicks were England's coat of mail, and Harestone was known as the Guardian of the Pass.' Lady Fenwick's accent changed again as she related her family's history. The washerwoman had become the refined matriarch of an ancient northern family. 'Obviously, one small tower could not stop a full army, but we delayed them on many occasions, and Fenwick men fought at Chevy Chase and Flodden, as well as Newburn and, more recently, Quebec and in America.'

'You have a long history, Your Ladyship.' Matthew thought it best to humour Lady Fenwick, although he could not see the relevance of ancient history to his present business.

'We do, Mr Pryde.' Allowing her hand to drop from the stone, Lady Fenwick walked purposefully across the lawn, scattering sheep and servants with a casual swing of her cane. She stopped at the ha-ha that marked the edge of her orchard.

'If you look upward, Mr Pryde, you will see the southern lip of the slap. That is what we call this pass: Hornshope Slap.'

Matthew looked upward. The hills rose steeply, rough grass marred with streaks of grey scree and loose boulders of indeterminate size.

'Can you see a cave there, above the scree?'

At first Matthew could see nothing, but eventually he saw a black smudge that could mark the entrance.

'The first Fenwick lived there, Mr Pryde. He was known as Wild Cerdic, and he wrestled the land from the Celts. His descendants fought the Normans, but King William granted us the house and land when we kept Malcolm Canmore out.'

Lady Fenwick bunched her fists as if wishing that she could grasp a sword and lay about her. 'At times the Slap was known as the Thieves' Road, there were so many mosstroopers crossing, but we Fenwicks fought them all.'

'I see.' Matthew had never been interested in history, but nodded politely as Lady Fenwick talked him through the story of her family. He heard about famous warriors who had faced the Scots, religious dissidents who preferred free thinking to the established Church and scandalous lords who had preferred a servant girl or neighbour's wife to their own. He also heard of the loyalty of the tenants, generations of whom had lived in the neighbourhood, son following father, daughter following mother, in the same village and often in the same house.

'Come with me, Mr Pryde,' Lady Fenwick ordered, and took him on an exhausting march around the estate, showing him the old boundary wall and the farmland, the stocks that had long been unoccupied and the whipping post that stood forlorn and rotting. 'These are good people, Mr Pryde, my people. Tenants who have been loyal for centuries, but things are changing now.'

The words caught Matthew by surprise, for it was the first indication that Lady Fenwick had returned to the present. 'We all have to accommodate progress,' he said carefully.

'Oh? Why?' There was a challenge in the words. 'When things have worked so well for so long, why should we embrace a change that is not proven to be better? Why change things that have always been?'

'We live in a changing world,' Matthew said cautiously, 'and many things improve.'

'And others get worse. Do you recall the terrible shortages at the end of last century?' A smile hovered at the lips of Lady Fenwick. 'Or perhaps you were too busy at school.'

'I remember,' Mathew agreed. The last few years of the 1790s had been harsh, with bitter winters and poor crops leading to severe grain shortages. He remembered the clamours of the peasantry and the worry that revolution might spread from France to Britain.

'There was little shortage here,' Lady Fenwick said. 'Do you know why not?'

Matthew shook his head. 'No, Your Ladyship.'

'The Lord provided for us. We do not interfere with His will, and He ensures that we have sufficient food and covering.'

Matthew could guess the answer to his next question even before he asked it. 'How did He ensure that, Lady Fenwick?'

'He sent a Lubeck ship to the Black Corbie. She carried grain by the ton, and although she broke her back, she did not sink until the men of Onswick had removed much of her cargo. We ate well while others starved.' Lady Fenwick had halted on a small mound that gave a fine view up the pass to Harestone House. She looked back, then slowly swivelled to look over the surrounding countryside. 'The Lord looks after us, Mr Pryde, and we look after England, on this frontier and throughout the world. We do not interfere with the will of the Lord. I will not approve the building of a lighthouse that might interfere with His will.'

'But Your Ladyship,' Matthew thought quickly. He could not out-argue Lady Fenwick's history, but he could try her Christianity. 'Perhaps He sent me as an instrument of that will. Had you thought that it might be His will to make things safer for passing mariners?'

Lady Fenwick frowned. 'Your use of the word "passing" is in itself informative,' she said. 'If that grain ship had passed, then my tenants would have suffered.' Lifting her stick, she pointed toward the village through which Matthew had ridden that morning. 'Come, Mr Pryde, let me show you something.'

Built of solid grey stone and thatched with heather, the cottages of the village clustered around an irregularly shaped green on which a crowd was gathering. Matthew frowned as he saw that the majority were watching one couple, a man and a woman. The man was burly and unshaven, the woman slender and cleanly clothed, with the remains of a fading bruise around her left eye. The man carried one end of a rope, which was tied in a slack noose around the neck of the woman, and shouted out that he was willing to sell his wife, if the right price could be agreed.

'That's barbaric!' Matthew looked at Lady Fenwick for support, but she merely smiled and tapped her cane on the ground.

'Wait,' she advised.

'What price do you want, Sim?' another man asked, leering at the woman, who looked away with an expression that could have been contempt.

'Five shillings and a quart of ale,' burly Sim said, 'and not a penny less.'

'Five shillings? And her with the hottest temper in the parish?' The leering man laughed and looked away. The woman said nothing, but her expression promised dire retribution on some future occasion.

'Slavery!' Matthew took a single step forward. It was not many years since Kate had persuaded Matthew that the abolition of slavery would benefit mankind, and he had never changed his belief. 'This is as bad as slavery!'

'Wait!' Lady Fenwick advised again, laying her cane across Matthew's chest to prevent him from interfering.

The burly man tried again. 'Maggie is a hard-working lass, a fair cook and a good bed warmer. A catch for any man, and a bargain at the price.'

'If she's so good, Sim, why sell her?' a tall, younger man asked.

When Sim did not reply, Matthew looked at Lady Fenwick, who shook her head. 'Wait,' she said for the third time.

'Five shillings, then,' the younger man said, and the woman looked up at him, then immediately dropped her head.

An older man stepped up and patted her arms. 'Nicely muscled,' he said, 'fine for working. Keeps the bed warm, you said?'

'Aye, fine in bed,' Sim agreed readily.

'Five shillings and threepence,' the older man upped the price, 'with the quart of ale to seal the bargain.' He reached for the rope as the woman looked at the younger man and winked.

'Women from Ederford are worth more than that,' she said quietly.

The younger man seemed to agree. 'Five and sixpence,' he said, 'and a gallon of ale.'

'It's an auction, a slave auction!' Matthew had heard of the practise of wife-selling, but never thought to witness such a thing.

'Six shillings!' The older man glared at his rival.

The woman raised her head again, smoothed her hands down her flanks and very gently thrust out one hip toward the younger man, who glanced from her to Sim and then to the older man. 'Seven and six, and a gallon of ale.'

The older man muttered something and took a handful of coins from his pocket, counting them slowly. At length he shook his head. 'Seven shillings and two gallons of ale!'

The husband shook his head, grinning, 'I've tasted your ale, Rob, and prefer the young lad's sixpence.' He handed the rope over to the younger man, who immediately removed the noose from the woman's neck. Handing over the money, he shook the previous husband's hand and kissed his new wife in a public display of affection that brought a roar of approval from the crowd.

'There now, everybody is happy,' Lady Fenwick spoke with some satisfaction. 'The wife is well rid of a brute of a husband, the young man has a good wife who will keep him satisfied and his belly full, while the husband has rid himself of an encumbrance to his drinking.' She looked over to Matthew. 'There are those who think that wife-selling is immoral and illegal, but it works, with no need for an Act of Parliament or a divorce, which would cost far more than all three could afford.'

Matthew nodded uncomfortably. 'I see.'

'I hope so,' Lady Fenwick said. 'Do you understand then that the old ways work? They have formed naturally over centuries, through tradition and experience and practice. Can you understand that what we do is right for the people that we are, while having new ways thrust upon us is unnatural?' She swept her arm around the village green, where a group of men were escorting the new husband to a small house from which drifted the aroma of ale and the sound of merriment. 'This bargain was decided well in advance, with only the sum to exchange being in dispute. The marriage had long finished and the husband knew the young man who would buy his wife. It only remained for the arrangement to be made public.'

'And the wife? Did she know?'

'Of course.' Lady Fenwick's easy laugh reminded him of Grace. 'She chose her new husband weeks ago. Think now, Mr Pryde, she has exchanged a drunkard for a vigorous man ten years younger than herself. Maggie Dodds has improved her life immensely. She would never be able to do that through the courts and the church.'

Lady Fenwick looked directly into his eyes. 'It is the same with a lighthouse, Mr Pryde. We know and understand the hazards of the Black Corbie, and we know the benefits that can accrue. Why change it for the unknown? With a lighthouse, we have no bounty from wrecks, no grain in times of famine, no occasional gifts of timber and brick, clothing and coal, exotic food and French wine.'

'No, Lady Fenwick, but you will increase your prospect of trade and will ensure that the coast is safer for all mariners.' Feeling that he was losing the argument, Matthew raised his voice.

Lady Fenwick shook her head again, still smiling. 'All mariners are in the hands of God, as Mr Grover would affirm. Instead of the Lord's favour we will risk the ogres of the Press, coming to force our men into the Navy, or French privateers, coming to burn and rob. It's not many years since American pirates plundered along this coast.' Suddenly she sobered, with her own voice rising above the hubbub of the village green. 'The old ways are under threat, Mr Pryde. First the colonials revolted and formed a republic from lands that we had wrested from Frenchmen and savages. Then the French defied the natural order; they committed regicide, revoked God, altered the calendar and created a Europe at war with itself, where priests and royalists were butchered like cattle.'

Lady Fenwick glared at Matthew, as if accusing him of personally attempting to republicanize the world. 'Now England is also changing, with engineers digging great navigation ditches through the land, while tradesmen and nabobs buy up land as if they were fit to stand next to the families who have been here for centuries.'

She stood silent for a few minutes, listening to the hum of village life. Laughter sounded from one of the cottages, and the sound of working looms.

'In Lord Chevington, Mr Pryde, we even have a Creole who owns property here. Although his family is long established, his money is earned in the sugar plantations of the Indies, and he is betrothed to my daughter, by God! Enough *progress* is enough, Mr Pryde, without adding a lighthouse to the equation!'

The unexpected bitterness took Matthew by surprise, but when he looked around, Lady Fenwick had resumed her composure.

'Come now, Mr Pryde, do not look so disconsolate. You have had an interesting time in the North, but now it is time to return to London.'

Matthew nodded. He knew that Lord Chevington, Nicholas Elmstead, had lived in the Indies, but strangely had never considered him a Creole, a man who earned his money from sugar plantations. He thought of Elmstead's obvious wealth and of the many black servants that he had, and then he thought of Grace Fenwick marrying into such a life. She was obviously an innocent young woman, if wild as the western wind. How would she cope with a husband such as Elmstead?

His sense of closeness to Grace made the prospect disturbing. He wanted to help her, to tell her what sort of man Elmstead was, but could not. Despite Matthew's gentleman's education and honourable occupation, he knew that he was only an escapee from the foundling hospital, hardly fit to speak to Grace Fenwick, yet alone offer her advice.

There was something else nagging at his mind, but he was unsure what. He struggled with a plethora of images and experiences, aware that he was missing something of importance. Matthew groaned; the science of mathematics was so logical when compared to human behaviour that sometimes he wanted to escape entirely into his books and theories.

'Ah, here is Grace now, come to see who is calling! I believe that you have already met my daughter, Mr Pryde?'

Grace's black and white stallion tore great chunks from the village green as it galloped toward them. She was laughing, with a long ponytail of hair protruding from her tricorne hat and a green riding cape flowing from her shoulders.

'Mother!' Grace reined in so abruptly that the stallion's hooves flailed the air a foot from Lady Fenwick's face. 'Well, Mr Pryde, did you manage to persuade my mother to have a lighthouse, then?' Dismounting in a scandal of skirts, she threw her reins over the saddle and smilingly ordered one of the villagers to hold her horse.

'Not yet,' Matthew replied, immediately aware of his strong attachment to this girl. He met her smile with one of her own. 'But I have not yet given up, Miss Fenwick.'

Grace's laugh smoothed away her mother's reactive frown. 'Good man, Mr Pryde. Never give up, never surrender, even if your position is hopeless. Follow the example of General Abercrombie in Egypt, or Admiral Nelson, and go for the enemy, tooth and nail!'

'I hope, Grace, that you are not comparing me to the French!' Lady Fenwick's attempt at severity was unconvincing.

'Certainly not, Mother. The French would not be half as terrifying as you.' Still smiling, Grace reached across and kissed Lady Fenwick lightly on the forehead. 'Have you given Mr Pryde the tour, yet?' She deepened her voice. 'The sacred history of the Hare Stone and how the Fenwicks defended England from savage Scots, fiendish French and daring Dons?'

Matthew looked away, expecting Lady Fenwick to explode with anger at her daughter's impudence. Instead the reply was mild. 'I have, Grace, but now he is leaving.' Her voice dropped an octave. 'Indeed, Mr Pryde, I would prefer if you catch the morning coach back to London. Without my approval, Lord Chevington will not present a bill in the House, and I certainly do not approve.' There was no humour in her smile. 'So there will be no lighthouse and therefore no need for you to be here.'

'Mother!' Grace looked scandalized. She lowered her voice. 'That's most unlike you, Mother! We cannot send Mr

Pryde away with such haste. It is positively impolite!'

Very aware that he seemed to be the cause of a family dispute, Matthew stepped closer, but a shout from one of the villagers ripped around the green.

'The signal fire! Look! The beacon is ablaze! Lord save us all but the French are coming!'

Thirteen

Northumberland, May 1804

Matthew had never experienced anything like the frenzied rush that ensued after that warning shout. Men, women and children crowded on to the green to stare at the smoke smudging the sky from the beacon on Harestone House. Youths yelled with excitement, men balled their fists and women pressed hands to their mouths or grabbed their children. The recently bought wife held her new man tightly, telling him that he was not to even think of fighting the French, while her drunken ex-husband lifted a stout staff and began a ponderous walk to Harestone. One young woman screamed in terror and begged her father to kill her, saying that he would 'be more gentle than the French'.

'I never thought they'd do it,' Matthew said, 'I never thought that they would get past Nelson!'

'Maybe the Navy has mutinied again,' Lady Fenwick gave her opinion. 'The rot started with all these republican ideas.' She sighed and immediately took charge. 'All right, we've faced invaders before. Grace, ride back to the house, quickly now, and find out who fired the beacon and from what direction the French are coming. Mr Pryde, it seems that you are not leaving yet. I have England to defend and I'll need every man, including you.'

'Yes, Your Ladyship.' Matthew was no warrior but he would do his duty. Thrusting a hand inside his cloak, he gripped the butt of his pistol. Damned if he would allow any Frenchman to invade England as long as he was here. Invigorated by the sudden surge of martial valour, he marched straight-backed beside Lady Fenwick. A swaggering drummer led what seemed to be the entire population of the village, with the young men boasting how they would repel the monsoors, and their sweethearts giggling or pleading caution.

'March on, Northumberland!' Lady Fenwick raised her voice. 'Rally at the Hare Stone.'

'Hare Stone!' A man echoed her words and started a ragged cheer as the mob began a shambling movement toward Harestone House.

As they neared the house, Matthew could see that the beacon was well ablaze, with smoke rising in a tall column until the wind blew it in a mad dance across the sky. The sound of crackling flames acted as a background to the rhythm of the drum and the excited murmur of the crowd.

'Your Ladyship!' A groom brought Lady Fenwick a horse.

'Three cheers for Her Ladyship!' some fool shouted, but without response.

Hoisting herself into the side saddle, Lady Fenwick urged her horse to the top of the stairs that led to the house entrance. Leaning down, she spoke to Grace for a moment, then, producing a small pistol from a saddle holster, fired a single shot in the air. After the initial shrieks from alarmed women, there was silence.

'Tenants, friends, fellow Englishmen and Englishwomen!' Lady Fenwick's voice was clear and loud. 'Once more our country is in peril, and once more the people of Hornshope are gathered at the Hare Stone to defend it!' She paused to allow the chatter to die down.

'It seems that the French have managed to evade Lord Nelson and have invaded our country! Shall we allow them to burn our houses and steal our women?'

There was a resounding 'No!' from the crowd, with much shaking of fists and rustic agricultural tools. One woman screamed in horror at the thought, until a man quietened her with a protective hug.

'Shall we allow them to kill our young men and enslave our elders?'

Again that loud No! with mothers clasping their sons to maternal bosoms and older men looking fierce and martial. The drummer beat a mad, brief tattoo.

159

'Shall we allow them to destroy our liberty and behead our beloved king?'

This time the cry was more muted, but it rose again as people realized what was expected of them. '*No!*'

Somebody began to sing 'God Save the King', but stopped after a few lines when only a few people joined in. Lady Fenwick waited until they were quiet again.

'It appears that the first beacon was lit at Onswick, so the French must be there. I want every man to collect whatever weapon he can find and follow me. Those of you who are members of the militia must march to Chevington Hall. I will send a messenger to Lord Chevington, instructing him to muster, although I suspect that he is already doing so.'

Lady Fenwick waited for a moment and then raised her voice to a shout. 'For England and Harestone!'

Matthew thought that the answering shout would have alerted every Frenchman as far as the Spanish border, then realized that his own voice had helped swell the noise and wondered at Lady Fenwick's power of inspiration. Grace grabbed his arm, eyes bright with excitement.

'Is it not thrilling, Mr Pryde? Boney himself could be only a few miles away, with all his army, guns, horse and foot! What stirring times we do live in, to be sure!'

'We do, Miss Fenwick.' Matthew resisted his inclination to hug her, contenting himself with a smile that disappointed them both. He nodded his thanks as a stable boy brought him Sally.

With Lady Fenwick leading and the drummer a few steps behind, the armed might of the parish shambled toward Onswick and a confrontation with the French. There must have been 150 people when they departed from the Hare Stone, and a further forty joined them as they followed the road to the coast. More than one mother was pulling her son away, while one youth's courage evaporated with every step until he finally slid into a copse of trees. A group of girls hounded him out with taunts that belittled not only his courage, but also his ancestry and manhood. As they neared the sea, the pace of the mob slowed, until Lady Fenwick rode around them with encouraging words.

160

By this time, Matthew expected to see the glitter of a cuirassier's breastplate or the high plumes of helmets. He listened for the bark of cannon and the harsh words of command as the French officers consolidated their control over their beachhead. Instead there was nothing save the bleating of sheep and the sough of the wind over a countryside swept clear of people. Rather than a village ablaze, the only smoke came from the beacon on top of the Heights and its fellow on the church tower.

'Not very good at pillage, are they?' one man voiced what sounded like professional disapproval at the lack of destruction.

Standing at the head of the steep, dog-legged track that led down the cliff, Matthew thought that Onswick looked as peaceful and prosperous as ever.

'So where are these French, then?' Lady Fenwick demanded of Matthew. 'I can see none. Unless they have landed elsewhere and our beacon only reflected the chain.'

Matthew's logical engineering mind grappled with the problem. 'The geography of the country seems to argue against that, Your Ladyship. Only the watchers on the Heights can see Onswick's beacon. The cliffs cut the village off from other parts of the coast, hence the need for a lighthouse.'

'There will be no lighthouse if the French have landed,' Lady Fenwick said. She sounded worried.

'Stand aside, Mother!' Still laughing, Grace pushed her horse down the narrow path. 'I will ride ahead and see.'

'You will not!' Lady Fenwick's temper cracked. 'Get back out of danger!' Raising her voice, she called for one of her servants. 'Take my daughter home, Alten, and make sure that she remains there until I say otherwise. You have my permission to use any methods you wish.'

Alten was a large man of about thirty-five. He grabbed the bridle of Grace's horse at once and, ignoring her protests that she was also a Fenwick and it was her duty to defend England from invasion, led her back up the path.

'Mr Pryde! Ride ahead and see what is happening.'

Matthew nodded and spurred his horse onward. He felt the pounding of his heart as he passed the first of Onswick's

161

houses, but there were no blue uniforms to challenge him, no jetting white smoke and crack of musketry, no French voices. He jumped in alarm as a burly figure slid from the shelter of the yellow-bricked garden wall.

'See her?' Robert Megstone said quietly, pointing out to sea. He carried a long musket in the crook of his arm. 'She's a Frenchie, sure as death.'

Matthew followed the direction of his finger and saw the topsails of a ship breaking the horizon. 'Is that it? Is that the invasion?'

'No invasion yet,' Megstone said quietly. 'Somebody panicked and lit the beacon, but that ship is heading here, and with some mission in mind.' He looked upward. 'And with the wind in this quarter, the Corbie can't help us.'

'The militia are on their way,' Matthew reassured him, 'and all the men from Harestone.'

'So I see.' Megstone looked up the path, where Lady Fenwick's army swarmed toward the village. 'We're safe now, then.' He did not keep the irony from his voice.

Lady Fenwick reined up beside Matthew, her expression asking a question. 'No invasion,' Matthew told her, 'but Mr Megstone here is of the opinion that the vessel out to sea is a Frenchman.'

Lady Fenwick's lips tightened as she scanned the horizon. 'I shall find out more about the beacon business later. In the meantime, let's prepare to repel these Monsoors. Do they think they can defeat us with one ship?' She looked at the gathered tenants, with their strained faces and old flintlock muskets, home-made pikes and unwieldy agricultural implements. She tightened her lips and stared at the ship, whose royals were now visible above the horizon.

'With the wind as it is we have at least two hours to prepare,' she said softly, 'so let us ensure that we have spiritual as well as physical help.' Raising her voice, she shouted for Mr Grover, who appeared in moments, holding his wig in place with his left hand as he pulled on a cloak with his right.

'The French are coming, Mr Grover, and I think that a service will be in order. Ring the church bells, pray, and inspire us all.'

'I am aware of the French ship, Your Ladyship, but I did not expect to find you here. Would it not be better to get away inland and let the soldiers face the invasion?'

'There are no soldiers here at present, Mr Grover,' Lady Fenwick explained as to a child, 'so we must do our duty like Englishmen until there are. Pray, do yours now, and ask for the protection of the Lord!'

The church bells attracted Lady Fenwick's followers as well as the people of Onswick, but Matthew doubted if any of them had ever attended such a sermon before. Sending the eager drummer to the tower to keep watch on the ship, Lady Fenwick ensured that all weapons were piled just within the iron-studded door, ordered that all dogs should be kept outside and nodded for Mr Grover to begin.

With such a short space of time in which to prepare, Matthew was impressed when Grover gave an inspired sermon about duty and faith, the closing words of which were: 'Then let us implore the divine protection before we leave this church. We face a brutal and godless enemy, but the Lord will put hooks on their noses and bridles in their jaws and turn them back by the way that they came.'

Grover ended with a rousing hymn that had the congregation on their feet, then released them, spiritually strengthened, to face the French. Checking that the pistol was safe inside his cloak, Matthew fought the nerves that set his limbs trembling. He had never thought himself particularly brave, preferring to deal with confrontation with verbal logic rather than violence. However, he doubted if reasonable words would convince the French, while many of the villagers were looking to him for leadership.

For the first time in his life Matthew recognized that he must assume the responsibilities of a gentleman. He had to step free from the mantle of the foundling hospital and act the part Maidhouse had drilled him for. Twisting his face into what he hoped was a ferocious grin, he drew his pistol and gestured toward the sea.

'Come on, lads, let's show monsoor that he can't land in England!'

The cheer was weak but audible as Matthew pulled himself on to Sally. If only Kate was here to see him.

The ship was much closer now, with her sails bulging under the pressure of the onshore wind and a row of chequered gun ports stretching ominously along her hull.

'Frigate.' Megstone was holding a long musket as he examined the approaching warship. 'Thirty-eight guns, I reckon, crew of maybe three hundred and no doubt a complement of soldiers. She's showing no colours as yet.'

'Let's face them, then.' Matthew kicked in his heels and walked Sally through the confused streets to the harbour. While most of the village's cobles bobbed beside the jetty, a few were out at sea. Hopefully they had the sense to scatter when the frigate appeared. As they watched, a wave broke against the harbour wall, sending spray high into the air. It remained for a long two seconds with the sunlight glinting on the droplets of water, then descended to the heaving waves.

'Swell's rising,' Megstone said hopefully. 'She might not come in.'

'She hasn't come this far to just look,' Matthew replied. He suddenly felt old and important, and wondered if he would enter the history books as one of the last protectors of England's freedom.

'Wind might change,' Megstone ignored his comment. 'If Lady Fenwick's wind comes when she's inshore, then it'll be goodbye Mr Frog. The Corbie will rip the keel off her.'

'We can't rely on that,' Matthew told him. Responsibility had chased away his fear so he could face the impending battle with some equanimity. He glanced behind him.

The defenders seemed to have divided naturally into the fishermen and seamen of Onswick and the up-country men who had marched from Harestone House. A chattering mass of women accompanied both groups, clutching household utensils, knives and even the occasional broomstick.

'The women are going to sweep them into the sea,' Megstone said sourly. He checked the lock of his musket for the fifth time and spat a stream of tobacco juice into the dull water of the harbour.

About twelve men had followed Matthew. Most were armed with muskets but two carried long boathooks and Clem Wharton, his scar prominent, had a brace of pistols thrust through the broad belt of his trousers. He also held a blunderbuss negligently under his arm. Fishermen flourished their weapons, aiming at the still distant ship, boasting of how they would send the Frogs running back home.

'Cut off Boney's tail, that's what we will do,' one elderly man said. He pointed to his left hand, from which two fingers were missing. 'I owe the French for that. Grapeshot took my fingers at the Saints!'

'Away!' another man said, chewing mightily on a wad of tobacco. 'Your wife chopped them off when she found you with young Betsy Foster! She was aiming for something else, mind, but your fingers were bigger!'

There was the coarse laughter of nervous men who knew every secret of each other's lives, and more gestures toward the ship that glided so purposefully offshore.

'Will she come right in?' Matthew wondered. There was a group of small boys shrieking around his feet and he called one over, threw him the key to his room and ordered him to bring down his spyglass. As the boy scampered away, full of self-importance, Megstone shook his head.

'She can't now. I said that the wind was changing. Even a ship of her power will keep away from the Black Corbie.'

'A landing party, then?'

Wharton replied, 'Aye. If we're lucky it will only be a quick raid. If we're unlucky she'll land a few hundred troops and head deeper inland. If we're really unlucky she'll be establishing a bridgehead for a major force that will be just below the horizon. Either way, Onswick will take it bad.'

The boy returned with his spyglass. Matthew gave him a penny and began to inspect the ship. 'There's no flag,' he said, 'nothing to say that she's French.'

'Except her build,' Wharton told him. 'See the rake of her bow? That's no English-built vessel. And why should a British warship come here?'

Matthew could sense his impatience for the spyglass.

'Officers in blue uniforms, lots of guns. They are mustering aft and dropping boats into the sea.'

Megstone's fists were white around his musket. 'That's the landing party. Here we go, then. Aye, where's Admiral Nelson when you need him, eh? Watching the south coast, that's where!'

Four boats sped from the frigate, their long oars flashing in the sun, a blue-coated officer in the stern of each.

'Let me see that glass, Mr Pryde!' The urgency in Wharton's voice chilled Matthew. 'Is that not a red uniform in that leading boat?'

As Matthew tried to focus, Wharton snatched the spyglass. 'Fiend seize them all! No wonder they don't display their colours. What do you make of that, Rob?'

Wondering, Megstone adjusted the spyglass to his eyes, swore and handed it back to Matthew. 'Time to leave, Clem, and sharp's the word!'

'What is it? What's the matter?' Matthew could think of nothing that could scare these two hard-bitten men. 'Is it Boney himself?'

'Boney? I'd stick a fork into Boney's arse just to see him jump,' Wharton said, while Megstone shook his head.

'It's worse than that, by God! Much worse. It's not Frogs, it's bloody lobsters! It's the Press Gang, that's what it is!'

Megstone was moving before he finished talking, taking Wharton and all the fishermen with them. 'Press Gang! It's the Press!' The panic spread, with some men dropping their weapons or pushing over their colleagues in their haste to escape.

'Wait! It might not be!' Vainly, Matthew tried to call them back. 'It might be a ruse!' But the men were gone. Brave men who were eager to fight the French ran in panic at one whiff of a Royal Naval Press Gang. 'Stop!'

Lady Fenwick led her horse through the rapidly thinning mob. 'It's no good, Mr Pryde. They won't be back.' She shook her head, a small smile on her face. 'And no wonder. Life with the Royal Navy is like a floating prison, but with less freedom and more chance of being killed.'

The boats were close now. Two headed directly for the

harbour, one for Grace's private cove to the north and the fourth skirted very close to the foaming rocks of the Black Corbie. There was at least one blue-uniformed officer in the stern of each, with a small knot of scarlet-clad marines and a dozen or so seamen in a variety of clothes. When the leading boat rowed into the harbour and turned sharply at the quay, the seamen lifted their oars in a fine display of seamanship that allowed the officer to land first.

'Follow me, boys!'

Matthew could hear them now as they clattered ashore, sword in hand and orders on lips. The marines followed, boots clumping solidly, and then the seamen, bare feet pattering.

'Search that inn –' the nearest officer pointed his sword at the Mermaid's Arms – 'and find me seamen! I want a score from this village, and no nonsense about protections, by God!'

Matthew realized that he was the only man left to defend the harbour, but the place was far from deserted. A score of women surrounded him, screaming insults at the seamen, waving brawny arms and shaking their brooms. He did not know who gave the order, if indeed anybody did, but the first stone clattered off the quay and fell harmlessly into the harbour. The next bounced from the musket-butt of a marine, and then came an entire salvo as the women found their range. Seamen ducked and weaved to escape the bouncing missiles, while the marines formed a stolid line and the officer's face turned an angry red as he roared his complaints. 'You women! This is the Royal Navy! Stand back!'

'Get back yourselves!' The fisherwomen had gathered handfuls of stones in their aprons and threw them with arms muscled by years of gathering bait and gutting herring. 'We'll have no Press Gang here!' Swearing with as much skill as they aimed, the women kept up a constant barrage that soon forced the seamen into a reluctant withdrawal. One man pressed a hand to the wound that pumped blood from his head and slowly sank down. A marine yelled as a fist-sized stone cracked against his knee.

'Cudgels! Bayonets!' When the officer saw that it was a

gang of women who were forcing back his men, he decided to save the reputation of the Royal Navy. With his head bowed before the barrage of stones, he led the charge from the harbour steps to the first line of fisherwomen and began to lash at them with the flat of his sword. The seamen and marines followed, using fists, clubs and the butt ends of muskets against the women.

Despite their fearsome reputation, Matthew knew that the Press Gang would use only moderate force against civilians for fear of casualties that might result in legal action. However, they were muscled, fit men driven to anger by the injuries suffered among their own number, so the struggle was short but ugly, and ended with the women in full retreat. The officer, a youth of around twenty, straightened his cocked hat and pointed to Matthew. 'Take that man on the horse!'

Until that moment, Matthew had felt slightly detached from the struggle. He had been quite prepared to fight against Frenchmen, but had no such animosity toward the Royal Navy. He was fully aware of the danger in which Great Britain stood, with over a hundred thousand Frenchmen poised to invade, and knew that only the skill of the Navy kept the country free. He was also aware that the Navy recruited largely by force, using the Impress Service to snatch men from homeward-bound ships, augmented by the occasional Press Gang on land. As a gentleman, he had considered himself immune from enforced conscription.

Now the prospect horrified him. He could imagine little worse than to be bundled on-board a warship for an unknown period of time, subjected to harsh discipline, poor food and low pay. All his support for the Navy vanished as the Press reached for him with tarry talons. Yanking his right foot free from the stirrup, he felled the first seaman with a kick of his riding boot, grunted as the swing of a cudgel cracked on his leg and retreated back up the path to the village.

'On, Sally!'

The second boat had also landed and more seamen rushed to join the melee. Matthew heard the bouncing clatter of stones, the high-voiced orders from a midshipman, the disciplined crunch of the marines' boots. He looked backward, hoping desperately that the second boatload had not cut off his retreat, and saw Grace, high on her horse and yelling encouragement to the women from Harestone. Alten was a few paces behind her, waving his hands in despair.

Matthew spurred toward her, even as a pair of agile seamen leapt on her horse and dragged her to the ground. He saw the women around her give way, and then Grace was alone, struggling on the ground with a knot of seamen around her and a file of marines keeping the Harestone women at bay, muskets level and bayonets extended. The midshipman cracked the black and white horse across the rump and it jerked upward and trotted away.

'Leave her alone!' Matthew rode straight into the seamen, bowling one over and causing the others to stagger. A man swung at him, the cudgel crashing against his shin so he swore in pain and kicked out. Grace was looking up at him, her face twisted and with her riding cloak torn at the shoulder. Leaning over, he reached down. 'Take my hand! Quickly now!'

She did so, her hand small but strong inside her tan covered gloves. Matthew pulled, gently at first, then harder as a red-haired seaman made a grab for Grace. She squealed as he hauled her upright, and then yelled again as he pulled her across the saddle in front of him, face down and legs kicking in a flurry of skirts and petticoats.

Matthew lashed out with the reins, catching the red-haired seaman across the face. 'You bastard!' The seaman staggered back, one hand over his face. Blood seeped between his fingers.

'Hold on, Grace!' Guiding Sally in a tight turn, Matthew kicked in his heels, swore as the midshipman leaped out of his way and thrust for the road that wound between the Mermaid's Arms and the church. There seemed to be more seamen beside him, and one frightened small boy running at Sally's tail. Recognizing the boy who had fetched his spyglass, Matthew shouted encouragement. The boy looked up, his eyes desperate, tripped over a raised cobble and sprawled on his face. A seaman swooped down, reached out a tattooed hand and lifted him by the seat of his breeches.

169

'We've caught ourselves a powder monkey!'

Matthew hesitated. Grace wriggled face down in front of him, alternatively squealing and laughing. He had to get her to safety, but he could not leave the boy as a prisoner of the Press Gang.

'Put me down! Please!' The boy was shrieking for his mother.

Matthew saw the boy's face twist in terror. He saw the tattooed seaman casually cuff him across the head, but then Grace tried to turn around and began to slip from her perch. Clamping an arm around her waist, he pinned her down.

'Stop that horseman!' A tall lieutenant pointed directly toward Matthew.

A column of marines appeared from the harbour, their scarlet tunics like blood trickling amongst the disordered mass of white-trousered seamen. There was no pity in the tense faces, no faltering as they moved to obey the order.

'Help me!' The boy was in tears, holding out an imploring hand to Matthew. He was about eight years old, with an ugly, pug-face and ears that protruded nearly at right angles from his face. 'Ma! Don't let them take me!'

The seamen were trotting up the slope, cudgels and cutlasses loose in their hands. The red-haired seaman was yelling obscenities and waving his fist. Blood covered one side of his face and dripped on to his canvas shirt. 'You! I'll see your backbone at the gratings, you lubber! I'll have you keelhauled, you bloody farmer!'

For a second Matthew hesitated. Lying in front of him, Grace was now sobbing with reaction, her body trembling, her cloak thrown back so her skirts shivered in the breeze. It was unthinkable to leave her with the seamen, but he could not leave the panicking boy behind. An image of himself as a twelve-year-old in Maidhouse seared his memory; the Navy would be far worse for an eight-year-old boy.

Cursing in a long repetitive monotone, he wriggled his feet free of the stirrups, dropped the reins and launched himself off Sally and on to the tattooed seaman.

His weight made the man stagger and drop the boy.

'Run!' Matthew roared. 'Run, boy, as if Boney himself was behind you!'

170

The seaman recovered quickly and wrapped an arm around Matthew's throat, squeezing viciously. Shocked at the sheer strength of the man, Matthew gave ground, as the seaman aimed blunt fingers toward his eyes, grunting foul breath.

As Matthew dropped his chin instinctively the seaman's fingers thrust into his mouth. He bit down, hard, tasting salt blood as his teeth ground on bone.

The seaman roared, nearly dislodging one of Matthew's teeth as he jerked his fingers free. He folded up, holding his injured hand, and fear made Matthew kick upward as hard as he could.

The contact jarred his leg to the knee, but the seaman dropped, rolling on his face.

The boy had not moved so Matthew pushed him roughly in the opposite direction to the advancing seamen. 'Run, damn your hide!'

At last the boy understood and sped away, his bare feet slapping the hard ground of the road.

Matthew looked for Sally, saw that she was well away, with Grace still lying across the saddle.

'Got you!' A seaman made a grab at his arm, but Matthew dodged and ducked away, heading in the wake of the fleeing boy. He heard the patter of the seaman's feet on the ground, heard the pant of his breath and hoped that life on board a ship had made him unfit.

The hope died instantly as a massive weight crushed him to the ground. Matthew felt himself pinned and helpless. Somebody stood on his ankle, somebody else grabbed at his hair, there was foul-smelling breath in his face, horrible oaths rasping in his ears, then he was hauled upright and the older of the two officers was leering at him.

'A prime seaman, this. Take him to the jolly boat.'

'Aye aye, sir. Usual precautions, sir?' A bald seaman had Matthew's arms twisted behind him and a knee pressed painfully into the small of his back.

'Yes. Carry on.'

'Aye aye, sir!' Releasing Matthew's left arm, the seamen pulled a knife from his belt and deftly sliced through the waistband of Matthew's breeches. 'Now you can't run anywhere, you lubber!'

Making a grab for his suddenly dropping breeches, Matthew began a formal complaint. 'You cannot press me. I am a gentleman!'

'Gentleman my arse!' the seaman said crudely. 'A gentleman would not have stood with these fishwives, throwing stones at the Navy. Stow your gab, you farmer bastard!'

Rough hands shoved him down to the harbour, but the seamen looked worried. 'Wind's changed, sir. It's coming from the north-east.'

The officer looked out to sea, where his ship rode a scant mile away, sails furled. The sea had risen in the last few minutes, with ugly waves curling above the harbour wall to fall and splinter into a million silver and white fragments. Further out came the sinister boom of North Sea rollers smashing into the monstrosity of the Black Corbie. Matthew remembered Megstone's forecast about Lady Fenwick's wind, but if it had saved the village, it had come too late to save him.

The officer grunted, swearing. 'Call back the search parties. We don't want to be stuck in this godforsaken hole.'

'Aye aye, sir.' The bald seaman saluted and scurried inshore, leaving Matthew by the harbour wall. He returned a few minutes later, knuckling his head in salute. 'Parties report that they can't find anyone, sir. Not a single man.'

'Damn! And the weather's getting worse!' The officer again looked to his ship. The boom of sea against the Corbie was louder now, a sound that seemed as regular and deadly as cannon fire.

With the seamen's attention directed to the changing weather Matthew took the chance to break free. Holding up his breeches with his left hand, he took three long strides to freedom, dodged around an upturned coble and jinked past the Mermaid and up the hill. There were rapid footsteps behind him, but fear powered his legs and he outdistanced them.

When he reached St Cuthbert's, Matthew began to relax.

He slowed, leaning against the churchyard wall, just as a large man appeared in front.

Matthew yelled as muscular arms folded around him.

'Easy, Mr Pryde, easy.' Megstone hauled him into the churchyard and stopped in the lee of a gravestone. 'You're safe now. They're much too concerned about the safety of their ship to chase one scrawny landsman.' He spat with the wind. 'But now you can see why we value the Corbie.'

Fourteen

Northumberland, May 1804

'I have to go to London, Grace,' Elmstead frowned and tapped his gold-topped cane against his boots, 'on parliamentary business.' He held his glossy black top hat in his left hand as a mark of respect to his fiancée.

'You have your duty to do.' Grace accepted his impending absence with surprising equanimity. They stood in the shadow of the Hare Stone, with Elmstead parading his latest carriage and Matthew a quiet spectator in the background.

'Are you still here, Pryde?' Elmstead injected surprise into his voice. 'I thought you would have left as soon as Her Ladyship rejected your request.'

'Still here, My Lord.' In formal company, Matthew allowed Elmstead the formality of his correct form of address.

'Not for long, I wager,' Elmstead replied. 'I'd take you with me, but, damn, I have to leave urgently.' He waved his cane and opened the door of the carriage. Matthew saw a picture of luxury that he would never have imagined, with silk damask upholstery, fur lap robes and even a walnut-cased carriage clock hanging inside. It made a stark contrast to the spartan accommodation of the stagecoach that he considered normal.

As Elmstead slammed the door shut, sunlight reflected on the gilded crest, highlighting the quartering. He leaned out of the open window.

'I doubt that we'll meet again, Pryde, so safe journey back to London.' His smile was broad and insincere. 'I am sorry that things did not work out for you.'

Grace caught hold of his fingers, smiling. 'Safe journey to you too, Nicky.'

'I'll be back within a month, Grace, God and Boney willing.'

They kissed briefly, then Elmstead gave a crisp order to the coachman and withdrew his head inside the carriage. The coachman cracked his whip and the great wheels began to turn, with the brace of barking Dalmatians running level with the four horses.

'Now there's style,' Matthew commented. He watched as the coach came to a sudden halt, sending a spray of gravel from the wheels. The coachman leaped off his seat and scrambled back to Harestone.

'Miss Grace,' he bowed deeply, 'My Lord's compliments, and he would seek the honour of your company for a few minutes.'

Grace sighed. 'Damn the man,' she said crossly, 'what has he forgotten now? Something of trivial importance, no doubt. Pray excuse me, Mr Pryde.'

Despite her assumed irritation, Grace hurried to the coach, where Elmstead was again leaning out of the lowered window. They spoke for a good five minutes, ending with mutual laughter, and then Grace sauntered back with a small smile on her face.

'Is that everything sorted, then?' Matthew asked.

'Of course. As I thought, nothing serious.' Grace shook her head, and then spun around to watch the coach roll past the outbuildings. The barking of the dogs faded as Grace raised her hand in a final farewell. 'You are an interesting man, Matthew Pryde. You are full aware that Nicholas does not like you, and yet you do not retaliate. Why ever not?'

Matthew looked away. He could not speak of his years at Maidhouse without reliving the pain. 'I've known His Lordship for quite some time,' he said at last. 'We understand each other.'

'Indeed?' Grace raised her eyebrows but said nothing. She looked upward to the pale spring sky. 'Come, Matthew. Ride with me a little.'

Once again Grace sat shockingly astride as she led Matthew on an exhilarating ride along the Heights. Scattering sheep before her, she followed the animal trails, whooping unrestrainedly when she reached the summit ridge and waited for Matthew to join her.

'Don't you like it up here?' With the wind whipping her blonde hair around her face, Grace surveyed the Northumberland countryside that spread out before her until the fields and moors merged with the distant Cheviot Hills. 'I love it on a summer evening, when the hill voices speak, the lapwing with its eerie song, the doves, so soft in their cooing, and always the sheep bleating. That's the true sound of the hills, that and the wind.'

When she looked up, the brown of her eyes was shaded and soft. 'There's something magical in the Heights then, they seem spirit-haunted, as if some wizard had enchanted the land with a spell of peace.' She laughed suddenly, tossing her hair so it formed a blonde cloud around her head before it settled around her shoulders. The scent of birch-water was fresh and clean. 'Do you think I am quite mad, Matthew Pryde?'

Matthew shook his head. 'No, Miss Fenwick,' he said seriously. At that moment he quite believed that these hills *were* haunted, and Grace seemed the sanest person he had ever met.

She looked at him, head tilted. 'It's all in the shadows, I think.' She spoke slowly. 'Or the clouds that trail above, while you can see the weather gleam clear above the hills, until the light fades and the Heights fade slowly into the dim of evening. I like to wait then, until the moon rises, with the singing stars lighting the restless road home.'

'You should have been a poet, Miss Fenwick,' Matthew told her seriously.

'Oh? Me and Wordsworth together?' She sighed and her eyes changed colour, her shoulders drooped. 'It can be sad up here too, Matthew, with the trees only gaunt fingers and the horses nodding. So sad, with the water rippling and the bare, bare hills.'

It was only instinct that made Matthew move closer and put a hand on her arm. He removed it immediately Grace shook her head.

'See? There's Harestone House down there.' Her mood

had changed again, her voice light and laughing. 'Does it not look small and insignificant? See the tower? That's my favourite place of all. I have the topmost room there. Some mad old ancestor used it as an observatory, but I claimed it for myself. I love to just sit and devour the view.'

'It's certainly different from London.' Matthew had struggled to match Grace's skill on horseback and now patted the heaving flanks of Sally. From this ridge he could see the spread of Lady Fenwick's estate and the road that led to Onswick and to Foulmire Cross. He could see where the open field system of Harestone ended and the neatly walled enclosures of Elmstead's lands began. Beyond that the ground rose to the irregular horizon of the Cheviots.

'Maybe you're right about the poetry,' Grace said, 'but this is very romantic countryside.' Ignoring the wind, she was staring north. 'You can imagine the old time horsemen raiding here, and the Saxons fighting the Danes, and the wild Scots invading and the Fenwick men out with their swords and shields. Oh, Matthew, I wish that I had been born then, rather than now, when life is so drab!'

'Hardly, drab, Miss Fenwick, with Boney poised to invade and the Press Gang raiding Onswick.'

'Drab, Mr Pryde,' Grace retorted. 'I want to do something that matters, not just engage in a brawl with a set of tarry sailors. I wanted to defend England against the French, face Boney himself and chase him away.' Abruptly turning her horse, she faced south, where the Heights slid into a slow descent. 'And see the prize, Matthew. All of England running south to Newcastle, York, Oxford, London.' She was silent for a moment. 'I would have liked to visit London with Nicholas.'

'It's an interesting city, Miss Fenwick.'

'It's an interesting city, Miss Fenwick!' Grace mimicked. 'Miss Fenwick! Why are you always so guarded, Mr Pryde? Why cannot you drop your barrier for a moment? After all, we have fought side by side now! We are comrades-in-arms, you and I, yet you give nothing away!'

Matthew reflected, slightly cynically, that only a minute previously Grace had brushed aside the encounter with the

177

Press Gang as a brawl. Now she had elevated it to something much more important. 'What do you want to know, Miss . . . Grace?'

'Miss Grace.' She grinned at him. 'That's better than Miss Fenwick, I suppose. What do I want to know? Everything, of course. I want to know everything.'

Matthew shook his head, fighting his compulsion to unburden himself to this girl that he had hardly met, yet that he felt instinctively he could trust. She was looking at him, eyes slightly slanted and already so familiar. 'No,' he forced away the temptation, 'I hardly know anything myself,' he said, 'so I cannot tell you.'

'Oh?' Again Grace raised her eyebrows. 'A man of mystery, are you? I like a challenge.' Her smile was pure devilment. 'I'll find out in time, be sure of that!' A rising sparrow hawk took her attention and she kicked in her heels, following the flight of the bird. Matthew followed slower, aware of the rough ground beneath the hooves of his horse and the long slithering fall only a few yards away.

'Come along, Matthew! I'll race you to those trees!'

A tiding of magpies marked the group of Scots pines that thrust up just to the south of the ridge. They were about half a mile ahead, part hidden in a dip, but with their foliage spreading pleasantly above the skyline.

'What are you doing? Counting them?' Laughing with pure pleasure, Grace whipped her horse to gallop along the ridge. 'Come on, London! Make a race of it!'

Suddenly determined to impress her, Matthew spurred on, feeling an unfamiliar thrill of excitement as Sally picked up speed. The hooves beat hollowly on the drum of the hillside, with Grace's laughter taunting him to greater effort. Since he had come to Northumberland he had been frightened by seals, attacked by unknown men, out-ridden in a coach race and nearly press-ganged. He wanted badly to win something, especially when his opponent was a girl. This girl.

Matthew glanced ahead. They were following a faint animal track that eased slightly downhill, arced around a patch of emerald grass and passed close by a solitary mountain ash.

Still laughing, Grace dominated the path, one hand working the whip, the other the reins as her horse kicked up great clods of earth that pattered against Matthew, further increasing his desire to win.

'Come on now, Sally! Catch her, girl!' Wrenching his horse aside, Matthew left the path, intending to cut the diameter of the arc and overtake Grace as she followed the circumference. Simple mathematics dictated that a straight line was the fastest route between any two points.

'Matthew! No!'

Grace's warning came too late as Sally's hooves sunk deep in soft mud. Matthew swore as he realized that the emerald grass concealed bogland. He looked back, but he was already quarter way in and it would be as hard to turn as to continue, so he kicked in his spurs and cracked the whip against his horse's flank. 'On, girl, on!'

'Matthew, be careful!' Grace was keeping pace with him along the outside curve of the bogland, one hand extended as if her frail strength could pull him from the mud. Her face was contorted with anxiety as she jumped from one foot to the other, offering help and advice that he could hardly hear as he struggled to keep Sally from foundering.

'Careful, Matthew!'

With every step sinking deeper into the mud, Sally plunged on gamely. Matthew swore, wrestling with the reins as he urged her onward. He could hear the keening of a buzzard, could feel the wind sucking sweat from his face, the strain of muscle between his knees as Sally fought the suction of the mud. Then, suddenly he was free, skiffing past the mountain ash until the pine trees were close and Grace was shouting in his wake.

'You cheated! I was all worried about you! That wasn't a fair race!'

'All's fair,' Matthew replied, 'in love and war.'

He saw the expression on Grace's face alter from anger to curiosity. 'And in which category would you place this event, Mr Pryde? War? Or love?'

She had been genuinely concerned when he was in the bog, but now she was teasing, with her eyes open wide and her lips parted. Matthew had never met a woman with whom he felt such an instant rapport, for although she mocked him, he could sense a different person beneath, and that perception was troubling.

'War, of course,' he told her, and saw something that might have been disappointment in her eyes. And that too was disturbing, for he had never before been aware of the feelings of another.

'Look at the state of your horse!' Grace's voice was sharp. 'We'll have to get the stable boy to wash all that mud off.'

The magpies were complaining above his head as Matthew dismounted and fondled Sally's ear. She lowered her head, nuzzled him softly and allowed him to blow gently into her nostrils.

'There, girl.' Matthew patted her trembling flanks. 'You did well.'

With her lower lip protruding in a childish sulk, Grace joined him for a moment, then grew bored and wandered off to poke at the piled-up pine cones on the ground and look at the view. 'I don't like this place much,' she said at last. 'It looks right into Horns Hope. A hope is a closed in valley, in case you did not know.'

Matthew remembered the tarry man at the ford mentioning the name. 'Horns Hope? Where's that?'

'Down there.' Grace accentuated her shiver. 'It's a horrible place, dark and miserable, with an atmosphere.'

'An atmosphere?'

'You can feel it.' Grace shook her head. 'Your friend Wordsworth may like to talk about romantic old places and crumbling abbeys and so forth, but he would not like Horns Hope. Mother told me once that I was never to go there, so of course, I did.'

'Of course.' Matthew nearly smiled. He could not imagine the headstrong Grace obeying any rule that did not suit her.

'That was the only time that Mother was really angry with me.' Grace wriggled with the memory. 'I'll spare you the details, but I would not have gone back to Horns Hope anyway. It's creepy, what with the grave and everything.'

'Whose grave?' Matthew was not really concerned about any grave, but he had to make conversation while he controlled Sally's trembling.

'Some ancestor, probably.' Grace looked away. 'Mother visits it a lot. I don't know whose grave it is. Don't care, really.' In another lightning change of mood, she grinned and pulled herself on to her horse. 'Come on, Matthew, let's ride on.'

As he left, Matthew remembered his first ride along the Heights, when he saw a lone woman riding into a closed valley. He could see the spur on which he had stood, and knew that the woman must have been Lady Fenwick. The thought was vaguely disturbing, but he did not know why.

It was nearly dusk before they returned to Harestone House, with the rising wind carrying large droplets of water that threatened to intensify into a downpour before dark.

'Maybe Mother will invite you to stay the night,' Grace suggested, looking skyward, but Lady Fenwick did not approve of the idea.

'Mr Pryde.' Still dressed more like a washerwoman than the most powerful woman in the area, Lady Fenwick took a firm grip of Matthew's arm and led him into the shadow of the Hare Stone. 'I think that you have spent quite enough time with my daughter. You do understand that she is affianced to Lord Chevington?'

About to protest his innocence of any amorous design, Matthew glanced at Grace and kept silent. He could not honestly say that he was not attracted to her, although nor could he say exactly what was the nature of his feelings.

'I do know that, Lady Fenwick.'

'Good.' Lady Fenwick's nod was firm. 'Then you will also understand that you may damage her reputation by your actions?'

Matthew felt the colour rise to his face. 'I certainly would not wish that, Lady Fenwick.'

'Good.' Lady Fenwick nodded again. 'Then you will oblige me by refraining from ever seeking my daughter's company again. Do I make myself clear?'

181

'You do, My Lady,' Matthew agreed, 'but I assure you that I would never seek to injure Miss Fenwick's reputation in any degree.'

'Nor shall you, Mr Pryde,' Lady Fenwick said. 'I shall make certain of that. This matter is now closed. Good day to you.'

The promised rain started at the exact moment that Matthew left the gates of Harestone House. Jamming the tricorne hat more firmly on to his head, he crouched in the saddle and guided his horse on to the now familiar road for Onswick. He rode instinctively, trusting to Sally's surefootedness as he struggled with his thoughts. He had failed with the lighthouse, failed to unravel the mystery of his background and now he would be unable to see Grace again.

Bowing his head before the wind, he enjoyed the memory of Grace's smile and wondered just what the attraction was in a girl – a young woman, rather – who was so obviously emotional, spoiled and even eccentric. He could not tell, but there was certainly something there, some connection that he could not fathom and something that he could never now explore. Matthew's smile faded as he thought of Grace in Elmstead's arms. He kicked in his heels to urge Sally on.

When he looked up, Matthew cursed. Sally had strayed from the path and was ambling down a narrow track into a steep-sided valley, scarred with gulleys that jostled water to a broad central stream.

'Horns Hope,' he told himself, pulling on the reins. He had no desire to stay here if it was anything like as sinister as Grace claimed. Yet it seemed no different from a score of other valleys that he had ridden through, with the remains of a fortalice hugging the slopes, a scattering of trees and the low bleat of scores of sheep. Despite himself he examined the valley floor, and saw the grave a few yards from where rain wept from the grey stones of the ancient ruin.

With Grace's words still in his mind, Matthew walked Sally closer and dismounted. Ignoring the rain that now sliced vertically down, he kneeled by the headstone and touched the fresh display of daffodils. While the grass in most of the Hope was long and harsh, around the small grave it was

182

neatly clipped and obviously had been carefully tended. There were no weeds and an area around the stone had been cleared and laid to gravel.

A master craftsman had prepared the stone, carving a pair of wide-winged angels who bore a figure between them, swathed in long white robes. Beneath the angels were the words: 'Much loved and never forgotten. Rest in the peace of the Lord' and the initials 'G F'. There was a date below: 13 August 1777.

G F. Removing his hat in a belated gesture of respect, Matthew knelt by the grave for a second in silent prayer. Presumably this was the grave of one of Her Ladyship's forbears, perhaps her mother. For a moment Matthew wondered why this unfortunate woman had been buried so far from the rest of her people, and with only her initials on the grave, then he shook his head. It was possible that G F had enjoyed happy times here, or perhaps there was family scandal somewhere, but he had neither the time nor the inclination to investigate. Grace's family was none of his business.

Leaving the lonely grave to the rain, Matthew remounted Sally and flicked the reins to return to the high road to Onswick. He was no nearer solving any of the mysteries that surrounded him than he had ever been, although he was constantly aware of something tugging at his memory, something that he had forgotten.

Fifteen

Northumberland, May 1804

Matthew kicked away the tangled sheet, unable to concentrate because of the constant booming of surf on the Black Corbie. The events of the last two days tumbled through his head in a mad procession, so that one moment he had a halter tied around the neck of Grace and was selling her to a frowning marine, and the next a boat-load of seamen were throwing stones at Lady Fenwick, who wore the blue uniform of a naval officer but rode a horse with the face of Bonaparte. Yet all the time he knew that he was missing something. If he could restore logic to his chaotic mind, he would exhume something signifi-cant, some small fact that nagged just beneath his consciousness.

It was only when the snarling seal had lifted the small boy and rapped his flippers against the iron grating of the beacon fire that the words came to him. 'Don't leave me!' the woman had pleaded. 'Women from Ederford are worth more than five and threepence!'

Matthew sat up with a jerk. 'Women from Ederford,' he repeated. 'It's a place! Ederford is a place!'

Ever since he had read the name in the tiny office of Timothy Flintock – *should he ever find out about Ederford* – he had believed that it had been either the name of a ship or of a person, perhaps even his own real name. The discovery that it was the name of a place changed things entirely. A place meant people that he could ask, and surely somebody would tell him something.

'I must go there!' He sat up in bed, unaware that he was speaking to himself. Rising swiftly, he pulled on his clothes and boots, thrust his hat on his head and was out of the door and halfway down the stairs before he realized that the inn was still asleep and his candle the only light in the gloom.

'Sir!' Silhouetted by the light of a lantern, Ruth peered out of the kitchen door, her nightclothes tangled and a white cap holding her hair in place. She blinked sleepily at him. 'Sir, there are gentlemen to see you, sir.'

'Gentlemen? At this time?' Matthew shook his head. 'I'm afraid I do not have the time. I must go to Ederford, madam, if you could kindly direct me?'

'You'll be going nowhere, my bucko, save London.'

The men barged past Ruth and into the parlour with Ruth, open-mouthed and tearful, protesting at their side. 'I'm sorry, Mr Pryde, but I can't stop them. It's Lady Fenwick, you see, Her Ladyship's orders.'

'What?' Too concerned with his own plans, Matthew could only stare at the men. There were three of them, burly and hard-featured.

'I see you're dressed.' The first man carried a stout cudgel and his breath stank as he peered closely into Matthew's face. 'That's good. We have a coach to catch.'

'I'm catching no coach,' Matthew said.

'Her Ladyship disagrees.' The second man came closer. He was even broader than the first and emphasized his sincerity by dragging a horse pistol from the belt that just managed to encircle his waist. 'Calm yourself, young sir, and come with us. We'll see you safe on the road.'

'I don't want to go on a coach.' Matthew backed away. Lady Fenwick must have sent these men to throw him out of Onswick, safely away from Grace and all temptation. Far away from this place called Ederford.

Smiling but unmoved, the men stepped closer. The third man held a lantern aloft, and despite the bandage that covered half his face, Matthew recognized the bellman. Lady Fenwick must have borrowed Grace's bullies to eject him.

Moving surprisingly quickly, the cudgel man blocked Matthew's path to the door. 'Come along now, Mr Pryde. Her Ladyship wants you to leave, so leave you shall. She brokes no refusal, you know.'

'But I don't want to go. My business here is not yet complete.'

'I am afraid that it is, sir. Her Ladyship owns this village, and she wishes you gone on this morning's coach.'

Matthew swallowed his frustration. He could sense that Ederford was drifting away from him, but faced with such odds, there could be no refusal. He had no choice. As the bellman and cudgel man stood sentinel over him, the pistol carrier accompanied Ruth to his room, returning a few minutes later with his portmanteau and case neatly packed. Ruth looked agitated as she followed, shielding the flame of her candle with a shaking hand.

'I'm sorry, Mr Pryde, but I hope you have a safe journey.'

Matthew lifted his hat. Politeness dictated no less.

'There we are, Mr Pryde. All serene. Nothing taken and nothing lost.' The pistol man adopted a tone of forced joviality as he opened the front door. 'Off we go, then, and don't worry about the bill; Her Ladyship will settle it all up.'

Escorted outside where the eastern sky was greying along the horizon, Matthew waited until Billy Anderson fetched Sally.

'There you go, sir,' Anderson said and stood to watch, arms akimbo and a leather apron around his waist.

Ruth threw him a nervous smile. 'It was good to meet you, Mr Pryde,' and then he was handed on to his horse with a man on either side. He could hear the waves of the harbour washing to his left and the familiar boom of the Black Corbie. For one brave second he contemplated digging in his spurs to make a bid for freedom, but his escort was too professional, with cudgel man pressing close to his left and the bellman steady in front.

'Where are we going?' He played for time, hoping for a chance to break away.

'Foulmire Cross, Mr Pryde. Her Ladyship has booked you a seat on the London coach, so you have nothing to worry about. There's plenty of time, so we won't hurry too much along the road. Just ride easy and swallow your spleen. We must learn not to flinch at our misfortunes.'

Matthew had long since learned not to flinch.

As they followed the road beneath the Heights, Matthew glanced from side to side, desperate for an opportunity to break free, but his escort knew their business and kept close by his side. They were heavy men but rode well, probably better than him. By their accents they were local, so would know every nook and cranny of this countryside, while he would in all probability ride straight into a marsh, or over a hidden precipice. He did not want to leave the area as a failure, but it seemed that fate, in the shape of Her Ladyship, had other ideas.

Matthew did not think of himself as an emotional man, but the frustration of helplessness made him feel like clawing the skin from his body. It was worse now that he had found one more piece in the jigsaw of his life. If Ederford was a place, presumably a village, then possibly he had lived there. It might be the name of the village where he had spent the first few years of his life, and where the woman who had acted as his mother lived. Perhaps she lived there still and could answer more of his questions.

There was a moment's hope when they passed the road to Harestone and cudgel man trotted away, but his friend pulled the pistol from his belt, levelled it at Matthew and smiled. 'Just sit tight, Mr Pryde, and you'll come to no harm.'

Hoping that somebody would ride past and create a distraction, Matthew prepared for a mad gallop, but the road remained quiet save for sheep and the buzzard that keened overhead. Cudgel man nodded to pistol man when he returned. 'Her Ladyship says to carry on,' he reported, and moved even closer to Matthew.

The coach was waiting when they arrived at Foulmire Cross, its dark paintwork spotted with mud and the guard glowering just as hard as Matthew remembered. He checked his waybill as the escorts bundled Matthew aboard.

'You're the late arrival then,' the guard said. 'On *Lady Fenwick's* orders.' He spat the name as if it tasted foul in his mouth.

Matthew could only watch as the bellman handed Sally back. She had been a good horse and a willing companion on the road, but he was allowed no time for a sentimental farewell. As soon as Matthew was inside the coach, the guard blew a long blast on his brass horn, the driver flicked his reins and the coach pulled out of the cobbled courtyard and on to the Newcastle turnpike. Matthew had hoped that he could disembark at the next inn, but the cudgel man heaved himself clumsily on to the roof and sat there, drumming his feet against the outside of the carriage.

As the coach rolled slowly south, crashing into every rut and splashing through puddles that sprayed muddy water against the closed windows, Matthew felt his frustration rising. He had failed to get Lord Chevington to present a bill to parliament, so there would be no lighthouse built. That meant the dangers of the Black Corbie would remain and more ships would be lost, more men would die. That also meant that he had let William Denton down in his first attempt to work independently. He had wasted time and money on a fruitless journey. He had failed to find Ederford and failed with Grace. For all his pretence at gentility, he was a failure.

'Are you all right, young man?' An elderly woman looked up from her sewing to smile to him. 'You look most downcast there.'

'Let him alone,' the woman's travelling companion, equally elderly but with a knowing cast to her eye, advised. Leaning forward, she patted Matthew's arm. 'I'm sure she will come round,' she said. 'It is your sweetheart that you are thinking of, is it not?'

Staring gloomily down at his feet, Matthew reflected that he had learned slightly more about his own background. He had been a baby on board *Pride of Matthew*, a London whaler, and had some connection with the village of Ederford, wherever that was. And now he was heading back south, with nothing resolved and less prospect of employment in his chosen career.

The coach jolted to another halt, the third since they had left Foulmire, and Matthew's fellow passengers raised a collective groan of despair.

'Oh, what is it this time? Has a horse cast its shoe? Or perhaps we've lost a wheel?' The sewing woman looked across to Matthew. 'We ended up in a ditch last time I travelled to York,' she told him. 'We all had to get off while the gentlemen helped pull the coach up. It was all very exciting!'

'Stand!' The word came from outside, crisp and hard and unambiguous. 'Stand and deliver!'

'What?' Matthew looked up. All of London knew that phrase, for it was what children shouted when they pretended to be highwaymen. He had never believed that he would hear it used in earnest.

'What's that? Highwaymen?' The old woman dropped her sewing and rolled down the window. 'Oh! Oh, this is even more exciting than losing a wheel! It's Captain Ellwood, I know it is! Oh, will there be shooting, do you think?'

There were two of them, one in front of the coach and one in the rear. The smaller had what appeared to be a triangle of black silk covering much of his face and a tricorne hat pulled low over his eyes. He held a pistol in each hand, one levelled at the driver, the other at the guard. His companion was taller and dispensed with any form of disguise. His face was long and lean and sported two days' growth of beard. He rode up and wrenched open the door.

'Out!'

Feeling slightly sick, Matthew left the coach, giving his hand to the two women as they stepped gingerly to the ground. It was full light, with sunshine dappling the woodland in which they had been stopped. Steam rose from the flanks of the horses, the nearest of which snorted and pawed the ground.

'They don't look very romantic, do they?' The sewing woman sounded disappointed.

Birds sang overhead and a mild wind flapped their travelling cloaks against the women's frail old legs. The taller of the highwaymen demanded purses and wallets, gold watches and loose change.

'And be quick about it!'

Despite having been brought up on stories of the chivalry of such people, Matthew felt only sick fear every time the pistol pointed in his direction. This man was no mere bruiser, but a professional outlaw who risked transportation or even hanging. He had nothing to lose by killing one of his victims.

'Oh, Captain Ellwood, I'm afraid that you can't have my purse. I only have enough money for the journey,' the sewing woman smiled to the highwayman.

'Down!' The pistol indicated that the outside passengers should come down. They did so unwillingly, with Matthew's large escort showing signs of truculence. The smaller of the highwaymen leaned over from his horse and swung a pistol hard against the man's head, so he staggered. Rapidly dismounting, the highwayman followed up with a quick kick to cudgel man's backside, then swung back on the horse.

There was a gasp from the second of the two women as Matthew moved instinctively forward, but the menace of a pistol brought him back into line. The escort pulled out a small purse and threw it on the ground. The second woman followed, but the sewing woman shook her head.

'I won't,' she said, looking at Matthew, who glared his distaste at both men. He did not care about the injury to cudgel man, but knew that a gentleman should try to protect the women.

The taller highwayman grunted and pointed his pistol at Matthew. 'You, unload your valuables!'

Matthew had dressed in haste, so his money was still in his case, save for a handful of loose silver. He was also aware that these highwaymen had to move quickly, in case other travellers caught them. They would naturally be nervous.

'I've only a little money,' he said, 'but if you let the lady alone, I will give you my watch.'

'You'll give us that anyway,' the highwayman told him, 'and never mind the old woman.'

The smaller highwayman pushed his horse toward his companion and murmured something in his ear. The second highwayman nodded, dismounted and scooped up the offerings that lay in the mud. 'All right! Back on the coach.' He pointed to Matthew. 'All except you! Chivalry has its reward, mister, and yours is to come along with us!'

'I'm damned if I will!' Matthew said, until the highwayman cocked the pistol that was levelled at his face.

'Oh!' The sewing woman looked at Matthew with something like envy, but did not linger. Cudgel man was just as eager to return to his seat as the highwaymen relieved the guard of his blunderbuss and sped the coach on its way with a resounding slap to the rump of the rearmost horse. Standing in the mud, Matthew watched the coach roll away, feeling a mixture of dismay and absolute horror. Although Captain Ellwood had a reputation for gentlemanly behaviour toward women, Mathew knew that highwaymen could be sickeningly violent at times. He glanced behind him, hoping for the advent of another traveller or perhaps a way of escape, but the tall highwayman was prodding him with his pistol.

'This way! Quickly!'

With both highwaymen ushering him on, Matthew began to run. He was aware of that pistol pointing at the back of his head and of the hot breath of horses on his neck. The smaller highwayman pushed him off the road and over an unenclosed common, where sheep grazed alongside scrawny cattle and furze tore at his knee breeches. There were a few scattered hawthorn trees, then a clump of bramble that the highwaymen avoided.

Already feeling the breath burn in his chest, Matthew saw a small cluster of buildings ahead. There was a low-walled cottage with the yellow glow of candlelight in a window, a group of tumbledown outbuildings and what might have been the remains of a bastle house, now crumbling into romantic ruin.

Without hesitation, the highwaymen rode through the gaping entrance of the bastle house. A mountain ash peered from its bed of nettles in one corner, while what remained of a circular stone staircase spiralled upward to a corbelled platform. 'Horses,' the taller man said, dismounting, and his companion obediently led the horses to the outhouses.

Gasping for breath, Matthew leaned against the stairway. 'What do you want with me?' He looked around. This was an isolated spot, perfect for a murder; he wondered if he should try to run.

The taller man holstered his pistol and removed his tricorne hat to scratch his short-cropped hair. He whistled, and a tousle-headed woman peered from the cottage doorway. 'Here,' the highwayman threw across the proceeds of the robbery, 'take care of that.'

The second highwayman walked back to Matthew, swaying from the hips. His laugh was as unexpected as the long blonde hair that flopped down when he removed his hat. He tore the black triangle from his lower face.

'You should have seen your face!' Grace said, grinning. 'It was a picture! And did you see that kick I landed?' She imitated her own action, swinging her leg upward jubilantly. 'Corker! Right in the breech! Serve the buffoon right, says I, for going against my will.'

For a moment Matthew could only stare as Grace laughed at him, then she explained, 'I know that you did not want to leave Onswick – God alone knows why, for there's nothing there for a gentleman – but Mother insisted. She had already taken my own servants, as you know, so I recruited this gentleman to rescue you!'

At length Matthew managed to find his tongue. 'Captain Ellwood?'

'Ask no questions, and hear no lies,' the highwayman said. 'But whoever I am, I keep the takings as payment.'

Matthew did not argue. The memory of the man's pistol pointing at his face was still vivid. 'Thank you for rescuing me, Grace, but why? And what am I to do now?'

'Finish what you started, of course.' Grace's reply was prompt. 'Whatever that was.' She came closer. 'You intrigue me, Matthew Pryde, although I cannot imagine why. And anyway, you helped me from the Press Gang.'

'There'll be the devil to pay if your mother ever finds out.'

'She won't,' Grace told him quietly. 'And if she does, why, then we'll pay.' The devil was back in her laugh. 'So what will you do now? And don't talk about lighthouses. I know that there's something else.'

The thoughts chased each other through Matthew's mind. He certainly could not push forward with the lighthouse bill, but he could investigate the village of Ederford. 'I can't stay at the inn,' he said slowly. 'Her Ladyship would be most unhappy.'

'All taken care of.' Grace was still smiling. 'Put your trust in the Lord and all will be well.'

'What?' Matthew stared. He had not expected Grace to show a religious leaning.

'You'll see.' She leaned forward so for a shocking second he thought that she would kiss him, but instead she pressed two fingers to his lips. 'You'll see everything, Matthew Pryde.'

It was the servant of the Lord who helped Matthew, when the Reverend Grover accepted him into his church like a sinner come to redemption. 'I thought that you'd be back, Mr Pryde.' As always, Grover's wig was sliding down his head and he carried an insect net rather than a Bible, but his sincerity was not in question as he ushered Matthew inside the churchyard. In the bright sunshine of May, the grave-stones seemed friendly, the trees welcoming and the small clusters of flowers patches of hope amidst a life that had turned drab grey.

'You'll recall that all the men in the village vanished when the Press came a-calling?'

'I do,' Matthew nodded. 'The Navy could only find one small boy.'

'Well, they were safe in the church. Come and see what I mean.' Winking, Grover led Matthew to the mausoleum that crouched beneath the now leafy birch trees, unlocked the gate and walked slowly down the thirteen stairs. There was a lantern hanging on a hook, together with a small tinderbox, and Grover scratched a light before walking to the far wall.

'See that flagstone?' Grover directed a pool of light on to the ground. The flagstone looked no different to any of the others, until Grover knelt down and, edging his fingers beneath, gradually pushed it up. 'It's not heavy,' he hinted, 'but still better when I have some help.'

'Of course.' With Matthew's belated assistance the flag-stone slid aside, revealing a dark hole into which Grover lowered the lantern.

193

'This leads to the cellars,' he explained, 'where we store the church records. Come along.' He grinned and, adjusting his wig, positioned himself beside the black square. Musty air wafted to Matthew. 'You'll have heard about priest holes, where Roman Catholic priests hid during the times of persecution?'

Matthew nodded, dimly remembering a history lesson. 'I have.'

'Well, this is nothing to do with them.' Grover laughed at his own joke. 'Come inside and see.' Twenty steps led to a long chamber, complete with box beds and a large collection of bottles. The air was stale and half a dozen candles provided light.

'We think that this was part of the original church, centuries ago, and that either the Vikings or the Normans destroyed it. Maybe even the Scots. They were always burning and looting around here.' He raised the lantern high. 'You can forget what Lady Fenwick claims: her ancestors were not particularly effective at guarding the slap. Anyway, we always knew that the Press would come some day, so we prepared for their arrival. Do you like it?'

Matthew did. Tight and secure, the room could shelter a large number of men until the Press Gang were tired of searching the village.

'Good. I know that you have unfinished business to attend, so consider this your home until you are ready to leave.' His voice dropped. 'I saw you turn back to help that boy the other day, Mr Pryde. That was the act of a real gentleman and a true Christian, especially with the Press so close.'

Matthew shook his head. He had acted instinctively. 'Anybody would have done the same,' he said.

'Perhaps they would,' Grover said, 'and perhaps they would not, but the fact is, you did it. So that's an end to it. I'll bring you food and a change of clothing.' He waited for a few minutes while Matthew sat on one of the beds. 'You look confused.'

'I am confused,' Matthew admitted. 'Why are you helping me? You want me out of the village as much as anybody does. You don't want a lighthouse built here.'

Grover sat beside him. 'No, Mr Pryde, I don't, but neither

194

do I think that you will ever succeed in having one built, not with Her Ladyship opposed to the idea. But there is another matter troubling you, Mr Pryde, is there not?'

Matthew nodded.

Grover lay on the next bed along and slid the wig until it covered his eyes. 'Tell me, Mr Pryde. You have my word that nobody else will ever know. Except the Lord, of course, and He knows already.'

Matthew hesitated. He was unsure how much he could trust Grover, but suddenly found himself relating the story of his life. It was the first time he had told anybody except Charles and Kate Denton, many years before, and now he had a few more details to add. Grover listened attentively, nodding when required, and when Matthew was finished he sat up, readjusted his wig and patted Matthew's knee.

'Well, Mr Pryde, it is hard for a man not to know who he is, or from whence his family originated. I understand your concern.'

Matthew nodded. It felt strange to tell another man about his life, and he suddenly felt vulnerable, as if a shield had been removed. He wished to be alone, yet felt a desperate need for human companionship, somebody he could trust.

'There is more on your mind, Matthew.' Grover did not leave. 'Tell me.'

'I want to find this place Ederford,' Matthew said. 'I want to see if anybody there remembers me.'

Grover's eccentricity seemed to drop from him as he nodded. 'Of course you do. I'll give you directions, Matthew, but I warn you that you won't learn much.'

Matthew stared at him. 'You know where Ederford is?'

'I can give you directions,' Grover repeated as he stood up, 'but don't raise your hopes too high. Man proposes, but remember that it's God that disposes.'

'It was a long time ago,' Matthew said, 'but somebody must know something.'

Grover sighed and patted his knee again. 'Things are not always all they seem, Matthew. I beg you not to expect miracles.' He stretched, shaking his head. 'Listen to me. I'm the man who talks about miracles every other day! You'll go to

195

Ederford tomorrow, Matthew.' There was deep sympathy in his eyes as he looked down on Matthew, and his footsteps echoed hollowly as he walked away.

Skylarks seemed to mock Matthew as he walked down the last incline to the ford. Nothing had changed since his last visit, save that now he knew at what he was looking. Each green mound that marked an abandoned cottage could be where he was brought up. He might have been carried over this very track as a baby, or toddled over the grass as an infant, yet he remembered none of it. What was worse, he felt nothing. There was no sensation of belonging, or of anything else.

Matthew stood in the centre of the ruined village of Ederford and looked over toward the tall tower that marked Harestone House. It was ironic that such privilege should exist so near to such pathos; the power of Her Ladyship opposed to the helplessness of the woman who had rescued him from the shipwreck.

She had raised him here, and then sent him to London for a gentleman's education. Now she was gone, and he was no closer to finding his origins. He did not know who he was, he did not even know her name, and he did not know what had happened. He had started off that morning with high hopes, despite Grover's advice to lower his expectations, but now he sat on a grassy mound and sank his head in his hands.

It was the eerie sound of the horn that broke the mood and Matthew looked up. The horn player nodded to him. 'Back again, Matthew?' He stepped closer.

'Back again.' Matthew checked inside his cloak to ensure that he had easy access to his pistol and cursed silently when he remembered that it was packed inside his portmanteau on the coach to London. He would never see that again, nor, more importantly, would he see his much more valuable equipment. 'This is Ederford?'

'This *was* Ederford.' The man was very light on his feet as he stepped to the centre of the village. 'Why the interest?'

'I might have lived here, once.' Matthew decided to tell the truth.

The man grunted. 'You might have? Are you not sure where you lived?'

'I'm not sure about anything much,' Matthew admitted.

The man nodded. 'Certainty is a sign of youth,' he said. 'The older we become, the less we know.'

'What do you know about Ederford?' Matthew had no patience with homespun philosophy. He wanted to solve this mystery that had troubled him all his life, then return to civilization.

'What do you want to know?'

'Everything.' Matthew put out a hand to prevent the man from playing his horn. 'For a beginning, who the devil are you?'

The man withdrew a pace. 'Some call me Old Horny, others Tarry Nat, but my real name was John.' He paused for a second, as if trying to recollect whether he had ever had a last name, decided that he had not and nodded as he said, 'Just John.'

'Well, John –' Matthew saw something stir in the back of the man's eyes – 'I have a shilling for you if you tell me what happened.'

John shook his head. 'A shilling? And what would John do with a shilling? Give it to the deer for milk? To the streams for water? To the heather for a soft bed?' He stepped further back. 'No, Matthew Pryde of London, you keep your shilling, and I'll keep my story.' He turned, but Matthew had expected the move and held him close. The tar was greasy on his jacket.

'No shilling then, John, but whatever you like, in return for your story.'

John wriggled, but Matthew was relentless. 'I'd like to go free, Matthew Pryde, that's what I'd like. I'd like to feel the soft rain and hear the birds talking.'

'Then that's what you shall have, John, just as soon as you tell me.'

John stopped wriggling, sighed and nodded. His resistance seemed to collapse as he sat down on the mound, looking very old and grey.

'I'll tell you, Matthew. You should know.'

197

'I should know? What makes you think that?' Matthew realized that he was pushing too hard as John cringed from him.

'It's all right, John. Just take your time.'

John looked pleadingly toward the hills and sighed again. 'It was a fine village, Ederford, a fine place to live, with clean water in the stream and good pasture in the hills, fields for barley and wheat and flax and always the noise of the looms. Clackety-clackety-clack, they went, as families worked together all the long day, clackety-clackety-clack, and children running and playing and squabbling, just as children should do. It was a fine place for the pipes, too,' John said, smiling. 'Ederford was famous throughout Northumberland for the quality of its pipers. We played at every fair and market from Berwick to Carlisle and Newcastle to the Esk.' He lifted his own pipe to show Matthew.

'I see.' Matthew tried to picture this quiet place as a thriving village, but heard only the sighing wind and the soft patter of rain. The looms were dead. 'And what happened?'

'Her Ladyship decided that Ederford should not be here,' John said slowly. 'And one day the men came from Harestone. Big men, with guns and crowbars and fire, and they knocked it all down. They sent the people away and tumbled their houses to the ground. They fired the thatch and broke the looms. They sent the people away, all the people, tall men and fine fat women and all the little children, crying in the night as their homes were burned. All the people.'

Perhaps the wind carried an echo of that day, for Matthew shivered as the picture came to him. He could see the burly men riding into the village, could hear the sound of children wailing, could see the villagers vainly struggling against the men with their muskets and cudgels, with women running to grab their children as the whiff of smoke drifted and flames curled from the thatch. He could picture the fear and horror and pandemonium as people were evicted from houses that had been home to generations of their family, destroyed on a woman's whim.

'Why?' he asked. 'Why would that happen?'

John shook his head. For a moment he looked as rational

as any man that Matthew had ever met. 'Why? That I do not know, Matthew. One day everything was as it had always been; the next all the people were out in the hills.'

'You were there?' Matthew no longer held John. The man sat still, staring into space.

'I was there. I saw everything that happened.' John walked slowly to one of the pathetic mounds of grass and nettles. 'I knew this house well. I knew the man and the woman. I remember what happened.' Kneeling, he began to stroke the ground. 'The man was in the fields when they came and the woman was at the loom. Then there was noise and anger. One hit the woman as she lifted her daughter. Then the man came running, all red in the face and angry, so they hit him with the butt end of a musket, then kicked him and kicked him and went on kicking him until the woman jumped between them, and they kicked her too, laughing.'

There was a long silence while John sat on the ground and the hot tears ran down his face. 'Laughing and kicking until she lay still. Johnnie ran to her then, but they kicked him too, and the roof fell in and the hot sparks rose and the smoke was choking Johnnie, so he ran away and never came back.'

Matthew had seen many broken boys at Maidhouse, boys whose minds could no longer cope with the bullying and who escaped into another world inside their head, or boys who took one step further and ended their sad lives. At that time he had been unable to help, for any display of kindness would have been construed as weakness and the bullies would have concentrated on him.

Matthew knelt at John's side. 'It's all done now, John,' he said, 'all done now.' He felt deep sympathy but was unsure what to say. He could only look away when John began to cry, great sobs that racked the man's body and tore huge tears from his eyes. A curlew circled overhead, its curved beak distinctive as it sounded its mournful cry.

'So you're Matthew Pryde.' John looked up. The tears had coursed pale streaks down the grime that covered his face, but he sounded rational again. 'You're Matthew Pryde come from London to ask about Ederford.' He rubbed his sleeve

199

across his face, leaving new black marks, tar amongst the tears and dirt.

'I am.' Matthew took a deep breath as the curlew continued to circle. He could see its yellow eyes watching him and wondered if anything here was what it seemed. That bird seemed to be the spirit of some lost soul. He shook away the fantasies. 'John, do you remember a woman with a young boy? A boy that did not really belong to the village but had been rescued from a ship?'

'Oh yes.' The clarity of the answer took Matthew by surprise. 'That was you, Matthew.' John nodded. 'I remember you.'

Matthew felt the shock within him as his heart began to pound harder and faster. 'Can you tell me what happened to the woman, John? Who is she? Where is she now?' In his urgency, Matthew took hold of John again until the man cowered away, his eyes hazed with memories.

'Widow Armstrong, that's who. Her man died of some fever and she lived alone, but she brought you back from the wreck, she did.' John's smile recalled happier days. 'A good woman, the widow, and she treated you as one of her own. Until the day the men came, and I never saw her again.'

'Where is she now?' Matthew fought his frustration as he attempted to bleed information from John's damaged mind. 'Widow Armstrong. Where is she now?'

John shook his head. 'She's gone, Matthew. She ran to the hills with the rest of us, and the hills took her in.'

'Took her in? What does that mean?'

John shook his head. 'She's with them. Part of the hills.'

'Part of the hills? What does that mean?' Matthew felt a slide of despair. 'You mean that she's dead?'

John nodded slowly. 'She is.'

Matthew closed his eyes. For most of his life, he had dreamed of being reunited with somebody from his past, either a blood relative miraculously discovered or this woman, Widow Armstrong, whose face was his earliest recollection. But that hope was now gone. Widow Armstrong was dead, and he would never learn who she was and how she managed to pay for him to be educated.

'Can you tell me about myself, John? Who am I? Why was I sent to London?'

But when Matthew opened his eyes he was alone in the village, save for the circling curlew and the soft swish of water over the ford. He had not heard John leave.

He was little better off. He had a name and the blurred memory of a face. He knew now that Widow Armstrong was no relative, as he had hoped, but only a woman with a kind heart. And he knew that Lady Fenwick had ordered the village removed for some reason, and had, directly or indirectly, caused Widow Armstrong's death. For a long moment he imagined Her Ladyship sitting on her horse in the ford, watching as her minions cleared Ederford. She would not be smiling, but would watch dispassionately, uncaring of the suffering that her whim had caused.

For one moment, Matthew considered rushing up to Harestone House to confront Lady Fenwick. He could challenge her over her actions, accuse her of cruelty and murder. But then what? Who would listen to him? Who would take the side of a young engineer against a gentlewoman whose line extended back as far as Creation? And what could he do?

There was nothing he could do.

'Hello, Matthew!' Even Grace's cheerful hail failed to lift his spirits, but he forced a smile as she splashed over the ford toward him. 'Were you coming to see me?'

'In my heart, Grace,' Matthew tried to act the light-hearted gallant, 'I see you always.'

'Do you?' Either the words or the sentiments pleased Grace, for she smiled broadly. 'Well, you won't see much of me here. I hate this place. Let's go elsewhere.'

When the three men behind her glowered at Matthew, he recognized them as the bandaged bell-ringer and his two companions and wondered if they would tell Her Ladyship about his reappearance on her lands. At that moment he did not care.

'Where are you going?'

'I was going swimming,' Grace told him easily. 'I often go swimming. I have my very own tower down by the sea,

201

with a romantic beach where nobody can see me. Come on, I'll take you there.'

Matthew blushed at the renewed memory of her slender, naked body. 'I can't go swimming with you!'

Grace laughed. 'I'm not asking you to, muttonhead! But we can sit in the tower and watch the sea together. Nicholas often joins me in the tower; he has the only other key.' She leaned closer. 'Nobody else, though. My bellman keeps them away!'

'I've no horse,' Matthew began, but Grace ordered the cudgel man to dismount. She handed his horse to Matthew.

'Now you have,' she said, and smiled. 'It's all right; he can walk.' Removing the sunbonnet that protected her head, she flicked back her hair. 'Come on, Matthew!' Replacing her bonnet, Grace trotted over what remained of Ederford, with Matthew following a few yards behind. He could hear the bellman swearing as he hauled his companion up behind him.

As they neared Onswick, Grace motioned to her followers to continue, as she took the path toward the tower on the coast. Matthew did not turn around when the bell began to clatter.

'Do you like it, Matthew?' Grace dismounted with that fluidity that he admired. 'Do you think that Wordsworth would approve? It's like having my own castle.' Her smile invited his approval. Unlocking the door with a flourish, she swept inside, gesturing for him to follow. When the door shut behind him, Matthew felt as if he had been transported into another world.

He stood on an Oriental rug in a square room with rose-painted walls. In one corner, a flight of wooden stairs disappeared to an upper floor, while opposite was a wardrobe, decorated with a Chinese dragon. Two of the walls boasted window seats that gave views of the sea and coast, while a fireplace in a third wall was set ready. A small pile of books lay on the deal table, while the two low chairs looked comfortable. Ornate lamps hung from brass hooks and there was a deep sea chest and a full-length mirror to which Grace at once stepped.

'You do like it, don't you? This is my own secret abode, my *whim*, as the rustics call it.' She laughed and removed her bonnet, watching her reflection as she allowed her hair to cascade over her shoulders. 'I had Mother build it for me a few years ago.'

Matthew nodded. 'It's very nice,' he approved. 'Her Ladyship does a lot for you.' He could not forget the image of the grassy mounds of Ederford, and wondered at the contrast in Lady Fenwick, the tyrannical mistress but indulgent mother.

'Mother will do anything I ask her, nearly,' Grace said. 'Now, Matthew, would you like a swim?'

The suggestion was so shocking that Matthew nearly jumped backward in alarm. 'You're betrothed,' he reminded her. 'It would not be right.'

'No, it would not,' she agreed, 'but wouldn't it be fun? Don't you like fun? Doing things just for the sake of shocking propriety? Like tying your garters in public?'

'I beg your pardon?' Even as Matthew protested, Grace placed one foot on a chair, lifted her skirt high to expose her stockinged leg and indicated the bright garter that adorned her left thigh.

'Like this?' Her eyes dancing with mischief, Grace adjusted the garter. 'I find that it always causes a stir.'

'I'm not surprised.' Matthew tried to look away, but the sudden sight of her smooth thigh held his attention.

'No? Most people are!' Grace looked sideways into the mirror and laughed again. 'Mr Pryde! You're looking! So you do like fun.' She replaced her foot on the carpet and allowed her clothing to slide slowly into place. 'My, but you are easy to colour-up, are you not? Your face is as red as a sunset.'

Rather belatedly, Matthew looked away. Grace was rummaging in the sea chest, pulling out packages that she placed on the deal table, shoving aside the books to make room.

Matthew stooped to pick up one of the books that had landed on the floor.

'Leave it,' Grace commanded as she opened the first of

the packages. There were legs of chicken and delicate slices of bread and cheese, last season's apples that must have been stored in an ice house and a china dish of some delicacy that Cook must have spent hours preparing. 'I had one of my men bring these here this morning,' Grace said casually. 'Just in case I decided to come.'

She looked up. 'Light the fire, Matthew, there's a man.' She indicated the tinderbox that lay in the marble fireplace beside the neat pile of logs.

Matthew smiled when she produced two plates, putting one at either side of the table. 'You're well prepared,' he said. 'Did you expect to meet me?'

'I would have searched for you,' Grace said quietly. 'I've had this in mind for a few days now.' She looked up. 'How's that fire coming on?'

The sparks had set alight wood shavings and small flames were beginning to lick at the twigs set beneath the logs. Kneeling close, Matthew encouraged them with gentle breath until the smallest of the logs were well alight. By that time Grace had the table all set. She offered him a chicken leg first, grinning when he lifted it with delicate fingers.

'Isn't this fun? Just you and me together and no servants or anybody else to bother about.' She bit into the white flesh with even whiter teeth. 'I don't always enter the water, you know, I often just come here to be alone for a while. You've no idea how tedious it is always having somebody at your beck and call: "Yes, Miss Grace" or "No Miss Grace" or "You're perfect, Miss Grace"!' Speaking through a mouthful of half-masticated chicken, Grace shook her head. 'Well, Matthew, I know that I'm not perfect, and I want somebody to tell me that, just once in a while. Perfect people do not tie their garters in public!'

Matthew could imagine Kate doing such a thing as a matter of practicality, but never in deliberate provocation. He smiled as he said, 'I suppose not,' and wondered if the differences in these women affected the way that he felt for both.

While Grace was wild, wilful, but strangely honest, Kate was challenging and caring. Grace introduced excitement, while Kate could calm him with a smile, or provoke him with one cutty-eyed glance. Matthew shook his head; he liked both, but in vastly different ways. Damn it! Here he was thinking about a woman who had been plain in her rejection while this prime armful was paying court to him.

'You see,' Grace continued, 'that's what I like about Nicholas. He doesn't mind telling me straight. He can be a very masterful man at times. Do you believe that? With all his charm and wealth?'

For a minute, Matthew was back at Maidhouse, with Elmstead giving orders that set juniors and fags scurrying around the school on pointless, humiliating and often dangerous exercises. He remembered Martlesham, a fair-haired youngster who he ordered to climb up the ivy that clung romantically to the wall of the clock tower. The boy had been terrified but had obeyed, while Elmstead and his cronies threw apple cores and stones at him. Martlesham had fallen and broken his left leg.

'Masterful?' Matthew nodded. 'Yes, I can believe that.'

'But I am not sure just how much he is committed to me.' She shook her head. 'Sometime I would like proof, if he is able to give it.' When she looked up there was a world of mischief in those disturbing brown eyes. 'I know he made a lot of money in the Indies. Tobacco, I believe, or perhaps it was sugar, I can't be sure.' Nibbling the last piece of meat, Grace inspected the bone for a moment before throwing it on the fire, where the fat began to spit and hiss. 'He says he might take me there, once we're married. I would be the mistress of half an island, with tropical fruit every day and a hundred slaves at my command.'

'And how do you feel about that, Grace?'

When she screwed up her face, Grace looked about fifteen years old. 'Don't care for it really. I would like the adventure of travelling, but plantation life sounds a bit dull. Provincial people and merchants' wives all pretending to aspire to a quality that, frankly, they will not have.'

'The slavery, I mean.' For a brief instant, Matthew was more interested in the answer than in watching Grace's expressions. He felt a strong desire to find out more about this girl that he felt he already knew so well.

'Slavery? Don't really care one way or the other. They're just servants, aren't they? But not paid. I suppose they're a bigger responsibility for the family, though. Owning them like property, I mean. It would make it harder to get rid of them when they are unreliable.' She lifted a slice of bread. 'Could always sell them when they get in the way, I suppose. Or free them.' Reaching into the chest, she produced a bottle of Spanish red wine and a corkscrew, which she handed to Matthew, and two glasses, which she polished on her skirt.

'Don't mind me,' she said, smiling her apology, 'just open the bottle and pour.'

Matthew did so, enjoying the satisfying glug-glug and the splash of ruby within the crystal. He passed a glass to Grace and sipped cheerfully. 'To you,' he said.

'To us,' Grace corrected, raising her glass and peering at him through the contents. 'And to an interesting friendship.' The wine increased the challenge in her eyes.

The fire was drawing well, sending its pleasant warmth around the room. Sitting back in his chair, Matthew stretched out his legs. He felt comfortable in the company of this fascinating, friendly girl. He did not care that her opinions were so at odds with his own; he just liked to watch her talk and move, listen to her voice and breathe in her perfume.

Grace smiled at him, her brown eyes friendly. 'Are you happy, Matthew Pryde?'

'I am,' Matthew admitted. He had not thought about lighthouses or engineering or even his own past since he had walked into this strange tower, with its crackling fire and delightful company, with its views over the sea and complete privacy. 'I cannot imagine a better sanctuary.'

'Nor can I,' Grace agreed. 'I like to watch the boats out fishing, but it's even better to see the fish. Do you know that we have dolphins here? And sometimes porpoises too? They come quite close to land and leap right out of the water.' It was the first time that Matthew had seen her so animated while discussing anything other than herself, and he listened as she spoke of shoals of herring and pods of grampus, gannets that dived vertically into the water and winter skies etched with skeins of wild geese.

'That's the best part of this place,' Grace said quietly. 'You have time to watch, and space to think.' She smiled, lifted his hunter and glanced at the time. 'I had no idea that it was so late. Would you excuse me for a moment?'

'Of course,' Matthew rose as she left the room, walking up the steps with an easy elegance that spoke of centuries of breeding. Unconsciously he enjoyed the swing of her hips, then looked away in quick embarrassment. He moved to the window, watching the waves commit spectacular suicide against the Black Corbie and fishing boats hauling in their longlines as they hoped for haddock.

'Matthew!' Her voice was loud and clear, echoing through the cosy confines of the tower. 'Find a towel for me, there's a dear!'

The wardrobe held no such article, so Matthew rummaged through the collection of feminine knick-knacks in the sea chest until he came across a towel that was large and white and scented with birch-water. He grinned and pulled it free, only then noticing the document that lay beneath.

Drawn in his own hand, the map of Corbie Island lay exposed and accusing. He stared at it for a long moment, wondering how it could have arrived in Grace's chest, and who could have put it there. Reaching out, he touched the crisp paper, remembering Grace's words: '*Nicholas often joins me in the tower; he has the only other key.*' Nicholas Elmstead would have enjoyed sending a parcel of rogues to beat him and steal the map, as much for devilment as for gain. Elmstead also wanted to impress Lady Fenwick. Matthew felt his anger rise as he stared at the map, feeling the remaining twinges where the three bruisers had landed their blows.

'Did you find that towel yet?' Matthew turned around as he heard Grace's footsteps patter on the stairs.

Her eyebrows lifted in mocking query, but it was not her expression that swept his attention downward. Except for a silver chain around her neck, she was completely naked. 'Let's go for a swim, Matthew!'

He had admired her from afar when he played peeping Tom with his spyglass from the Corbie, but close to she was not a slender girl but a full-grown woman. The light from the fire gleamed from limbs and flanks and reflected from eyes that were as mischievous as anything Matthew had ever seen in his life. For a long moment, Matthew could say nothing as he stared at her.

'What's the matter, Matt, have you never seen a woman before?' Her voice gently taunting, Grace turned, showing off all her curves and secrets. 'Or have you just never seen a gentlewoman?' Thrusting out a hip, she looked over her shoulder, pouted and laughed. 'Come on, Matthew! Clothes off and let's go.'

Matthew could not move. He felt his eyes examine her body, admiring every smooth line, every hollow and shadow, yet he knew that there was something wrong. This woman was virtually offering herself to him, standing before him in a secluded place with no possibility of interference, teasing him with her body, and he did nothing. He looked on her dispassionately, aware that she was immensely desirable, but feeling no desire. There was a barrier between them that he could not breach. At last Matthew found his voice, but he spoke an excuse, not a reason. 'You're betrothed,' he said. 'It's not right!'

'You've already told me that,' Grace reminded. She stepped closer, pushing against him so he withdrew to the wall. 'I know that I'm betrothed, and we both know that Nicholas is no friend of yours.' Her voice lowered as she put her arms around him, gently unbuttoning the first button of his waist-coat. 'I know all about Maidhouse, Matthew, and what happened there, and what I don't know, I can imagine. Think about it, Matthew, you can retaliate now, in a way that would hurt him more than anything else.'

The feel of her pressing against him was more than Matthew could stand, but he could back away no farther and she was still there, slipping his waistcoat off his arms, smiling into his face. Against his conscious will, Matthew put his arms around her, feeling the softness of female flesh, and then the door opened.

'You bastard! Unhand my woman!'

Nicholas Elmstead stormed into the room.

208

Sixteen

Northumberland, May 1804

'What?' Matthew dropped his hand at once, even as Grace stepped back, giggling but making no attempt to cover herself.

Ignoring her, Elmstead took two quick strides to Matthew and slapped him full across the face, following with a back-hander that made him stagger. 'I'm not sure if I should horsewhip you now or bring you into the public street and do it!' He was roaring, his eyes wide. 'By Gad, I always thought that you were no gentleman, Pryde, but this beats all! Sneaking into the private tower of Miss Grace when you know full well she likes to bathe alone, and grabbing hold of her!'

'I did no such thing!' Matthew looked to Grace for support. Maidhouse had trained him never to speak ill of a lady, so he could not speak the truth.

'Well, madam? What do you have to say for yourself?' Elmstead was in his full travelling fig of long cloak and tall hat, with soft grey gloves and his gold-topped cane in his hand. Now he pointed the cane at Grace. 'Speak, woman! Tell me how this man broke into your private retreat.'

'Speak? I cannot get a word in edgeways!' She seemed to find the whole scene amusing. 'But if you two gentlemen will excuse me for just a minute, I must put my clothes on. Rather chilly, you see, with the front door open and your coachman goggling outside, Nicholas!'

It was a mild rebuke, but Elmstead reacted immediately, slamming shut the door with a back swing of his heel and turning his back as Grace scuttled upstairs. He glowered at Matthew, breathing deeply. The arm holding the cane twitched and Matthew prepared to retaliate, but Elmstead controlled himself.

'Well, Pryde, you're a dead man now. Pistols or swords?'

Matthew could only stare, feeling his limbs collapse beneath him. Three minutes ago he had been quietly searching for a towel; now he was facing a duel with a man who would enjoy killing him.

The journey back to Harestone had been chilly, with Grace riding alone and Elmstead keeping to the seclusion of his carriage. Neither had spoken to Matthew, but Lady Fenwick accepted the situation with surprising calm. Presumably her family had experienced many similar encounters over the past thousand years.

They sat in the drawing room, with no servants present and Grace appearing demure in a dove grey gown that would not have been out of place in a nunnery. She sat with her head bowed and wiped an occasional tear from her eyes. Nearest to the fire, Matthew felt sick. He noticed that after she had recovered from her initial surprise that he was still in the parish and not safe in London, Lady Fenwick barely addressed him.

'Pistols or swords?' Elmstead had recovered his composure and now acted like a gentleman, keeping a precise distance from Matthew as he again issued the challenge.

Matthew shook his head. He was still stunned, unable to properly comprehend the seriousness of his situation. He felt that he had blundered, or had been led, into something over which he had no control. He felt as if these northern lords were manipulating him. 'Neither. I will not fight you.'

Lady Fenwick sighed. 'You must fight, Mr Pryde,' she said with a voice that was quiet, yet the words were clipped, as if she was holding back her anger, 'or His Lordship will accuse you of attempted rape. You will hang.' She leaned closer, her eyes intense. 'Be assured that you *will* hang, Mr Pryde.'

Matthew started. 'Rape? I attempted no such thing!' When he looked at Grace for support, she turned away.

'We only have your word for that,' Lady Fenwick said quietly, 'while your accuser is a gentleman, a magistrate, a lord and a Member of Parliament. Who will the judge believe?'

Grace was looking at him now, eyebrows raised and a smile on her lips. About to ask her to tell them what happened, Matthew closed his mouth. He could not ask her to interfere. He had been raised as a gentleman and must do the honourable thing.

'I choose pistols, Lord Chevington.' He tried to conceal the tremor in his voice.

'Pistols it is, then,' Elmstead agreed. 'I would have enjoyed pinking you, Pryde, but I'll get the same satisfaction when I put a ball through your head!'

Lady Fenwick stood up. 'Then it is agreed. Do you have a pair of pistols, Mr Pryde? No? Then Lord Chevington will provide them. How about a second? No, I thought not.' She tightened her lips. 'It's a little irregular, but I'm sure the Reverend Grover will act for you. He is a man of the cloth, but also a gentleman, and I'm sure I do not know anybody else who would wish to stand at your side.' She looked at Grace. 'And as for you, young lady, go to your room. We have matters to discuss.'

'Yes, Mother.' Grace stood at once, allowing her hip to brush tantalizingly against Matthew's shoulder as she passed. She placed a gloved hand on Elmstead's shoulder. 'Thank you for rescuing me, My Lord, and for showing your commitment to our engagement.'

'Your room, madam,' Lady Fenwick repeated, but Grace had time for one triumphant glance toward Matthew before she swayed through the door.

'Ten o'clock tomorrow, Pryde,' Elmstead said. 'It must be on neutral ground, so shall we say at Ederford?'

Matthew met his eye, wondering why he had chosen that particular venue. 'Ederford is acceptable,' he agreed. He felt sick.

Grover proved to be a surprisingly knowledgeable second, showing no hesitation in demanding first choice of Elmstead's pistols and ensuring that the ground was paced out to the required length. 'I do not approve of duelling,' he told both parties sternly, 'but if this affair has to take place, then it will be fought according to the rules.'

Matthew accepted his pistol, one of a matching pair that Grover removed from a walnut box. He remembered discussing duelling with Joseph Manton during the months he had spent in his workshop.

'Any pistol can be used in duels,' Mr Manton had told him gravely, 'but the *code duello* prefers single shot weapons with a smooth bore and no sights.' He had shaken his grey head. 'Not that there are many rifled pistols on the market, anyway.'

Matthew examined this pistol, hiding his thrill of satisfaction that it was one of Manton's own.

'Is your man firmly set on this barbarity,' Grover asked, 'or is there any path back to sense without the need for bloodshed?'

'The honour of my man was deeply hurt, as was the honour of his intended,' Rutledge, Elmstead's second, said formally. 'He insists on this meeting. An apology will not suffice.'

'My man will not apologize,' Grover said, glancing at Matthew. 'Let us get this tomfoolery over with so we can all get home. Please God both parties are poor shots and honour is satisfied without injury.'

Both parties took a practice shot to show their intention to prove him wrong.

The curlew still wheeled overhead as the seconds paced around the deserted village and the principals stood in splendid isolation on opposite sides of the ford. While Elmstead produced a silver flask and took a series of short pulls, Matthew pondered over the strange fate that had brought him here. He could die on the same spot where he had spent the first few years of his childhood, without ever knowing his real name or who had sponsored his education. The irony made him smile, and Elmstead frowned and looked away.

'So the two participants meet in the centre of the ford,' Grover decided. 'I shall stand with this handkerchief,' he showed a bright square of silk, the scarlet an uncomfortable reminder of the blood that might soon be flowing. 'When I drop it, both parties will turn and take twenty paces, counted by Mr Rutledge, then they will turn and fire whenever they are ready. Agreed?'

'Agreed,' Elmstead said at once. He glowered at Matthew over the hilt of his pistol. Matthew glared back. Now that the duel was about to begin, he no longer felt afraid. He remembered all the cruelty of Maidhouse, all the taunts and bullying, the pain and fear, the humiliation and frustration. Now, perhaps, he had a chance to retaliate.

'Wait!' Rutledge lifted a hand to delay the proceedings as a small group of riders approached from Harestone House. Lady Fenwick rode slightly in front, with Grace, her bellman and two bodyguards slightly behind. They arrived in a body, but while Lady Fenwick remained on horseback, the others dismounted.

Grace tossed the reins to the broken-nosed bellman, who threw Matthew a look of pure malice. Grace's other bravos appeared as friendly, with one running a finger across his throat in a gesture that could not be misinterpreted.

'Is there no way that this tomfoolery can be ended?' Grover asked again, and sighed when both parties shook their heads. By now Matthew was determined to go through with the duel, whatever the outcome. If he was killed, then all his problems were ended, but if he managed to shoot Elmstead he would have at last succeeded in something.

'Take your positions, gentlemen.' Rutledge gave the order in a firm voice.

Both principals marched to the centre of the ford, glared at each other for a moment and turned around. Cool water swirled around their booted feet. Matthew could hear the sound of Elmstead breathing behind him, could hear the rustle of his silk cravat and smell the faint aroma of sweat. In front he could see the humped mounds of Ederford with the patches of nettles swaying in the slight breeze. He would have to allow for windage when he aimed, he thought, and concentrated on listening to the orders.

Lady Fenwick remained slightly aloof, her face devoid of any expression, while Grace and her three pugs remained in a tight little group. Grace wore a dark green riding cape, Matthew noticed, and she was smiling.

Matthew checked the lock of his pistol for the third time. His hands were trembling again and he tried to swallow away the lump that had risen in his throat. He wanted to ask Grace why she had acted as she did, but could not. He wanted to drop the pistol and run, but if he did he would be an outcast for ever.

'Good luck, Nicky!' Grace's voice was clear, but Matthew hardly noticed. There was a familiar whistle in the wind and he saw subtle movement to his right. A head poked from a clump of bracken and John the piper looked toward him. For a second their eyes met, then Matthew looked away. He had to concentrate on the matter in hand. He was an engineer; he had to work out the mathematics of this duel, the angles of windage, the weight of powder and ball. Oh God, but he might de dead in a few minutes' time.

Lady Fenwick bent over and murmured something to the pugs, two of whom began to circle in the direction of Matthew. When one grinned evilly to him and lifted a flap of his waistcoat to reveal the barrel of a pistol, Matthew felt a new ripple of fear. The inference was obvious. Even if he did win the duel, the pug would ensure that he did not leave Ederford alive.

A gust of wind sent ripples over the ford, while the curlew circled overhead, its curved beak a reminder of the goblins that the old folk said lived in the eaves of houses. Matthew shivered; where had that story suddenly come from? He had heard it as a child, sitting in a cottage in Ederford, and he did not want to die. Could he drop the pistol and run? Hardly. Yet the pugs were coming closer, taking up position a few yards to his right, opposite Grover. The pistol man put his hand in his waistband and cocked his piece, the sound ominous.

The silk handkerchief was held high, the scarlet vivid against the dull green of the hillside. Then it dropped and Matthew was pacing forward, feeling the ground uneven under the soles of his boots. He counted as he paced: one . . . two . . . three . . . every step taking an eternity and the breath harsh in his chest.

Silence save for the wind. Even the curlew was quiet, but

Grace was holding her mother's arm, her eyes huge with excitement. Four . . . five . . . six steps and John was moving closer, his mouth gaping open. Somewhere on the hillside a sheep bleated plaintively. There was movement to his left and Matthew anticipated that the pistol man was levelling his weapon, perhaps shielded by his friend. The thought made him straighten his back in anticipation. Scared as he was, he was damned if he would cower.

Seven . . . eight . . . nine . . . the words as remorseless as a clock, with barely a pause between each. His life ticking away and nothing achieved, nobody to mourn his passing, not even his own name to carve on his grave, if anybody paid for a stone. He might end here, tumbled into a pauper's pit, unheeded, one of the nameless dead to sour these Northumberland fells.

. . . Ten.

Sweet Jesus!

Matthew stopped and turned, hearing the thundering of his heart within his chest, feeling the tremble of his legs as he wanted to cut and run, silently screaming for help that he knew could not come. He had been trained as a gentleman; now was his chance to prove it – probably his only chance, for this could be the end. Despite the need for concentration, he glanced to his left and saw that two more men had joined the pugs. One was Robert Megstone, the other scarred Clem Wharton, and Wharton had a pistol of his own, thrust hard into the side of one of the pugs. He faced Matthew and nodded once, before jerking his head to his side, where stood the young boy that Matthew had rescued from the Press.

'My son.' Wharton mouthed the words, but his meaning was clear as the bell of St Cuthbert's.

The relief was so intense that Matthew could have wept. With that danger removed, he could concentrate solely on Elmstead, remembering all the advice that Joseph Manton had given him, many years ago. He remembered to stand sideways on to present as small a target to his opponent as possible; remembered to keep cool and control his breathing. Keeping his head high, he extended his arm, aware that Elmstead was doing the same at precisely the same time.

Twenty paces had sounded quite far, but Elmstead seemed devilishly close, so that the muzzle of his gun appeared as wide as a cave, his eyes cold and hard and calculating.

Matthew was resolved to die like a gentleman. As he raised his arm, remembering the pain of the gauntlet and the humiliation of the warm bath at Maidhouse, the years of bullying and the life of constant fear that he had lived, he also remembered the pugs that Elmstead had set on him and the theft of his map. Now he had the perpetrator of all that horror in the sights of his pistol and for the first time his chances were even. There was the drift of John's horn and a faint puff of white smoke from Elmstead's pistol, with an accompanying crack that seemed strangely muted.

Head shot or body? Time seemed to pass slowly as Matthew waited for the ball to strike. He could see Elmstead's face looking strangely distorted, eyes narrow, mouth open, and his white cravat fluttering above a dark waistcoat. Go for the body; there was more chance of a hit and he would have left his mark before he died. His practise shot showed him that the pistol fired to the right, so he adjusted to the left and allowed for windage. He aimed his pistol at the left side of Elmstead's waistcoat and squeezed the trigger.

It was curious that Elmstead's ball had still not reached him, for they were both standing erect with the white smoke drifting between them and the audience watching. He felt a tickle on the side of his head, as though a butterfly had brushed against him, and then he lay on the ground, smiling into the broad face of a woman, and the smoke from the fire was comforting as the bustle of Ederford spread all around. The woman washed him with water that turned to scarlet.

'Matthew!' Grover was bending over him, his wig askew and concern on his face. 'Matthew!'

There was warm blood on his face and he was lying on his back, arms outstretched and the smoking pistol still gripped in his fist. There was a medley of sound: the keening of the stock-and-horn pipe, women chattering, somebody groaning, the snorting of alarmed horses, the chuckle of the stream and that curlew's mournful call.

'Can you sit up?' Supportive hands lifted him and somebody thrust something between his teeth. He swallowed, choked on fiery brandy and swallowed again, coughing. Grover was staring into his face and there was John at his side, nodding.

'What happened?' Letting the pistol drop, Matthew put a hand to his face, feeling the blood. There was pain too; a dull throbbing that seemed to increase with every breath he took.

'I'm not sure yet. He hit you, that's for certain, but I don't know how badly.' Grover bent closer, but it was John who gave the first opinion.

'Just a nick, Matthew. He's cut the skin and given you a bang on the pate, nothing more. It'll hurt for a week and then you'll have a nice scar to show to your girl.' John's accent and attitude had altered once more. No more the lunatic wild man, he sounded lucid and intelligent.

Struggling to sit up, Matthew saw a similar knot of people around a prone Elmstead. 'Did I hit him? Is he dead?'

'Do you want him to be dead?' There was concern in Grover's voice.

Matthew considered. Now that the duel was over and he had taken his shot, his feelings toward Elmstead had changed. 'I do not know,' he admitted. He certainly did not like the man, but did he want to kill him? 'No,' he answered more firmly, wincing as movement sent deep stabs of pain across his head. 'No, I don't want him dead.'

'Good,' Grover nodded approval. John rose and loped across to where Elmstead lay, to return a few minutes later.

'You hit him all right,' he reported. 'I think that you broke one of his ribs, judging by the noise he's making.'

'Will he live?' Suddenly Matthew did not want to be responsible for a death. He tried to rise to his feet, but pain forced him back down.

'Can't be sure yet.' John's smile was bleak. 'That's the trouble with you young men. You take irresponsible actions and regret it when it's all too late.' He shook his head. 'Let's get you somewhere warm and dry first, then we'll worry about Nicholas Elmstead.' At that moment John sounded like the most rational man there.

'Who are you, John?' Matthew asked, just as the pain increased in his head. He yelled, once, as Grover lifted him to his feet, then bit hard on to his lower lip, for gentlemen did not flinch.

The next few days were a blur for Matthew. He had vague recollections of a nightmare journey on the back of Grover's horse, of being lowered into a bed and of concerned faces hovering over him. There were examinations and bleedings, leeches applied to his arm and foul-smelling potions plastered to his head. He heard snatches of conversation that made no sense and heard a hundred times the crack of Elmstead's pistol and felt the feather of his ball tickle his head. Then there was blackness and a deep roaring, the inane gibber of insanity and the tortured horror of captivity without end. A thousand thoughts returned to torture him, unrelated faces stared into his and the boom of the Black Corbie sounded like the harbinger of death.

'We could have a floating light moored offshore,' the voice was saying. 'Moored just off the rock, until a beacon house for the articifers can be built on the largest island. That would do away with any necessity to rely on Her Ladyship for support. We could feed and supply them by sea, and issue the workers with Protections against the Press Gang.'

At first the words meant nothing to Matthew, but eventually he realized that somebody was discussing engineering. He listened, glad to be back in a world of facts and figures, where practical problems could be solved by realistic methods and there was no mystery about origins, no need to worry about honour and no women to cause complications.

'Matthew's ideas about dovetailing and the lower curve of the house are solid. Based on Smeaton, of course, as are all the best ideas. I would like to use a trainer, that's a timber-framed rule, to ensure that each stone in each course is correctly positioned.'

Matthew tried to sit up in bed, groaning at the pain in his bandage-swathed head. He concentrated on the conversation, attempting to reach consciousness through the application of his profession. He knew that a trainer had a socket on one side, which fixed the implement to a steady-pin that was placed in the exact centre of the stone, and it was used to ascertain the radiating direction of the stones from the centre outward to the circumference of the lighthouse. He must pass his information to whoever was speaking.

'The trainer is vital,' he said. 'We must not forget it, but we'll need vertical joggles too, to act against any horizontal movement.'

William Denton looked down at him. 'So you're back, young Matthew. And what do you mean by it, eh? Risking your life with some gentlemanly idiocy when you have important work to do?' There was genuine anger in the man's eyes. 'By God, Matthew, you're lucky that you're out of your apprenticeship or I'd cancel the whole damned thing!'

Matthew looked around him. He lay in a wide bed in a warm room with a bookcase along one wall and a heavily curtained window opposite. As well as William Denton, Charles Grover sat nearby, and a surprisingly respectably dressed John, who smiled and nodded to him.

'What happened?'

'You nearly got killed, you young fool, that's what happened!' William Denton was not ready to allow the subject to drop.

'It's all right, Matthew.' Grover sat on the edge of the bed. 'You were recovering fine when a fever set in. John here helped get you back to rights. He has experience in that sort of thing.'

John looked away.

'And Mr Denton? When did you arrive, sir?'

'Two days ago, Matthew.' William Denton stood up. In appearance he was similar to his cousin, but carried himself with more authority. 'We took coach as soon as your portmanteau and case arrived in London without you. Kate was worried – God knows why!' He shook his head. 'So I arrived in time to hear what you had done. Duelling over some blasted woman!'

'Yes, sir.' Matthew was still dazed. He felt the bandages that covered his head. 'But Mr Denton, did you not get my letter? I said that there was little hope of a bill being presented to the House of Commons.'

'Even less hope now, surely, with you trying to kill the Member of Parliament!'

The memory returned to Matthew. 'Elmstead? How is Lord Chevington? Is he all right?'

'Recovering nicely,' Grover said. 'Still in bed and raving fit to frighten the French, so I've heard.'

'Her Ladyship does not like you, young Matthew,' William Denton spoke gravely. 'You have incurred her severe displeasure.'

'I can understand that, although the fault was not entirely my own.' Matthew told of his friendship with Grace and how Lady Fenwick had sent him away, how he had returned and how Elmstead discovered them alone together in the tower by the sea.

'A bad man, Nicholas Elmstead,' John said quietly. 'He was always a wild young fellow, always getting into trouble, mingling with the worst of the smugglers and illicit whisky-makers of the hills. His father was glad when Her Ladyship got him a place at a school well in the south.'

'Maidhouse,' Matthew said. 'I was also there.'

'Indeed. Interesting coincidence.' William Denton looked over the top of his spectacles in a manner strikingly reminiscent of his cousin. 'Pray forgive our bad manners in interrupting, John. Please continue. You were telling us about Lord Chevington?'

'Well,' John screwed up his face, 'he came back just as undisciplined as ever and at once began causing trouble among the village girls, so his family sent him off to the Indies. He came back a changed man, it seemed. Successful, with so much money and charm that he improved the estate and secured a title, somehow.'

'He was not always Lord Chevington, then?' William Denton asked.

'Not at all. The title is recent.'

'Lady Fenwick told me that, too,' Matthew confirmed.

'Lord Chevington does not like you either,' Grover pointed out. 'You seem to have a knack for making enemies, young Matthew.'

Matthew nodded. 'Maybe I should have killed him when

I had the chance.' The memory of the duel was too shocking to recall. 'But how is Grace? Her Ladyship's daughter? I must see her again.'

Grover looked over to William Denton and frowned. 'That would hardly seem to be advisable, Matthew, considering the trouble that she has caused you.'

'It was not her fault,' Matthew defended her at once. 'She was an innocent party in all this.'

Grover raised his eyebrows. 'If there's one thing Miss Grace Fenwick is not, it is innocent. Leave her with Nicholas Elmstead, they are well suited to one another.'

As Matthew began to protest, William Denton put out a hand to keep him quiet. 'Grace Fenwick?' William Denton said quietly. 'I understand from your conversation that she is the daughter of Lady Fenwick. Is that correct?'

'It is,' Grover answered for Matthew. 'Grace is Her Ladyship's only daughter.'

William Denton shook his head. 'And you are close, Matthew?'

'We are friends,' Matthew agreed. Remembering Grace's behaviour in the tower, he was not sure exactly how close Grace wished them to be. He tried to make sense of their relationship. 'But she is betrothed to Elmstead, so has to appear on his side.'

Grover shook his head. 'You may be a fine engineer, young Matthew, but you know little about the fair sex.'

William Denton sighed. 'There was a time that I had hopes of you and Kate, but I fear that you are aiming higher now.' He looked toward the fire. 'Poor Kate.'

'Poor Kate?' It had been a number of years since he had last seen Kate, for ever since his rejection, Matthew had ensured that he avoided her company. He still felt the pain. Now he thought of her companionship at a time when he had desperately needed a friend, and remembered how much he had relied on her. 'Why poor Kate? What has happened to her?' He sat up in bed, wincing as a score of blacksmiths began to work on his head, and very aware that the eyes of everybody present were fixed on him.

William Denton removed his spectacles and began to polish

221

them with a corner of his handkerchief. 'Nothing, Matthew, except that she seems to have lost you for ever.'

'I lost her some years ago,' Matthew said quietly. Leaving the bed, he sat down quickly as dizziness hit him, and then began to pull on his clothes, which had been folded neatly over a hard-backed chair. An image of Kate came to him, her practical common sense and the manner in which she had been able to understand him; her intelligence and learning; her constant kindness to her father. Then Grace took her place. Grace of the wild, madcap laughter, the sense of constant fun and the ability to do whatever she desired.

'I see.' William Denton nodded slowly. 'You have given up on her. My niece is no longer good enough for you when you have the daughter of Lady Fenwick in tow.'

Matthew stopped with his breeches halfway up his legs. 'Given up on her?' He stared at William Denton in complete confusion.

'You think about that, Matthew,' William Denton said quietly, 'while you go to visit this other girl.'

'This other girl?' There was pain as Matthew shook his head. 'No, you don't understand. Grace is more than just another girl. There is something special there, a bond that I do not comprehend.' He struggled to find words that could describe his feelings. After the enforced repression of Maidhouse, any emotional revelations were difficult, but he had to tell somebody, and it seemed that these men were his friends. 'As soon as I saw her, it was as if we had always known each other. And she's so, so different from anybody else. She's not like Kate, and I don't feel for her as I do for Kate.'

William Denton removed his spectacles and began to polish them. He raised bushy eyebrows toward Grover. 'As you do for Kate? Should that not be as you once did for Kate?'

Confused, Matthew shook his head again, gasping at the pain. 'God, no! I still do, but she cares nothing for me.' He stopped as the image of Kate blended with that of Grace. 'God, I don't know. Kate, Grace, they're so different. But I must see Grace at once. I must see her.'

'I see.' Again William Denton looked over to Grover, who was watching a house spider crawl along the ceiling.

222

'Young people nowadays,' Grover said quietly. 'We must give them their head and clear up the consequences.'

Denton sighed and glanced toward John. 'Now, John, tell me what you think of this plan of ours for a lighthouse.'

The words captured Matthew's attention, as no doubt William Denton had intended. He hesitated between rushing off to tell Grace that he was alive and investigating the task that he had set himself.

Obviously aware that his snare had succeeded, Mr Denton touched Matthew's shoulder. 'What do you think, Matthew? After all, you have seen the site and performed the ground-work.' Mr Denton helped Matthew make up his mind by pushing two sheets of paper toward him. On one was a revision of his original plan. On the other, the lighthouse soared above the Black Corbie, sketched in straightforward black and white, with every elevation marked and the island penned in immaculate detail.

Matthew studied the plan for a full three minutes before speaking. He noted that William Denton had added a floating light off the rock, and a building in which to house the artisans while the work was being completed. There was also a site on the island where the pre-constructed masonry blocks were to be assembled before being fitted on to the foundations.

'It's fine, sir,' he approved. 'But without a bill for parliament, it will never happen.'

'That is so,' William Denton agreed, 'but this is a good exercise. If the Black Corbie does not go ahead, there are other dangerous areas on this coast. The Farne Islands for one, and Lindisfarne for another.'

'Indeed.' John patted down a crease that had formed in the centre of the plan. 'Her Ladyship is not a woman to change her mind, unfortunately. There is little chance of her being persuaded.'

'Yes.' Matthew frowned at John. 'John – do you know that this is a lighthouse that we are discussing?'

'John is well aware of the subject matter,' William Denton said. 'Indeed, he has given us some valuable assistance.'

Grover leaned closer. 'John did not always live on the

fells. He was an engineer once, with the Board of Ordnance.'

'I didn't know that.' Matthew looked up. There was always something to surprise him in Northumberland. Nobody seemed to be exactly what they appeared. 'An Army officer? But John, you told me that you came from Ederford.'

'I did.' For a second the madness returned to John's eyes, but he shook it away. 'And before that I was from Chevington Hall.'

Matthew looked to Grover for help, but the vicar's face was expressionless. 'Chevington Hall? A servant?' He grappled with the concept of identity as John shook his head.

'No, Matthew. I owned Chevington Hall – the old one, not the new. Nicholas Elmstead is my son.'

'You are John Elmstead?' Matthew at last succeeded in pulling on his breeches. He stared at John. 'But – how Ederford? And Chevington Hall?'

'Chevington is an old property, Matthew, and an honourable one, but it was never rich. It was tradition for the elder son to serve in the Army until his father died, when he returned and took over the running of the estate. My father would have liked to place me in one of the better regiments, the cavalry by choice, but the funds just did not run to that, so instead I joined the engineers. A Royal Engineer, you see, does not have to purchase his commission. Hardly a career for a gentleman, perhaps, but honourable and requiring more practical sense. Anyway, I could not see myself running with the fast set.' A short bow to William Denton erased any sting that the words may have held.

'So,' John continued, 'the Board of Ordnance sent me to the Royal Military Academy at Woolwich to study fortifications and siege warfare; I learned to be a sapper. I met Marie in the West Indies. She was the daughter of a plantation owner, and we married. Nicholas was the result, but Marie died in childbirth, and a lone soldier cannot raise a family, so I sent him to be reared by his mother's relatives. They came to Chevington for the privilege.'

Grover was nodding. He removed his wig and mopped

the sweat from his close-cropped head. Noticing the direction of Matthew's eyes, he hurriedly replaced the wig and attempted a look of solemn dignity.

'Then,' John continued, 'I was sent to Hindustan, where I served with John Company. We were in some fort or another; there were so many that I cannot remember the name. The French were helping one of their Rajahs besiege the place, and there were batteries and assaults, bombardments and murderous sallies. William Black, the chief engineer, took a fancy to me, a young captain with no hopes of advancement. He sent me to all the dangerous spots to enhance my career. There was one day . . .' John's eyes suddenly widened and his voice changed. 'We were working in the tunnels and the French launched a raid. Our men met them head-on with tomahawks and bayonets.' His voice rose. 'Blood and gore and death, one man with his arm hanging by a thread, another with his head split in two and still screaming . . .'

John sank on to the bed, his eyes dark with memories as he recalled the events. 'There was an Indian soldier with a bayonet in his stomach and his entrails coiling around his legs, but he was still fighting. Then it was my turn and a Frenchman knocked me down. I lay there helpless, unable to move as a fire started. Fire and flames and smoke so dense that we could see nothing. Only then did I know that we were trapped inside the tunnel. The roof collapsed and I was down there with a broken leg and no air, with the fire coming closer and the man with half a head burning slowly and the man with no stomach on fire and screaming, screaming, screaming . . .'

'John!' Grover was holding him secure as John shook with the memories, his hands covering his face and his legs kicking.

'Open the window, Matthew! Let John see the air!' William Denton took charge.

Momentarily forgetting his own weakness, Matthew ripped back the curtains. The resulting flood of daylight helped to quiet John, and Grover kept a wiry arm around his shoulders as William Denton poured a generous measure of brandy into his mouth. John coughed, choked and staggered to the window, staring outside.

225

Glancing toward Matthew, for everybody knew that the sick should be kept in a warm and stuffy environment, Grover pulled the window open so that cool air flowed around John.

Matthew said nothing. He had spent all his life preoccupied by his own troubles, but here was a man who had experienced far worse. Here was a man who had lost not only his name, but also his house and a good part of his sanity.

'You're a brave man to come indoors, John,' Matthew said.

'I could not come indoors,' John told him. 'They brought me back to England and placed me in Bedlam, so that my raving could entertain half the world, but one day one of my old comrades arrived and took me away. He brought me home and handed me into the care of Marie's relatives.' His smile was bitter as he looked at the light northern sky, where the oystercatchers were whistling and a score of kittiwakes danced around the cliffs. 'They locked me away, so that my son could not see me, and I cried for release.'

Matthew could not imagine the horror of a man afraid of confinement being held prisoner inside his own house. 'I hardly saw Nicholas, but I knew that he was spoiled. I could hear him tormenting the servants, but he would not see me, until I broke free.' His smile was bleak. 'After all, I am an engineer; picking locks is easy enough, given time and a rusty nail. I ran for the hills and lived around Ederford, where there were kindly people and sweet water.'

'Ederford?' Matthew came closer as once more his own needs overcame the troubles of another. 'I want to know about Ederford. What happened there? Why did Her Ladyship destroy the village? Who was the woman who looked after me there? Can you remember? Widow Armstrong, you told me.'

'Why was Ederford destroyed?' John looked upward again. 'You will have to ask Her Ladyship, because I'm damned if anybody else knows. And I've told you all that I can about the Widow Armstrong.'

As Matthew sat with his head buried in his hands, Grover spoke quietly to him. 'Well, Matthew, it would seem that there are still questions to be answered, but your time remaining here is short. I will accompany you to Her Ladyship if you wish to ask what she knows, but you may not like what she tells you.'

Matthew looked up. He did not reply to Grover's suggestion, but addressed his master. 'I appreciate your arrival, Mr Denton, although I am not sure why you came. I fear that we both had a wasted journey.'

William Denton shook his head. 'The journey is not yet complete, Matthew. There are problems to be straightened out, and only you can do that.' He looked over to Grover. 'I would take the good Reverend's advice and ask Her Ladyship again.'

'I'll do that,' Matthew agreed. That way he could see Grace once more and ask about her feelings for him.

'Wait, Matthew,' Grover stood up and replaced his wig. 'I said that I would accompany you. You might need my help.'

Seventeen

Northumberland, May 1804

It was early evening when they arrived at Harestone House, a host of swallows swooping over the lawns. The house cast vaguely sinister shadows that slithered toward the scattered outbuildings, while the Hare Stone itself seemed to act as a repellent sentry at the door. A servant greeted Grover like an old friend, stared curiously at Matthew and ushered them both through the house to the great hall where Lady Fenwick was busy with the estate accounts. She looked up from behind a pile of papers, poised with quill in hand.

'Good evening, Reverend,' she said, 'and what the devil do you mean by bringing that man into my house?'

Grover bowed politely. 'He has a question to ask of you, Your Ladyship.'

'Has he indeed?' Lady Fenwick snorted. 'Well, Mr Grover, he can leave at once and take his question with him.'

'It may be to everybody's advantage if he finds out the answer.' Grover sat down without being asked, but Matthew remained standing. His heart was pounding as hard as his head and Lady Fenwick was as formidable as ever.

'He shot my daughter's intended,' Lady Fenwick said bluntly. 'Why should I even speak to him, let alone satisfy his curiosity?'

'It may save some complications, Your Ladyship.' Grover glanced from Matthew to Lady Fenwick. 'Mr Pryde here is curious about the village of Ederford.'

Matthew saw Lady Fenwick stiffen. Her eyes strayed to his face for a second, then returned to Grover. But her long fingers began to drum on the tabletop until she stilled them.

'Curious? It is a deserted village, Reverend. Nothing else.'

Grover bowed again. 'Indeed, Your Ladyship, but Mr Pryde has been informed that he lived there once, as a small boy.'

Lady Fenwick's fingers began to tap again. 'Has he indeed? It seems that somebody in the parish is long of tongue, Reverend. Long of tongue and short of sense, I fear.' For the first time, she faced Matthew directly, and he flinched at the cold fury on her face. 'Well, Mr Pryde, it seems that you are of an inquisitive mind. Let me warn you that we do not always find out things to our advantage when prying. Do you understand?'

'I do, Your Ladyship.' Matthew forced himself to face her malicious stare. 'But there are things that I wish to know.'

Lady Fenwick inclined her head. 'What things, pray?'

'About Ederford, Your Ladyship. I believe that I was shipwrecked at Onswick and brought to Ederford as a baby.' He searched for some expression on Lady Fenwick's face but there was nothing there but distaste. He could hear Grover moving behind him and the soft, relentless ticking of the long-case clock that stood against the far wall.

'So I have been informed,' Lady Fenwick replied. She held Matthew's eyes.

Matthew swallowed. 'I also believe that Your Ladyship had Ederford removed and all the houses destroyed.' Now that he had started, Matthew could not stop the words from pouring out as he voided the hurt that had haunted him all his life. 'I had been sent away by then, Your Ladyship. I don't know why, but the woman who looked after me, the woman who paid for my education and gave me a chance in life, was hounded from her home to live in the hills. She died there, Lady Fenwick. The Widow Armstrong, the only woman who ever cared for me, died because you ordered Ederford cleared.'

The fingers were tapping again as Lady Fenwick's eyes bored into Matthew's. She did not flinch. 'And now that you have said your piece, Mr Pryde, kindly state your question so I can choose whether or nor it deserves an answer.'

The sheer callousness shocked Matthew. 'My question, Your Ladyship, is *why*? Why did you order that village destroyed? Why did you send these people to live in the hills? Why did the Widow Armstrong have to die?'

Grover stepped forward then. 'Mr Pryde is a little upset, Your Ladyship. Lord Chevington's pistol ball has kept him in bed this last week and more. But I do think that everybody would benefit if he heard the truth.'

'The truth, Reverend Grover?' Lady Fenwick's fingers stopped their tapping. 'And in what manner would the truth benefit Mr Pryde? Or me?'

'Mr Pryde has taken a . . .' Grover's hesitation lasted for a full ten seconds, 'a romantic notion to your daughter. He seems to think that a liaison is possible.'

'Does he indeed? A liaison with Grace?' There was a hint of amusement in her face when she looked from Grover to Matthew. 'Is this true, Mr Pryde? You believe there is some attachment between you, a castaway tradesman, and Grace, my daughter?'

Matthew took a deep breath. 'I feel a deep friendship for her, Your Ladyship, and I believe that she shares similar feelings for me. But that is not what I have come here to discuss.'

Lady Fenwick leaned back in her chair. 'I see.' The fingers resumed their drumming on the table. 'You, a mere artisan, make eyes at my daughter, invade her privacy and declare some sort of impossible attachment. Then you come here and dare to bandy words with me?' The malice did not fade even when she smiled. 'Did you not learn by my daughter's conduct at the duel? She has thoughts only for Lord Chevington.'

'My Lady,' Grover leaned across the table, 'Mr Pryde perhaps should learn the truth about Ederford.'

Lady Fenwick sighed and nodded slowly. 'Very well, Reverend. I will tell him.' When she faced Matthew, she made no attempt to conceal the expression of utter disdain on her face. 'You see, Mr Pryde, it was not I who ordered the clearing of Ederford, but your apparent sweetheart, my daughter.'

'Grace?' Matthew shook his head. He refused to believe that laughing Grace could do such a thing. 'Why would she order that?'

'That is no concern of yours,' Lady Fenwick began, but again Grover leaned closer.

230

'It may be helpful,' he said quietly. 'Trust me in this, Your Ladyship.'

Still trying to accept that Grace could have been the cause of the Widow Armstrong's death, Matthew glanced from Grover to Lady Fenwick and back. He realized that there were undercurrents here with messages being passed to which he was not a party.

'Helpful? I just want to find out what happened. I want to find out who I am and why the Widow Armstrong cared for me!'

Lady Fenwick ignored Matthew's outburst. 'You may be right, Reverend Grover. Indeed, I hope that you are right.' She leaned back again and pressed the fingers of both hands together to form a pyramid on the table.

Matthew looked from one to the other. 'Will somebody tell me what is happening?'

'My daughter, Mr Pryde, did not like the view from her window,' Lady Fenwick spoke quietly, not facing Matthew. 'She said that the village of Ederford was an eyesore.' She turned in her seat to face him, her eyes completely void of expression. 'So she ordered it removed and the people cleared.'

Matthew felt the colour drain from his face. 'Grace did that?' He closed his eyes and his vision of Grace altered. The laughing, devil-may-care girl disappeared and another person took her place. Now he saw the woman who ordered an entire village to remain indoors because she wanted to swim in private, and sent a duo of bruisers to ensure compliance. He remembered her pleasure at the view from the top of Hornshope Heights. He remembered her interest in the duel and excitement to see blood spilled.

In a startling bout of insight, he also remembered the quick confabulation between Grace and Elmstead the day that Elmstead had driven off to London, and his sudden and oh-so-inconvenient return just as she had positioned herself in the most delicate situation imaginable. He also remembered that she had checked the time on his watch before rushing away to undress, and her complete lack of surprise at the unexpected return of Elmstead.

231

Matthew stood up suddenly as the colour returned to his face. He remembered Grace declaring that she would like proof of Elmstead's commitment to her. Grace had manipulated him to fight a duel to obtain that proof.

'So, Mr Pryde, now you know.' Lady Fenwick's eyes had not strayed from his face. 'And do you still hope for some romantic attachment with my daughter?'

Unable to talk, Matthew shook his head. All his previous feelings had altered, crushed by revelation. He felt as if a hood had been drawn from his eyes, leaving him able to view a new and cruel reality. Yet while part of him wished to run from Harestone House and never return, somewhere deep inside him something reminded him of the attraction he felt for Grace. Even now he could see every detail of her face, but not in the same way that he could visualize Kate. There was a difference that he could not describe, a disturbing attachment that he could not erase.

'I must leave now, with Your Ladyship's permission.'

Lady Fenwick waved a hand in dismissal. 'Leave,' she said.

Bowing stiffly, Matthew stalked out of the room. He had to see Grace last time, to try and understand the bond that they shared. 'You!' He addressed a startled servant, who flinched as though he had been struck.

'Yes, sir?'

'Where is Miss Fenwick?'

The man shook his head so rapidly that his powdered wig nearly fell off. 'In the Stuart wing, sir, looking after Lord Chevington. He was shot, you see.'

'Take me to them.' For once, Matthew felt no discomfort in giving an order. He was not acting the part of a gentleman or hoping to become an engineer, but was following his own instincts. All his life he had been aware of the mystery that surrounded him, and he knew that at least part of the solution lay within this house.

'If you would follow me, sir?' The servant bowed deeply and led him through a succession of corridors that brought him to a part of the house he had not previously visited. There were carpets on the floor, great oil paintings adorning

232

the walls and furniture of a style and substance that he had never imagined.

Eventually the servant stopped outside a panelled door. 'In here, sir. If you'd permit me?' A sharp rap on the door brought an instant response.

'Wait!' Grace's voice was unmistakable. There was a pause, during which Matthew examined the nearest portrait. It showed a tall man, with Lady Fenwick's steady green eyes and long nose. He held a long musket in his left hand and clutched a brace of wild fowl in his right, while a gaggle of dogs played around his feet.

'Her Ladyship's father, sir,' the servant had noticed the direction of Matthew's gaze. 'A good man, so I've heard.'

'Not a man to destroy villages, then,' Matthew said.

'Indeed not, sir.' The servant bowed again. 'Or place mantraps in his grounds.' He lowered his voice. 'If I may say so, sir, your shot was a little to the left.'

Matthew stared his confusion.

'You missed the vital organs, sir.' Tapping again, the servant received permission to enter and ushered Matthew inside. 'Mr Pryde to see you,' he announced, and withdrew with hardly an expression on his face.

'What the devil?' Elmstead lay propped up in bed, bandages covering his exposed chest. With no wig he looked older, his close-cropped hair already showing signs of grey. Scrabbling for a pistol from his bedside drawer, he pointed it waveringly at Matthew. 'You can't come in here!'

'It's all right, Elmstead,' Matthew dismissed him with a casual disregard that would have been unthinkable only a few weeks previously. 'It's not you I have come to see.' He glanced around the room, comparing its luxuries with the spartan accommodation that he would accept as comfort. There was an Oriental carpet on the floor, polished panelling on the walls, heavy drapes to keep out the dangerous fresh air and an assortment of elegant furniture, from the mahogany dressing table to the oval mirror that reflected the light from the chandelier.

'Hello, Matthew,' Grace dropped in a short curtsey, her eyes searching his face. 'I trust that you have quite recovered from your wound?'

'Quite, thank you,' Matthew replied. He fought the sudden impulse to hit her and bowed instead, then repeated the movement in the direction of Elmstead. 'And you, My Lord? I trust that the exchange of shots has ended any dispute between us and that honour is satisfied?'

Elmstead's glare could have curdled milk, but he dropped the pistol on the bedside table and bobbed his head in a parody of acknowledgement. 'I see that you still persist in bothering my intended wife.' His voice was hoarse.

'Not for much longer, my Lord,' Matthew had his anger under control. 'Indeed, I believe that you make a well-matched couple. You, my Lord, are a bully, and you, Miss Fenwick, used pretended friendship to inveigle me into a position where your intended could challenge me to a duel and probably kill me.'

Grace's laugh mocked him. 'Oh, Mr Pryde! And why not? You came into Onswick so full of conceit, so sure that you were going to build your damned lighthouse. As if we cared for a lighthouse or anything else! Who are you to change our way of life, Mr Pryde? A nobody, that's who! Nicholas told me all about you at Maidhouse, his little fag who he enjoyed tormenting! Well, Mr Pryde, so did I!'

The attack forced Matthew to take a step back. When he looked up, he saw himself reflected in the oval mirror. Dressed in his shabby best, with old-fashioned breeches that wrinkled around the knees and pinchbeck buckles on his shoes, a waistcoat whose pocket bulged with use and shiny patches on the elbows of his jacket, he looked a failure. Even his eyes were faded, a dirty brown when compared to the laughing brilliance of Grace or the enigmatic green of Her Ladyship. It was no wonder that people sought to torment him, for he looked like a failed clerk or a rejected suitor.

As the fight drained from him, Matthew bowed one last time and backed to the door. He could not stand against landed gentlemen. He was only an orphan with a dark past, and he should accept that. He had to accept inevitable defeat.

'Oh Matthew,' Grace stepped forward, her eyes light with malice, 'I enjoyed watching Ederford collapse. We came at dawn, you see, and drove them into the hills, and as they

ran, I had my bellman ring them a hearty farewell!' It was
her laughter that rankled; that husky, terrible laugh that
Matthew hated himself for still finding attractive.

If Grace had not insisted on that last spiteful jibe, Matthew
would have retreated as a vanquished man. Now a lifetime
of repressed anger shattered his self-control. He hardly felt
his back straighten and he barely recognized the shout as his
own. 'You killed the Widow Armstrong!' He saw Grace's
face change, saw Elmstead sit up in bed in renewed alarm.
'You murdered my mentor!'

Elmstead scrabbled for the pistol, groaning as he thumbed
back the hammer. He stretched across the bed with the bandages white against the crisp hairs of his chest. 'You'll die,
Pryde! I should have ordered my men to kill you in Onswick,
rather than just hammering you.' When he raised the pistol,
the muzzle was steady. 'Now I'll finish the job!'

Matthew did not hesitate. Stepping back from Grace, he
feinted to his left, jinked right and threw himself on top of
Elmstead. There was an instant of satisfaction as he rammed
his left elbow against the bandages, so Elmstead howled,
and then he grabbed at the pistol. Elmstead pulled the trigger,
but Matthew shoved his hand against the lock, wincing as
the hammer fell on to his fingers. He swore, shook his right
hand to relieve the pain and saw the pistol skitter across the
carpet.

'I'll kill you myself!' Grace was no longer laughing as
she lunged downward, her blonde hair flopping free across
her face. She scooped up the pistol, but struggled with the
hammer. Her eyes were wide and brown, the loose green
gown she wore flapping around her legs and bare feet. She
aimed at him, mouth open, breasts heaving visibly as she
bent forward. Light from the chandelier reflected in the dark
barrel.

Matthew heard the soft snick as Grace managed to pull
back the hammer. She hesitated when the door opened, and
he swept his hand sideways, knocking the pistol from her
grip.

Grace mouthed inarticulately as she jumped at him, slapping with both hands. Each blow landed on his bandaged

235

head, like a succession of hammer-blows that increased the pain and rocked him backward. He landed on top of the pistol, twisted and snatched it up. The weapon felt good in his fist, not as well balanced as a Manton but cool and comfortable. As Grace kicked out with her feet, he shoved the barrel against her stomach.

'No! Enough now!' That was a familiar voice, but not that of Grace. 'You can't shoot your own sister!'

Matthew turned, pistol in hand. He saw Lady Fenwick standing in the doorway, arms extended. He saw William Denton with his mouth open. He saw Charles Denton with an arm around Kate. She held out her hand.

'Give me the pistol.'

Matthew handed it over.

Eighteen

Northumberland, May 1804

T hey made a tight little gathering around the fire in the great hall, with the frowning portraits looking on and the collection of arms and armour reflecting the light. Matthew sat in the centre, shivering with reaction as he sipped his brandy, while to his right Charles Denton held Kate tight by his side. Grover sat upright on a hard chair on his left, with his wig square on top of his head and one hand supporting the arm of Lady Fenwick, while Grace sat sobbing at her other side, all her bravado gone. In the background, William Denton stood and said nothing.

'Sister? What do you mean, sister?' Matthew looked from Kate to Grace and back, but neither replied. Instead it was Lady Fenwick, as straight-backed as ever, who looked at him.

'Well then, Matthew Pryde,' she said, her eyes narrow and pitiless, 'so now you know all the truth.'

'Not all, Your Ladyship.' Kate held Lady Fenwick's gaze. 'There appear to be many gaps in Matthew's life, and many questions that remain to be answered.'

Lady Fenwick's lips curled slightly. 'That may be so, Miss Denton, but I am certainly not obliged to answer them.'

'Indeed not, Your Ladyship,' Kate replied evenly, 'but neither am I obliged to withhold what I know.' She raised her eyebrows in a gesture that could have been copied from her uncle. 'I have unravelled your little deception.'

Matthew did not hide his puzzlement. He looked from one to the other, returned his attention to Kate and wondered when she had arrived in the north and why she was here. 'Deception? I don't understand . . .'

Charles Denton adjusted his pince-nez glasses and nodded

gravely to him. 'Just listen and let Kate do the talking, Matthew. I find that is usually best.'

Kate had waited politely until Matthew finished. 'I think there is a lot to answer, Your Ladyship.' When no reply was forthcoming, she faced Matthew. 'Have you seen the grave in Horns Hope, Matthew?'

'I have,' Matthew replied, 'but I really don't see the significance.'

'Of course not. You reason like an engineer, you don't think like a woman.' Kate's smile revealed those uneven teeth that Matthew had always found so attractive. 'Can you remember what it says?'

Matthew shook his head. 'A Biblical reference and some initials with a date. It might be the resting place of Lady Fenwick's mother.'

'It's not.' Kate disposed of that suggestion with a firm shake of her head. She withdrew a sheet of paper from a bag that sat beside her, shook out the folds and said, 'This is what it says: "Much loved and never forgotten. Rest in the peace of the Lord." There are also the initials "G" and "F" and the date 13 August 1777.' She looked up. 'Don't you think that the initials are significant? "G" and "F", the same as Grace there, Grace Fenwick.'

'A family name,' Lady Fenwick was rallying again. 'Common enough.'

'Quite so, Your Ladyship,' Kate agreed, 'quite so.' She refolded the paper and replaced it in her bag. 'However, now think of the date. August 1777. The same year and only one month before the ship, *Pride of Matthew*, came ashore on the Black Corbie.'

Matthew looked up. 'How do you know that?'

'Mr John Elmstead is quite lucid now, Matthew. He remembers the event very well.'

Lady Fenwick looked away. 'That means little.'

Kate nodded. 'Little in itself, but I have access to an unlimited number of volumes of books, Your Ladyship, and I have ascertained that your mother, who was named Grace, died at sea in 1775. I have heard that you were not close. So that small grave does not belong to her.'

238

'What does all this mean?' For the first time, Grace stopped sobbing and looked up. 'How can I be that man's sister? Mother, tell them!'

Lady Fenwick said nothing. 'You seem to think that you have all the answers, Miss Denton. Continue.'

'As Your Ladyship pleases,' Kate said quietly, ignoring the look of pure poison that her words inspired. 'I believe that grave belongs to your daughter, Grace.'

'Impossible. Grace is sitting behind you even as we speak. Sit up, girl, and stop that damned snivelling!' Lady Fenwick's hands curled as though she would like to strangle somebody.

Kate sighed. 'Grace Fenwick died in August 1777 – or at least your daughter Grace Fenwick did. That is why you visit that lonely grave so often.'

Lady Fenwick threw a furious glance at Grover, who shook his head in confusion.

'Oh no, Lady Fenwick. The good Reverend ensured that the entry was erased from any parish records.' Kate drew another square of paper from her bag and held it close to her.

'Then how?' Lady Fenwick asked, frowning as Grace began to howl. 'Keep silent, girl! This has nothing to do with you!'

Kate opened the paper. It was blank. 'Then how did I know? I did not know, but I did guess. And I'm right, aren't I?'

'Damn you for an interfering hussy!' Lady Fenwick snarled.

'I thought I was right.'

Matthew looked up. 'So when your own Grace died, you found an orphan, or perhaps bought an abandoned child to pretend that it was your own? You had to keep the Fenwick line going, didn't you? The line that extends in an unbroken sequence to the days of Wild Cerdic.' He looked over to Kate. 'That's what it's all about, Kate. Pride in her aristocratic blood.' He remembered Lady Fenwick's history lesson when first he came to plead for her help. 'It was all false, wasn't it? You want the appearance of a blood line, not the reality.'

'I had not worked that part out,' Kate admitted, looking at him with her head to one side. 'Perhaps there is hope for you yet, Matthew.'

Matthew smiled back. 'I don't know how you think that Grace is my sister though, Kate.'

'Oh, Matthew.' Kate pressed her lips together. 'Look in a mirror, can't you? It's obvious! The same eyes, the same mouth, the same build even. And both from the same ship-wreck, too!'

'I was the only survivor,' Matthew said quietly.

'No, Matthew, I believe that there was at least one other.' Kate looked at Lady Fenwick. 'Well, Your Ladyship, I can guess at the truth, or you can tell us exactly what happened.' It was a direct challenge that made Matthew catch his breath, but Lady Fenwick barely blinked.

'Better from me, I think, Miss Denton.' She took a deep breath and, reaching to her side, squeezed Grace's arm in the first sign of human compassion that Matthew had ever seen her display. 'You will know that the Black Corbie claims vessels from time to time. It is part of our heritage. Well, in September 1777, twenty-seven years ago, the Corbie took another. She was a whaler, with the name *Pride of Matthew*, and she broke her back . . .'

Lady Fenwick remembered the night, with a wild wind whipping clouds across the face of a hunter's moon, and the sea roaring against the outstretched wings of the Corbie. She had been walking the sands, weeping over the loss of her child, for although infant deaths were common, the birth had damaged her so she could never bear another. She would never be a mother, and the Fenwick line would end with her. She watched the sails move closer and heard the terrible sounds of the ship dying on the predatory rocks. The foremast fell first, then the main topmast, and finally the mizzen, and pieces of ship came ashore. Spars and timber, barrels and a hatch cover, lengths of rope and scraps of canvas.

Lady Fenwick watched unmoved, unable to open her shield of grief to allow in compassion for others. She saw the waves wash over the body that lay beside the hatch cover, ignored it and walked on, until she heard the sound. It was unmistakable, the tiny mewing of an infant, the sound that her own baby had made when she had wanted food.

'There was a baby washed ashore. I saw it lying on the beach, all alone and crying in the surf.'

The mother had turned over in the surf. Her clothes were shredded and she was bleeding from a score of wounds, her face torn open and her hands a mass of watery blood. 'My baby,' she had said, pressing the wailing infant to her breast.

Lady Fenwick had bent over, seeing her own baby lying still in its coffin, seeing the white linen sheet that covered her and the closing of the polished lid. She could hear the doctor again, saying that she could not have another. She had no difficulty in wresting the baby from its mother. 'Mine now,' she said, 'I'll look after her.'

'I picked her up,' Lady Fenwick said, her voice low. Matthew could hear Grace sobbing, but could not take his eyes from Her Ladyship's face. 'And I took my baby home.'

Leaving the mother to die in the waves, Lady Fenwick had covered the baby with a corner of her cloak and ridden hurriedly to Harestone House. The doctor had agreed to say nothing, and soon afterward left for a more lucrative career in London. None of the staff would argue with Her Ladyship, and nobody else knew the truth, so Lady Fenwick raised the baby as her own. She called it Grace and soon the servants accepted that it was her baby, and nobody mentioned Lady Fenwick's frequent trips to the grave. It was three years later that she heard that another baby had been recovered that day, and she mounted her horse in a hot rage and galloped to Ederford.

'I raised the baby as Grace, and she was mine.' Lady Fenwick looked over to Grace and lifted her chin even higher. 'She *is* mine.'

'There's nobody would dispute that, Your Ladyship,' Grover agreed, but Lady Fenwick stared coldly at him.

'Then I heard about another survivor from the wreck.' Lady Fenwick transferred her poisonous stare to Matthew.

The baby lay in a pile of rags in the cottage of the Widow Armstrong, who grinned with black teeth and picked it up.

The smell of urine and vomit was hidden beneath the stench of raw whisky. When Lady Fenwick held the child, the resemblance was unmistakable. The eyes that stared at her matched those of Grace, and the snub nose was identical to that of her daughter. This was Grace's brother, an identical twin.

'You can't keep him,' Lady Fenwick said.

'You can't take him,' Widow Armstrong answered, and she belched stale whisky into Her Ladyship's face.

Lady Fenwick pondered. If she allowed the child to grow up near Harestone House, the resemblance would eventually be noticed. People would ask questions and her parentage of Grace would be questioned. For a terrible minute Lady Fenwick was temped to have this baby kidnapped or killed, but she knew that she could not. This was the brother of a child she looked on as her own.

Returning to Harestone House, Lady Fenwick ordered that the new vicar should visit her. He was an eager young man who had no desire for advancement, but a passion for scientific research. She ordered him to buy the baby from the Widow Armstrong and send it to a London orphanage, where it would be cared for but disappear as only another unknown. Then she relaxed and watched her own child grow up.

With only one child and no possibility of another, Lady Fenwick could afford to indulge Grace's desires, so that she could have anything she liked on demand. Before she was eight, Grace was in charge of her mother, and all the servants moved in fear of her whims. When Grace demanded the top room of the house, Lady Fenwick ensured that it was given to her, and when Grace demanded that she had a private place for bathing, a tower was built for her by the sea. Even Grace's demand for the destruction of Ederford was obeyed, despite the anguish of the tenants. It was then that John Elmstead heard the Widow Armstrong's story, and, in one of his periodic returns to sanity, sought out Lady Fenwick.

John's ultimatum had been stark. Give the Widow Armstrong's child a chance in life, or the story would be known. He would provide half the money as well as the name of the same school that his son attended.

'Of course, I could not allow a child to be brought up in

such poverty,' Lady Fenwick said, 'although I entirely doubt your claim that the boy, Mr Pryde here, is brother to my Grace. I arranged for him to be brought up in one of the finest schools in the south, and then for a career in the Honourable East India Company to be purchased.'

The East India Company was a fine solution. It answered John Elmstead's desire for a good chance in life, and the boy might vanish in Hindustan and never return to cause problems. It came as a shock when Timothy Flintock informed her that Matthew Pryde, the name that they had chosen, had turned down the offer. By that time John Elmstead was rarely lucid, so Lady Fenwick had no hesitation in stopping all funds and allowing Matthew to make his own way.

'When he refused that offer, I was nonplussed. My solicitor informed me that a reputable engineer had offered him an apprenticeship, so I left matters in his own hands.' Lady Fenwick looked at Grace. 'I had enough problems with Grace. By indulging her so much, I had raised a spoiled child. But look at her now, like a ripe fruit, ready for the plucking and with a young Lord in tow. Is that not success? Until Matthew Pryde comes back with his interference and his lighthouse, spoiling all my plans.'

'I just want to know who I am,' Matthew said quietly. He was also looking at Grace, this sister that he did not know he had.

'Who you are?' Lady Fenwick's voice rose shrilly. 'You are nobody! Nothing! An orphan from the storm, yet you dare to try and break the line of the Fenwicks, one of the oldest families in England? Get out of my house, and take your ramshackle entourage with you!'

Matthew nearly quailed before the force of Lady Fenwick's fury, but Kate put her hand on his arm. The touch burned. 'Not yet, Your Ladyship, not yet. In a small while we will leave, but first I have to tell you Matthew's real identity, and that of his sister.'

A sudden gust of wind blew smoke down the chimney and caused the fire to flare, and then Kate stepped out of her chair and stood beside Matthew. Her hand remained on his arm. 'When *Pride of Matthew* left London for the

Greenland fisheries, she had on board the owner and his wife. They had their family with them, brother and sister. She dropped the owner's wife off at Leith, and they remained in Edinburgh for a few months on some business of their own, to be collected when the ship returned home. It was on the homeward voyage that *Pride of Matthew* hit bad weather, and the rock sunk them. I have seen the ship's manifest in the files of the company, and I know the names of the owner.'

'Oh, God!' Matthew felt Kate's hand tighten on his shoulder. 'Who am I, Kate?'

'Your father was called Martin, and he was owner and master. Your mother was Sarah, and your name, your real name, is Matthew Pryde.' The words were quiet. 'The ship was named after you. Grace's real name is Sarah, after her mother. She is undoubtedly your sister.'

'Oh, God in heaven!' Matthew sagged with the knowledge. He was Matthew Pryde. His father was a shipowner and master and he had a sister. He looked at Grace and their eyes locked, held and slid away. He did not know how he felt.

Lady Fenwick had moved quickly, holding Grace close to her. Her voice was high pitched as she broke into Matthew's mood. 'You won't take my Grace! You won't take away my daughter!' Lifting a heavy poker from the fireplace, she faced them, eyes wide.

'Indeed not, Your Ladyship,' Matthew said quietly. He knew who he was, and little else mattered, but now he had obligations to fulfil. 'I do not think that anybody here will ever attempt that.' He looked at his sister and saw only a frightened young woman. It was no wonder that he had felt such an immediate bond, for they were bound by blood. He closed his eyes, remembering that moment when she had presented herself to him, yet he had felt no desire. The thought of what might have happened made him shiver. Yet they were so far apart in character and upbringing that they could never be close. He looked at Kate and saw again the girl who had befriended him as a youth, but full-grown and so sensible that for a second he nearly felt overawed.

'Why did you go to so much trouble, Kate? Over me, I mean?'

Kate did not avoid his eyes. 'I once thought of you as a friend,' she said, 'and do we not help our friends in need?'

Matthew nodded. 'A friend, indeed.' He sighed, and spoke to Lady Fenwick, who still clutched her poker and glared at the company. 'Nobody in this room will mention what has happened, Your Ladyship. After all, we are kin, of a sort, for your daughter is my sister. However, I would be obliged if you could speak with Lord Chevington. I believe that he has a bill to put to the House. Mr Denton and I have a lighthouse to build here.' Putting up his right hand, he squeezed Kate's hand that had remained for so long on his arm. 'And I believe that I have a woman to woo.'

Author's Note

The character of Grace Fenwick is based, in part, on Janet Anstruther, an eighteenth century Fife lady who built a personal bathing folly by the Firth of Forth. She employed a bellman to keep the local villagers away and reputedly cleared a village that spoiled her view.

Throughout the eighteenth century, ships were in danger from storms. Every winter had its quota of shipwrecks. At the end of the eighteenth and beginning of the nineteenth centuries, engineers built a series of lighthouses around the coast of Britain.

The Royal Navy protected Great Britain from French, Spanish, American, Dutch and other enemies, but it was an unpopular service. It was necessary for the Navy to obtain recruits by force, often by the Impressment Service. When a Press Gang descended on a village, the local women often defended their men.